THE
OLD HOUSE
IN THE
COUNTRY

CHI VARNADO

ALSO BY CHI VARNADO

The Dance Centre Presents Giselle

The Dance Centre Presents The Nutcracker

The Dance Centre Presents Coppélia

A Canyon Trilogy:
Life Before, During and After the Cedar Fire

The Tale of Broken Tail

ADVANCE PRAISE FOR
THE OLD HOUSE IN THE COUNTRY

"Even though the locale is different, this story line is very parallel to my own experiences of growing up in a rural setting with siblings. It's compelling to read how, with compromise, a realization of dreams and wishes of a previous generation is accomplished... through love and determination!"
—Beverly Silvers

"I loved this book and felt like I was with them on a really important trip. At the end, I got a bit teary. The story parallels mine in many ways. Thank you! The entire novel is remarkably concise. References to the fire and the ballet studio show that Marli has a solid career and family life. The losses caused by the fire, and of her parents, and menopause—have made her long to keep her family heritage and happy memories alive. She strives to reconcile her ancestors' racism and misogyny with the love and well-being she and Ellie experienced in their ancestral home. I ponder this stuff a lot so the story really hit home for me. It made me realize that I love my life in spite of its messiness."
—Debbie George

"*The Old House in the Country* contains dramatic themes about family conflicts, culture clashes, loss, and nostalgia. It is not, however, a maudlin or a heavy read. The novel is buoyed by female characters who are flexible, optimistic, and adventurous. A likable and engaging cast of women move this story along at a good clip. The sisters and their friends embark on a project that is part fantasy, sometimes a test of courage, and in many ways a life passage of the kind that happen to adults if they are lucky and brave. Readers will be happy to accompany these women on their journey and might be inspired to let a little more of the unexpected into their own lives."
—Susan Nelson, San Diego Book Award Judge

"The pictures painted with words give insight to so many aspects of life. The reader is introduced to family dynamics, geography, the differences in other parts of the country and the interaction of friends. This story is insightful on many levels and maintains interest right to the end."
—Julie Iavelli

GnomeWood Press
P.O. Box 404
Ramona, CA 92065
GnomeWoodPress.com

Book cover and interior design by Monkey C Media
Edited by Adrianne Moch

First Edition
Printed in the United States of America

ISBN: 978-1-7341423-6-5 (Trade Paperback)
ISBN: 978-1-7341423-7-2 (E-Pub)

Library of Congress Control Number: 2021905357

For Ellis M. Varnado

1

ALL ABOARD!

*T*he bustling city of New Orleans greeted the two sisters, three days after they'd boarded the train in San Diego. They dragged their wheeled suitcases and walked the six-and-a-half blocks to the motel. Marli shouldered a day backpack while Ellie clutched a Gucci bag under her arm. The warm, humid afternoon reminded Marli that wherever you were in Louisiana, a swamp or muddy river was never far away. Sweat streamed down between her shoulder blades—yes, they had indeed arrived. They were now officially enveloped in the Deep South of their father's homeland.

Ellie claimed one of the double beds and removed her sandals while Marli unfolded the luggage rack from the closet and lifted her suitcase onto it. She unzipped the green canvas bag and wondered how her sister would react to the quirky, handmade urn. After pulling the paper sack out from under the layers of clothes, she slowly unrolled it. As she reached her hand inside and carefully pulled out the plastic bag that held the vessel, an uneasy feeling crept up her spine and flushed over her face. Up to this point, she alone had been responsible for keeping their father's ashes.

Knowing Dad the way she did, and sharing his frugal nature, she'd opted for a different sort of urn. She respected his making do with what he had and his ability to create new things from old parts. Why spend money on some new contraption when you could come up with something on your own that would work just fine? It was for this reason she had selected the old trophy, the kind with two winged handles, from a thrift store. While rummaging through his house, she'd found a dated, glass jar lid that covered the top of the trophy. It was not a tight fit, but she had an idea. She came across a roll of dark brown duct tape in his shop that matched the color of the trophy and then wrapped the neck of the jar and the glass lid together, all the while hoping for his approval from the other side.

"Hey, do you want to see it?" Marli asked.

Ellie lifted her focus from the pamphlet listing local New Orleans entertainment. "See what?"

"The urn. You haven't seen it yet." She nervously cradled the package in her arms. "I already told you about it so don't freak out, okay?"

"O-k-a-y," Ellie said, hesitantly.

Marli took the unique urn out of the plastic bag and held it up for her sister to see. "I think he'd appreciate the fact that I found this lid in his house, don't you?"

"Um, I guess so." Ellie stared blankly at the relic displayed in her sister's hands.

Marli couldn't quite read her expression. Maybe she didn't have an opinion. Or could it be she didn't care? Or maybe she was shocked. That could be it. She probably just didn't want to hurt her feelings.

Ellie finally spoke. "I wonder what Aunt Mae and Caroline will think when they see it at the cemetery."

"Don't you think they'll understand how fitting it is, you know, his frugality and all? And this duct tape around the lid—that came from his shop," Marli explained. "You think it's all right?"

"I suppose."

Why was Ellie so reticent about this? Marli would have liked to hear some kudos for her efforts, but perhaps it was better to leave it alone for now. She rewrapped the vessel and put it back under her clothes. "I'll pack him back in here real good."

As if on autopilot, they grabbed their purses and headed out, walking down Royal Street to window shop and people-watch. Later, after dinner, they wandered over to the bank of the river. Before long, four stoned teenagers stumbled over to a nearby bench.

"Hey, you got a light?" the girl with blue hair asked.

"No, sorry," Ellie answered, shooting Marli a disapproving glance.

The two women watched the kids dance and goof around to the hip hop beat coming from their boom box. One of the guys muttered something about not liking the particular song, but he seemed to be absorbed in the music anyway and swayed back and forth in a rather uncoordinated manner. As a dancer, Marli was intrigued by their relaxed movements. The giggling and guffaws displayed a small slice of the New Orleans street scene. Dusk settled and darkness crept in around them, urging the travelers back to their room for a good night's sleep in real beds.

⁓

The sisters were taking the railroad all the way from San Diego to Mississippi to honor their train-loving father's wishes. They planned to lay some of his ashes to rest in the Pickens cemetery, next to his parents and brother. He had hoped to ride a "choo choo" train one last time, but had been too feeble in the months preceding his death—much to his dismay. Marli was glad she'd insisted on the rail trip, for Dad's sake.

At first, Ellie had said, "That's just too long to be gone. Maybe we could ride one way and fly home. That's about the best I can do. Besides, what about our kids?"

But Marli had put her foot down. "The kids are all older now. And we have husbands. They can pitch in. It won't be for that long and I want to do this for Dad. I think it's important to slow down and *be* with this thing and not rush through it. Remember, the day after he died—we worked hard and cleaned out his apartment, so we wouldn't have to pay the next month's rent? Well, that *one* day was it. Everyone was too busy to slow down and let it all sink in. We just resumed the rat race."

"So what are you getting at?" Ellie asked.

"All I wanted was for everything to stop," Marli began. "Isn't anything worth stopping for? I thought his dying was. I needed that, but it wasn't to be. I felt so alone. I know I'm fortunate to have the friends I do. They really rallied and kept me company. You can fly if you want, but I'm taking the train."

"It's way more expensive that way. You're being ridiculous."

"But I need to take my time with this now, especially since Dad loved the whole train thing so much. This feels like the way we're supposed to do it. That's all."

Ellie finally acquiesced. Train tickets were purchased and hotel reservations made as the sisters mapped out their trip. They would be gone two weeks, delivering their father's ashes to his Mississippi homeland and revisiting some of the places that were part of their heritage. They would ride the rails from Southern California to Mississippi, and when they were finished with their business, they'd travel back through Chicago—for a change of scenery.

The slow pace of the South lured Marli back as she relived the Mississippi summers of their childhood: the deafening drone of cicadas in the backyard; mosquitoes hovering over the pond; sultry days lingering on, endured from the front porch swing of Grandma's house. That place in time seemed so far away, yet drew her in ways she couldn't put into words. It just did.

"I'll flip you for the bottom bunk," Ellie had offered at the beginning of the trip, already with quarter in hand. The two passenger seats by the large picture window faced each other and folded down into a twin bed at night. The upper bunk offered very little headroom.

"Okay, tails."

Ellie flipped the coin, but it fell on the floor.

"Look at it first, before you pick it up. Whatever it is, it counts."

"It's tails," Ellie said, glancing down before picking up the coin and putting it back into her purse.

"Hot-diggity-dog!" Marli rubbed her palms together happily. This meant for the next three nights they'd spend on the train heading eastward, Marli would get to sleep the first and third nights on the larger bed next to the big window. She looked forward to the extra headroom, so when insomnia would inevitably take over, she could sit up and enjoy the view. Ever since perimenopause had begun making its presence known, her sleep had been affected. No longer was she able to fall asleep within minutes of her head hitting the pillow and stay asleep for the better part of the night. And now, fully menopausal, she never knew what kind of night lay ahead. Luckily, her five-foot four-inch gymnast/dancer body allowed her to curl up almost anywhere—including, at times, the backseat of her car.

The sisters were both rather petite, intelligent, educated women. Marli, the oldest by three years, had always considered herself the less attractive one in spite of her pale blue eyes. Her sister's sea-green eyes had always seemed to draw more male interest. Perhaps this was the reason that Ellie paid more attention to her appearance than Marli was ever willing to. As a teenager, her sister would style her hair and put on makeup before school. Marli just made sure her face was clean and hair pulled back into a braid after her morning workout. These habits remained with them ever since.

On that first night of their rail adventure, the full moon shone into their compartment and lit the mountain ranges to the north, as the locomotive swayed back and forth, blowing its whistle every fifteen minutes or so. Marli wondered why that was necessary out in the middle of the desert. It's not as if the coyotes and deer couldn't hear the train approach without its pompous warnings. Nevertheless, she found the gentle rocking soothing, enough to allow sleep to come and send her gently into dreamland. Even when she'd surface above REM, she felt content and relaxed. *This* was definitely the way to go. It had been a hard sell to convince her sister to travel 5,000 miles in any manner other than on an airplane.

"Dad didn't get that train ride he wanted," Marli had said. "This way, he gets his last wish."

Of course, Ellie had been hesitant. As a top-notch real estate agent, she had to be at the beck and call of her high-rolling clients. It was all about getting top dollar for million-dollar homes in fancy neighborhoods. That took a lot of wining, dining, schmoozing, and looking the part. Marli knew her sister was good at what she did, but at what personal cost? Was there anything real left underneath that "for show" facade?

This train trip was proving to be an adventurous undertaking, especially when the two women had disembarked for a walk in the outskirts of El Paso.

"Hurry up! We're gonna miss the train. I already heard them blow the whistle." Marli urged her sister to walk faster.

"Just wait a minute! I'm going to sprinkle some of his ashes here by this rail spike. I'm almost done." Ellie tossed a handful of ashes into the breeze, straightened up and stuffed the baggie into her sparkly Gucci bag before picking up the pace.

The one-hour layover was hardly enough time to explore the "Warehouse District" of El Paso, as the locals referred to it, on foot in the August heat. But they were determined to do a little sightseeing anyway. The next stop wasn't for another twenty hours and they desperately needed to stretch their legs and breathe some fresh air. Openable windows were no longer standard in newer trains, or modern motels for that matter. The passengers were at the mercy of the locomotive's air conditioning system, whether functioning well or not. Marli missed the good old days of natural ventilation.

"Wait for me!" Ellie called to her sister who was now sprinting ahead of her along the tracks, toward their home away from home. The conductor pulled the box down out of the doorway so the stragglers could step back onto the train, and shot them an impatient look.

"That was too close! Let's not do *that* again," Marli said as they made their way up the stairs, down the corridor and into their tiny sleeper car. The engine pulled and jerked each car into motion. The bump, bump, bump combined with the back and forth swaying of the double-decker dictated the rhythm of the ride. That aspect of the old-fashioned mode of transportation had not changed. It was hypnotic and soothing and exactly what Marli had hoped for.

The sisters had smuggled two bottles of Merlot onto the train, buried under clothes in each of their suitcases. The legality of bringing alcohol on board appeared ambiguous. The agent they purchased their tickets from had assured them it was fine to bring it along, as many did. But after boarding, the conductor made an announcement declaring it against policy and any open container would get you thrown off the train with no refund, even if they were out in the middle of nowhere.

"What? You've got to be kidding," Ellie said.

One evening they decided to chance it and poured the wine into their water bottles, ready to claim it as cranberry juice for their "hereditary urinary problems," or something along those lines. Before uncorking and pouring, they simply locked their door and closed the compartment's heavy curtain.

"I want to get out and walk around San Antonio when we get there, like we did with Dad that time," Ellie said.

Marli thought back to when, just ten years before, in the summer of 1998, her family had driven their ten-year-old truck and camper across the country. Dad had wanted to share his roots with the grandchildren. He, along with Ellie and her daughter, drove his ancient, decrepit, 1972 Ford RV to meet Marli's family in Texas. They then caravanned the rest of the way.

"I remember asking him if he was sure that thing was gonna make it," Ellie said.

"Oh yeah! He said, 'Of course it will. It won't be any problem. If it breaks down, we'll just pull over and fix it. Besides, Richard will be there to help me.'" Marli laughed, picturing her history professor husband. "He barely knows how to change a tire and I don't think he's ever performed an oil change."

"But Dad said *he* knew how and that's all that really mattered." Ellie shook her head and grinned.

Marli took a long pull of the red liquid in her plastic bottle and remembered the eight of them wandering along the restaurant-lined San Antonio River Walk. "I hadn't realized the allure of that city before we went. I really didn't know anything about it."

"I'd been there before, but it was still special sharing it with Dad that way." Ellie coughed and wiped the red dribble from her chin. "But I think one of the most memorable things about that trip was the whole Galveston fiasco with his RV. Remember how we kept escaping to the beach to avoid listening to his ranting about the damn fuel pump or whatever it was? I don't know how Richard put up with it. You've sure got one patient husband there." She turned and looked out the window.

That was true. Richard was the only one who would volunteer to help Dad work on anything. The old man had always seemed to need someone around to "hold this" or "move that." Even though he was a very capable mechanic, trained as an electrical engineer, he couldn't help letting his frustrations get the best of him.

Marli grabbed her stomach and imitated his groaning. "Oh, my belly! Oh, my belly!"

Ellie laughed, spewing wine onto her blouse, remembering how their father could carry on so. She joined in, "Oh, Lord in heaven, help me. I can't do it alone. God dammit, son of a bitch!"

Marli cracked up. "For a Southern Baptist, he sure did raise Cain, didn't he? Hey, remember that contraption he built in front of the radiator to squirt water on it so it wouldn't overheat? That was probably one of the reasons he cursed so much that day." Barrel cactus and ocotillos whizzed by their cabin window.

"Yeah," Ellie said. "The repair job would have been a lot easier without *that* thing in the way."

Richard, in his usual patient manner, had helped him with the repair while also trying to keep him calm. This was ultimately what Dad needed, someone to keep him company while he did the work. Both Marli and Ellie were unable to provide this for their own father for any longer than ten minutes or so, since they had officially overdosed on this type of service to him during their childhood. To do so would completely overwhelm them. Their tolerance for these tirades was quite simply used up. They knew better and could usually duck out of "helping" before too much resentment set in. Richard didn't have the same background with their dad, so he was more willing and patient.

Then Marli remembered what they'd been discussing before they'd gotten off on this tangent. "Better check the schedule to make sure the San Antonio stop isn't in the middle of the night."

Ellie stood up to get the small pamphlet off the top bunk. "Oh crap. It is. We get there at 2:00 a.m. But I still want to do it."

"But it may not be in the safest area. A lot of the depots seem to be in the rundown part of town."

Later that night, the train slowed and bumped along before coming to a stop.

"Wake up, Marli. We're here," Ellie whispered.

Sure enough, it was dark and deserted. They stood waiting for the door to open and then descended the steps down to the platform. A few people got off and disappeared into the darkness while the sisters stood with their hands in their coat pockets.

"Let's put some ashes on the track behind the train," Marli suggested. They hurried back into the semidarkness and emptied their fists. "I don't like this. Maybe there're creeps hiding behind those buildings." Just like when she was a kid, goosebumps rose on the back of her neck. They ran back under the lights of the dimly lit station.

"You might be right. But I really do want to check it out." Ellie walked ahead along an old sidewalk. They veered around a large branch. "Just a little farther."

The wind rustling through the tree scared both of them enough to turn around. They hurried back to safety just like they were little kids again, giggling once they got there.

"Good," Marli said. "I don't think it's worth getting mugged on the streets of an unfamiliar city."

"We should've made some friends and gone out as a group." Ellie took off her coat before climbing into bed.

"Yeah, that would've been a good idea. Food for thought, next time."

"Well, goodnight, Marli. Tomorrow—New Orleans!"

2

INTO THE SOUTH

The following morning, after a luxurious night spent in a full-size, non-rocking bed, Ellie checked the schedule to see if they could join a tour group to one of the old plantations. They'd heard their ancestors had owned a cotton plantation, so they wanted to visit one. Marli was looking forward to seeing some of those old Southern mansions.

Her interests and preferences in architecture were eclectic. Visiting the South each summer had fostered in her a passion for large, columned front porches; two- or three-story pointed roofs; attic space crammed with antiques; and large living rooms, kitchens, and pantries. Even now, when she'd think about it, she could still hear Grandma's back screen door whine, and catch wafts of that musty, dank, mothball scent of the pantry behind the sprawling kitchen. The paradox came with her belief that small was better and less wasteful. She enjoyed a simple line and efficient use. The weather in Southern California, where they lived, really didn't warrant extravagantly large houses. A small dwelling would suffice because it was temperate enough to be outside most days. But the South presented other challenges, like bugs and humidity.

It turned out, unfortunately, that none of the tours ended in time for them to make their train up to Jackson, Mississippi. Perhaps they could visit a plantation there. So they spent the morning wandering around the French Quarter instead and enjoyed a leisurely brunch of beignets and coffee.

⸻

After arriving in Jackson, they took a taxi across the city so they could pick up their rental car. Marli, who was prone to car sickness, sat in the front seat of the speeding cab. Almost any driver drove too fast for her comfort. Her right foot must surely have worn a divot in the floorboard as she pressed down on the imaginary brake pedal. This reminded her of riding with Uncle Parker. His large, boat-like Oldsmobile drifted and rocked as he barreled down long stretches of county roads. But she could feel almost oblivious to the sultry, bug-infested atmosphere outside while sitting comfortably inside that air-conditioned car, battling nausea as she looked out the backseat windows.

And now, belted into the passenger seat of their rental, greenery and cars whipped by outside the vehicle, turning her stomach again. She simply wasn't comfortable being hurled through space at seventy miles-per-hour. She sensed she might have been born in the wrong century.

It was odd that Marli wasn't the one driving. She almost always insisted on it. No matter who she was with, *she* was the one in control of the vehicle's path and speed, and therefore her stomach. But her sister had filled out the paperwork and used her credit card when she took over this portion of the trip. For the time being, Marli accepted it, almost with relief, since she sometimes tended to get lost. Besides, if she wasn't the one driving, Ellie would definitely be the best choice of anyone she knew. They had both been taught to drive by the best teachers ever. Safety first was their parents' motto.

Ellie had checked the AAA guide for plantation tours in Jackson, but again, none fit with their schedule. "How about the Governor's Mansion? They're offering a tour there at two o'clock."

"Okay. Why not? But that means we have to go right now." Marli navigated to the best of her ability, trying not to look down at the map for very long and risk getting carsick. After spotting their destination, Ellie drove around the block twice, trying to find the entrance onto the grounds of the formidable gray structure with its overly manicured grounds. They finally found an attendant who explained they weren't doing tours that day.

"Figures," Ellie muttered.

"Why don't we go park over there so we can think about what to do?"

Ellie pulled into a metered space and began reading the AAA guide again. Marli took a swig of water and rolled down the window. The heavy, damp air christened her face. They had stopped in front of an old church, just across the street from the Governor's Mansion. Statues in the courtyard graced the front, and arched stained-glass windows blended into the dark gray exterior of the building. Dense green grass and voluptuous vines decorated the foreground, muted by the subdued light cast by the cloudy sky.

"Look Ellie. Isn't it beautiful? It seems ancient. I want to go inside." Marli opened her door. "And *this* is free."

"Go ahead. I'm going to sit here and read." Ellie leaned the seat back and reached for her book.

Marli found herself relieved, suddenly aware of her desire to be alone. Perhaps her sister needed space as well. She walked up the path and through the courtyard, admiring the serenity of the statues and potted hydrangeas. She moved slowly, respectfully, and noticed the tall wrought-iron gates. After pushing open the enormous, lacquered wooden door, she stepped inside and stopped to let her eyes adjust.

Her soft-soled sandals muted the sound of her steps as she passed through a foyer and into a larger room containing more sculptures. Each one, she thought, must have a story to tell. The coolness of the floor crept upward, enveloping her feet, and she wondered if this church had been here pre-Civil War. A beautiful oak staircase beckoned from the corner, but it felt "off limits" somehow, so she walked straight ahead. She passed an ornate fountain, adorned with angels playing in the trickling water, and then into the sanctuary. She stood in front of the altar and looked upward, inviting God. Smiling, she took one purposeful step at a time toward the back in a walking meditation. Marli sat down in the last row and pulled her legs up into an easy pose, rested her open hands on her knees, and prayed. After a few cleansing breaths, she settled into a meditation, in spite of the musty aroma permeating the entire space. It felt peaceful and right. This place welcomed her.

"Are you almost ready?"

Marli opened her eyes and struggled to come back from somewhere within.

Ellie stood nearby, looking around. "It stinks in here. I'm going back to the car. It *is* pretty though."

Marli sensed that Ellie simply wasn't in the mood to linger, that's all. She took her time leaving and thanked the sacred space for holding her. She took a different way out, through a garden, and passed a woman sitting at a desk.

"This place is beautiful," Marli reverently whispered, and drifted back to the car to join her sister.

They drove northward, up the 55, past small, neglected communities and shacks on stilts. As they neared Canton, where their motel reservation awaited, the landscape opened up onto mowed fields, populated towns, and well-maintained businesses. In a couple days, Aunt Mae and Cousin Caroline would be meeting them. After checking in, Ellie chose the bed by the window and began to read her book again.

"I noticed a workout room downstairs so I thought I'd go exercise. It's been a while." And for Marli, it had. Four days with no aerobic activity is a long time for a dancer. She'd been teaching dance and gymnastics for almost thirty years and her muscles screamed for attention.

"All right," Ellie mumbled. "I'm going to stay here and try to finish my book."

The mini-gym was empty, thankfully. Marli preferred to work out alone. The room was small, so she moved a chair out of the way and unfolded a mat. She methodically performed her Kundalini yoga, rapidly breathing in and out through her nose using *breath of fire*; did her sciatica stretches; worked through an exercise routine she'd been doing and revamping since she was fifteen; and then relaxed into right, left, and center splits. She still had energy to burn, so she hopped onto the treadmill and jogged for another twenty minutes. Ellie walked in just as she finished.

"You want to go to dinner soon?"

"Yeah, just let me take a quick shower first." Marli stopped the machine and put the mat away before wiping the sweat off her forehead with the back of her hand.

"That would be a good idea." Ellie chuckled, lightening the mood between them.

Marli noted the effort.

The motel was on the outskirts of Canton near a restaurant, only a short walk away.

"I need a salad, how about you?"

"I agree," Ellie said.

"Hey, our appointment in Yazoo City is tomorrow, isn't it?"

"Yes, it is. I sure hope this attorney can help us sort out the property issues. He supposedly deals with land and trusts and things of that nature."

One of their missions while in Mississippi was to get Dad's property transferred into their names. Unfortunately, he had neglected to put it in his will.

3

YAZOO CITY

*M*arli and Ellie left the motel midmorning to have time to visit the old homestead before their appointment with the attorney. Taking the 55 north from Canton brought them just outside Pickens, where they had spent their childhood summers. Ellie took the exit off the highway and turned left over the old rickety bridge. They found the gravel road and followed it before turning into the driveway that led to "the old house out in the country," as Dad called it. This was an old habit of his, even though there was not much house left at all anymore. They knew the remains were almost completely hidden beneath the overgrown vines and fallen trees that made up "the woods" as it was known as around here.

Oppressive, muggy heat greeted Marli when she opened the car door. "We're gonna be sweaty messes by the time we see the lawyer."

"Yeah. Let's just look around for a little while. Where was the house, anyway?" Ellie asked.

"Somewhere in that tangle of jungle over there." Marli pointed past the uprights of the gas line that crossed the property. "Hey, remember that old, abandoned car we found last time we were here?" She thought about their trip back, over ten years ago, and how that car's frame had been completely stripped. There were no wheels, the windshield was bashed in, and ripped clothes and trash littered the ground. "It was kind of creepy, wasn't it?"

"Definitely. Very creepy. I'd suggested we leave since it was getting late. Then we found the set of keys in the grass."

"And then we went to report it to the sheriff."

Ellie squirmed. "All sorts of illegal actions were flashing through my mind, including rape and murder."

By the time Marli had backed their camper around to pull out of the driveway she had lost sight of Dad's RV. It had been many years since they'd been here back in their college days, and neither sister knew their way around very well. But Dad did.

"We wondered where on earth you could possibly be. You couldn't just disappear. I was so worried about it getting late and kept thinking about that ominous stripped car back at the crime scene and all—" Ellie looked toward the area they'd seen the keys, those many years ago. "I remember crossing the old rickety bridge and pulling over on the side of the road to wait for you guys."

"It *was* a little scary, I have to say." Marli listened to her sister continue.

"After about twenty minutes, but it seemed like forever, I finally spotted your truck's headlights in the side mirror. And then you got out and walked up to the driver's window."

"Yeah, Dad looked relieved and wondered what took us so long."

Ellie shook her head. "Do you remember what he had in his hand?"

"I do. A pistol! I told him to 'put that thing away before someone drives by and sees it!'"

Ellie clarified, "He just wanted to be ready, he'd said. As far as I was concerned, we couldn't get out of here fast enough!" Ellie sighed. "Let's talk about something else."

"Agreed."

They automatically started walking down the driveway before instinctively turning left down the path toward the pond. It was as if the body of water held some sort of gravitational force. Ellie swatted, in vain, at the mosquitoes, and Marli brushed a hanging vine away from her face. Tiptoeing along the path, looking out for poison ivy, they headed toward a small wooden dock.

"Someone's kept this place up," Marli said.

"I don't even remember this being here."

"I think it was. At least, ten years ago I think it was. Maybe not before that." Marli sat down on the old gray planks and dangled her bare feet in the water. "It feels nice. You oughta try it."

Ellie glanced at her watch. "We better go. I just wanted to see the place before the meeting."

They drove westward for half-an-hour before pulling into town. Marli remembered how, as a young teen, Yazoo City teemed with life. Every storefront boasted the best merchandise in town, luring you in with the promise of the latest fashion designs, the tastiest Cajun catfish with hushpuppies, John Deere's fastest riding lawnmower tractor, and the most stylish hairdo at the beauty parlor. Stuckey's advertised the frostiest malt, while the best prices could be found down at the Piggly Wiggly. Southern women with well-sprayed bouffant hairstyles tugged their children along sidewalks and discouraged their young-uns from staring at or getting too close to the elderly, unemployed men sitting on benches. Gentlemen wearing business suits tipped their hats and opened doors for ladies. When Aunt Iris brought Marli shopping here, they had picked out a light blue, polyester pantsuit, which became the fanciest thing she owned. Beyond the sidewalks, on the outskirts of town, the oil well riggings stood like prehistoric dinosaurs moving in slow motion. Their long, skinny heads with elongated tongues took turns with the angular rumps, pitching forward and rearing back, pumping oil up and out of the ground. "Y'all this and y'all that," floated over the din of the mosquitoes and cicadas that hovered above the lush green blanket of the Deep South.

But now, in August 2008, Marli and Ellie drove around and around the town, searching for an open restaurant—anything would do at this point. Their stomachs growled. Neither had been back here in over ten years. The moist, heavy air felt familiar, but the lack of people and traffic was bewildering.

"Everything looks closed here," Marli said. "Isn't this downtown?"

"Yeah, what's up with that?"

"There's a cafe, up there on the levy." Marli pointed and Ellie turned the rental car up the side street.

"It's a Mexican restaurant!"

"Wow, they'd never even heard of a taco or burrito the last time we were here." Marli thought back to a decade ago.

They'd spent the afternoon at "the old house in the country," just outside of Pickens. Dad had led them down to the pond to skip rocks across its surface. Uncle Parker's old aluminum boat was still there among the reeds, obviously used periodically by the locals.

The oil well stood tall in the clearing. She remembered its slow, steady movements, but it was seldom reliable enough even to create the tiny royalty checks that were dispersed between so many relatives. Marli wandered off behind a line of brush and looked off toward the neighbor's soybean crop. She'd taken pictures of the pond and the cotton plants around the oil well.

The group walked past the gas line station where they'd parked, and ducked through a barbed-wire fence. Ellie and Dad headed one way while she and Richard went another, looking for signs of the old house. The kids followed. It was difficult to find. The jungle had taken over.

She'd yelled, "Here it is! We found it."

Naked Ladies, also known as Amaryllis, presented their voluptuous, pink, tubular blossoms in profusion around the crumbling foundation.

Marli crouched down to smell them. Then, one at a time, they climbed in through a window opening. All the glass was broken and shards littered the ground. Dad went in from the other side. The whole structure was falling down and precarious. Marli and Dad tiptoed up the dilapidated stairs and carefully inched their way across the ancient oak bedroom floor, now exposed to the green canopy above.

Marli remembered finding an old chest of clothes up there when they were kids. Caroline tried them on and put on a little fashion show. She looked stunning in those beautiful antique dresses.

Dad had said, "This place was actually salvageable back then. I really wish I'd done it. Who knows? I still might."

She'd responded with how it was fun to think about, but not very practical.

"No, I guess not. But who cares?" he'd countered, distractedly.

Marli now pondered that option as they parked the car and entered the restaurant.

———

After lunch, Marli and Ellie still had an hour to kill before the meeting with the lawyer, so they decided to walk down Main Street.

"Where is that music coming from?" Marli wondered out loud.

There was nobody around. The sisters peered into each storefront they passed, wiping the dust away from the glass. There were beautiful wood-plank floors inside; canopied front door coverings; and age-old window displays with tricycles, Radio Flyer wagons, and mannequins dressed in seventies-style clothing. Ellie had an itchy rash on her arm, which she attributed to the poison ivy they must have encountered earlier while traipsing around the old homestead. She wanted to find some cortisone cream. The next storefront window displayed an old book of handwritten prescriptions from the early 1900s along with tins of powdered remedies and bottled tinctures. They cupped hands around their faces to see through the dusty glass door and it moved! The drug store was actually open!

Ellie went in to make her purchase while Marli stood there, captivated by the antique bottles, silver medicine spoons, pestle and mortar, and a large book containing old unreadable scrawl next to a tiny pair of spectacles. She again sensed that perhaps she belonged back in time, with these simple yet beautiful implements of the trade.

The door whined when Ellie came out. As they walked down the sidewalk, Marli noticed a small speaker on a lamppost.

"So *that's* where the music's coming from."

This felt so odd. There were huge urns spewing beautiful flowers, antique lampposts, and piped-in music here in this fossilized town. Of the thirty or so stores along Main Street, only two or three were open. Ellie walked ahead and Marli stopped at a gap between two old brick buildings. Here, there were tiered, bleacher-like board benches, with an aisle in between, leading down to a wooden stage with a lush, overgrown weeping willow backdrop. Old decaying planter boxes, now containing weeds, graced the outdoor foyer area and a rock-embedded stream flowed beneath.

"This is wonderful," she gasped.

The romantic, old-world appearance of the place fascinated Marli. Her mind reeled with the possibilities: staging outdoor performances, planning where dancers could change, and turning the building next door into a terrific dance studio… The creative juices began to flow and her head filled with ideas. Ellie turned back after her older sister had gotten sidetracked. Marli started to explain, but the words didn't come. Ellie was ready to walk ahead again.

"I need to sit here awhile and let all this sink in."

Ellie sat beside her on the bench. An old, dilapidated truck rattled across the street and slowed to cross the railroad tracks at the far end of town. The road became dirt down there. An instrumental version of "Moon River" played over the empty Main Street. Tears welled up in Marli's eyes as she imagined what was and what could be. An old man wearing dirty, rumpled overalls limped by, ducking between buildings, on his way to who knows where. She felt discombobulated in this depressed place. This area had borne the brunt of the economic down-turn, but somehow someone had enough hope to sugarcoat the town with fresh flowers and outdated Muzak. The bizarreness of this place, frozen in time, washed over her as she tried to make sense of it all, but couldn't, because it was time to go meet the lawyer.

———

"How do you do, ladies?"

"Hello, I'm Ellie and this is my sister, Marli."

"That's an interesting name," he said. "How'd you get that?"

"Well, my given name is Mary Ola, but somehow it transformed into Marli," she explained. "A nickname."

Ellie asked, "Are you related to the senator? You have the same last name. Landers, isn't it?"

"Yes ma'am, I'm his brother."

The aging, heavy-set attorney parked himself in the cushy office chair behind the large desk that occupied the center of the room, while the women sat in folding chairs facing him. The space was small and smelled of stale, humid air. This was the only law practice Ellie had been able to find in the area that dealt with trust and land issues.

"Your dad's friend, Nathan, works here ya know," he said.

"Well, actually, Nathan's father was our dad's best friend growing up," Ellie corrected him.

"Well, anyway, I know Nathan's family would be interested in your property, if y'all wanted to sell. I don't know what they'd pay for it though." The lawyer went on. "I've gone over the papers y'all sent me and we'll need a few more things. You see, your dad neglected to pay property taxes on your old family homestead the last time they were due. Under Mississippi law, the title is seized when taxes are not paid. Plus, he didn't put the property into his trust."

"But the will shows that Marli and I are his sole beneficiaries," Ellie said. "He'd been so weak and distracted during the last few months of his life. But we did pay the taxes, albeit a little late."

"Well, I'm gonna need the original will with the actual signatures. Also, you'll need to get a signed document from at least one of the witnesses to the will and preferably both," he drawled.

Marli shot Ellie a concerned glance, attempting to convey what a pain this thing was shaping up to be. "How would we find them, assuming they're still alive?"

The man scooted over in the groaning chair and turned on his computer. He came up with a couple of rather labor-intensive possibilities as to how they might be able to locate these individuals. Unnerved, Ellie gathered up the pile of papers needed to continue their quest while Marli attempted to lighten the air.

"Why are almost all the businesses here closed up and the streets so deserted?"

He responded, "High unemployment rate—they don't want to work—welfare and disability take care of 'em—"

Marli knew what he was referring to. The poor colored people, as they were called here, were still attempting to climb out of the deep hole Mississippi's white population had put them in and kept them in for far too long. People like their attorney may believe times had changed, but from this outsider's perspective, things hadn't changed nearly enough.

The attorney shuffled out of the room and shortly reappeared with Nathan, introducing his partner and son of their father's childhood best friend.

"It's so nice to meet y'all," said a fit-looking Nathan. He stretched out his hand to shake, radiating natural self-confidence and genuine interest. Marli sure hoped they could trust him. After all, it was he who was interested in their family's homestead.

4

MISSISSIPPI LAW

Ellie

*B*ack at the motel, Ellie reminisced about their extended family trip ten years earlier.

They had just pulled into the yard of what used to be their great grandparent's place, on Grandpa's side, down in Osyka.

She remembered Marli saying, after climbing out of the truck, "This adventure sure requires an awful lot of sitting."

"At least you get to drive," Ellie had complained. "Dad hasn't left the driver's seat since Texas."

"Well, you know him. I bet he will, though— it's too long a drive not to."

An older fellow puttered in the yard and came over to see who they might be.

"Howdy. I'm Will Vernet. My grandparents used to live here and had a brickyard down by the train tracks."

"Is that so?" the man drawled. "I'm Reese Butters. I bought the place, oh, 'bout nine years ago. I didn't know it had all that history on it."

Ellie struggled to make out the oddly pronounced words and figured the thick Southern drawl was going to rub off on Marli. She could feel it coming. It would happen all right. Anytime they came back here as kids her sister would return home with a touch of it. It was a little annoying. And it always seemed to take her a while to shake it, too.

Mr. Butters invited their family in and introduced them to his wife. They had iced tea, of course. It wouldn't be proper Southern hospitality without that. By the time the kids were ready to jump out of their skin from sitting so long, Mr. Butters offered to give them a tour of the property. Dad said it didn't look anything like it used to. But he also admitted he didn't have a very clear memory of what it really was like back then. He hadn't spent much time there.

After Mr. Butters went inside, the group walked back to their trucks. Dad said, "This is a fairly new house. Remember, I told you before, this was the place where my grandmother lived her final days. She was old and alone when the house caught fire. She never got out."

Fortunately, the kids had run ahead; she and Marli had heard that story before, but that didn't make it any less bothersome. At least her sister and her family had gotten out before their house burned down in 2003. She'd never given fire that much thought until it happened so close to home. It had been devastating to Marli and her family, losing everything. But somehow her sister had moved on—a changed woman. She shivered just thinking about it. Ellie didn't figure Dad had really known his paternal grandparents all that well. He'd spent his childhood north of here, in Pickens. That's even north of Jackson. It would have been a long trip back in those days.

She enjoyed seeing all the green the state had to offer, in contrast to Southern California, which didn't get nearly the rainfall. Osyka was a jungle, down in the swamp, but it opened up a little as they had driven northward through Jackson and on up the 55 into Pickens.

The next day, the sisters met Nathan out at the old place just as the sun was coming up over the pond. The deafening drone of the cicadas permeated the dense green forest and a trickle of sweat ran down the small of Ellie's back.

"Thank you for meeting us this morning. We really appreciate you coming out here before work," Marli said.

His family's land hugged around theirs in a U-shape, so he knew where the boundaries were. "Oh, it's quite all right. I come huntin' and fishin' out here during the season, but I don't often traipse through the woods in the summertime like this. I brought this stick to beat around in the underbrush to scare out the snakes. There are definitely water moccasins and copperheads out here."

Ellie hesitated. "I'll make sure to walk right behind you, maybe even in your same tracks." She followed him closely, eyes scanning back and forth.

Nathan waved his free arm, the one not holding the viper waker-upper, and pointed from the pond over toward the oil well and then to the soybean crop on his property. Then he swung around to indicate the old house site in the thicket past the gas line station on their dad's land. The painted pipes connected hip-height above the ground with various knobs and dials attached.

"I think the gas company retrenched that line recently, so I'm not too sure where it actually goes now," he said.

"They better not have," Ellie said. "Our dad denied them permission."

"Yeah, I remember that," Marli said.

"Well, y'all might have to look into it." Nathan turned into the woods, beating his stick at the grass ahead of him.

Tromping along behind, Ellie looked at Marli, more than a little concerned about coming across some cottonmouth hungry for a bite of native Californian. She was being diligent in scanning the dense groundcover, holding her breath every time she saw a potential danger—usually nothing more than a curved stick.

Suddenly, Ellie flashed back to that abandoned car frame she and Marli had just talked about yesterday, and the memory replayed.

Ten years ago, they'd caravanned into town and pulled up outside the sheriff's office to report the crime.

"It's locked," Dad had said.

"Well, knock on the door," Marli suggested.

He knocked and a woman answered. Dad introduced himself and a sheriff appeared.

"We have to keep the doors locked these days. There have been some hold-ups at a couple convenience stores lately and a man was killed just last week. It's gotten pretty bad around here," said the deputy.

This did nothing to take the edge off Ellie's nerves. She knew Dad wanted to camp out there at the old place that night. He filed a report and Ellie thought it might behoove her to gain this potential ally.

"Our dad wants to stay out there tonight," she said. "But that doesn't seem like such a good idea right now, does it?"

"Oh no," the woman replied. "There's a campground over in Durant. You'd be much better off over there." She proceeded to give them directions.

Once back at the trucks, Ellie recommended they go find the campground.

"It's not that far away," Marli added.

Oh good. At least her sister was on her side about this.

"Now wait a minute. Nothing's gonna happen. Remember?" He made his hand into the shape of a gun.

"No way," Ellie said. "Even that lady, Mrs. Butters, in Osyka, said times have changed up here and we should be careful."

"Oh, she doesn't know," Dad said dismissively.

"Well, I don't want to subject the kids to that. We're going to Durant," Marli insisted. "You do what you want."

That managed to change his mind. Thank God. They drove through the Mississippi darkness on to Durant, found the campground, ate supper in the campers, and bedded down for the night. Ellie got a much better rest that night, knowing some burglar wasn't going to come back and steal the rest of that abandoned car only to find them there as a new target.

Ellie jolted back when Nathan snapped a branch in two with his long stick. She wondered how long she'd been caught up in her memories.

"Is that an oak?" Marli asked, gesturing to a broad, towering tree above them.

"Yes ma'am, it is." Nathan pointed out a deer blind. "I usually just let 'em pass, but I let my son take one last time."

Ellie, still a little unnerved by her thoughts, asked, "Have things changed a lot here? I mean—as far as crime goes?"

Nathan stopped and turned around. "Yeah, they have. You've probably noticed some of the businesses have their doors locked. It's definitely *not* as safe anymore." He fanned the stick around his feet. "But I'd still rather be here than anywhere else. My roots and family are here."

"Of course," Ellie conceded.

"You know," he said, changing the subject, "these are mostly ancient woods. It's probably been close to a century since any of this has been logged."

"These trees are beautiful," Marli said, gazing upward.

"We're havin' a guy out next month to look at our woods for thinning out. You want him to look at these, too? It'd be worth some money."

"It would be a shame to cut this, but maybe he could clear out a little," Ellie said. She hadn't thought about the place actually making money before.

Walking through the undergrowth, carefully planning each footstep, the sisters made their way behind him. A mesmerizing

30

haze hovered over the pond and expanded through the woods, permeating the space between the trees. Sunlight trickled down through the canopy into broken shards of refracted light, softened by the high humidity. The drone of the insects amped up as the morning progressed and the mosquitoes were out for blood. Ellie swatted at them constantly. The three hikers ducked through a barbed-wire fence and headed into the neighbor's cornfield.

"It looks like possums have gotten into some of these stalks," Nathan said. "I don't know who these folks are on this side. I think they must be leasing this farm." He led the women along the edge of the property before climbing through another fence where it became his family's land.

Marli leaned down to examine a soybean plant and felt the long seed pods. "These leaves are a little brown around the edges. Is that normal?"

"Well, they were probably just sprayed," Nathan said. "We have to do that here, ya know. Those damned environmentalists would have y'all believe it's not safe and would just as soon have all our crops die. They have no idea what it takes to have productive farmland here."

Ellie watched Marli restrain herself when she simply said, "Oh."

After all, her sister was one of those "damned environmentalists." Ellie wanted to keep the peace and remain on his good side, especially since it was *his* law firm that was working on getting the property transferred from their dad. She was happy Marli did not bring up her usual spiel about eating local and organic and all that. Back home, her sister practiced her own small-scale farming: gardening, making cheese and yogurt from their own goats' milk, and eating home-grown food from her garden or what she traded for with friends.

Nathan pointed out poison ivy when they turned back into the dense woods. Upon examination, Ellie noticed it looked different than the poison oak they were familiar with. She realized they'd plunged through quite a bit of it this morning, as well as yesterday when they'd hiked around the pond.

After Nathan left, the sisters ducked back into the woods to the old house site and picked some Naked Ladies for their Dad's small memorial service at the Pickens cemetery the next day.

"I'm so glad they happen to be blooming right now," Ellie said. "It's perfect timing."

5

HONORING DAD'S WISHES

*M*arli couldn't believe Dad wasn't around anymore. Sometimes it seemed like he was still here—just off visiting somewhere else for a while—and at other times it was like he'd been gone for an eternity. Time existed in such a multidimensional way for her. She remembered Dad saying, about his brother some twenty-odd years before, "I still can't believe he's really gone." Uncle Parker had been a popular and well-respected attorney in Belzoni, Mississippi.

Dad's sister, Aunt Mae, and Cousin Caroline arrived from Atlanta and were meeting them at the motel in Canton. Marli now thought back to finding the old urn-like trophy at a thrift store, and how Dad would have probably appreciated her attempt at frugal creativity for his sake. While she was getting ready for the trip, she'd taken his ashes outside on the porch. Richard held the vessel as she tipped the bag to pour the dense, granular silt that was once Dad's body. The wind picked up during the process and carried some of her beloved father's spirit through their canyon.

Dad had grown up in the small rural town of Pickens during the Great Depression. He was the middle child of a storekeeper father and a schoolteacher mother. The three children were raised as Southern Baptists during an era in which religious worship took place in small, wooden churches scattered throughout the South. Later, he earned an engineering degree from Mississippi State.

Growing up in a strict and segregated community hadn't exactly prepared him for the eye-opening experiences Southern California had to offer. Dad had worked as a stress analyst at Convair, in San Diego, before serving in the Navy from 1944 to 1946.

In 1947, he'd attended photography school in Dallas, Texas. Then, after working in a photo laboratory in San Diego, he felt ready to embark on his own. By the spring of 1949, he was building his own lab in San Diego's backcountry.

Marli's parents' interest in photography, in part, was what helped bring them together. Dad systematically taught Mom shutter speeds and apertures while she helped him see the beauty in nature. She'd pose for this handsome photographer, leaning against massive, curved boulders or standing under blossoming oaks, and he shared the science of developing film with her. Even though he was thirteen years older and had much more experience, she seemed to have the more natural eye for creating a work of art.

Ellie and Marli were surprised how lax rural Mississippi law was concerning burials compared with California.

"What are the specifics for the burial container?" Ellie had asked.

"Oh, it don't really matter," the Pickens undertaker said. "You could even dig the hole yourselves if you want to." She had assured him they didn't.

Aunt Mae and Cousin Caroline arrived the day before the funeral and stayed in the same motel in Canton, just thirty minutes south of Pickens. After supper, the four women walked back into the lobby and sat down on the couch. The cable news blared loudly until Caroline got up and changed channels. She smoothed out her flowered skirt and shook her head. "I can't believe anyone would want to watch that."

"Hey now, I watch it every evening," Aunt Mae said, flustered that her daughter would interrupt her, now that her tired old body was seated comfortably. "I find it informative."

"That station? It's very biased, you know Mom." Caroline was her most educated and cosmopolitan daughter and served as a neurologist at a prestigious hospital on the East Coast.

The sisters, of course, nodded their heads in agreement, but didn't care to get involved in the mother-daughter dispute.

"Oh Caroline, could you go up and get those photographs out of my luggage? Let's show Marli and Ellie the pictures we found."

Caroline took the elevator up. Aunt Mae sipped from her water bottle and distractedly set it down on the lid. Everyone watched as it rolled off the table onto the floor. An African American woman was setting out dishes for the next day's breakfast and Aunt Mae signaled her to come over.

"I spilled my water here. Do you think you could go get something and clean this up?"

The woman paused.

"Oh, don't worry about it. I'll get some napkins, Aunt Mae," Marli said, and gave an apologetic shrug to the woman as she got up. This felt like a color issue. Marli figured she'd simply take care of the chore herself.

As she mopped up the spilled water, Aunt Mae said, "Why Marli, you don't have to do that. She was perfectly capable."

"Well, she was busy setting up for tomorrow. And besides, this really isn't her job."

Marli walked over to throw away the napkins and apologized to the lady for her aunt. These bygone behaviors and attitudes that her dad and his sister had clung to were a little irritating, not to mention downright embarrassing. She shook her head and joined her family on the sofa. She knew, though, that her aunt had meant no harm.

The incident got her thinking back to when she was a kid, sitting in the sun parlor at Grandma's house.

Uncle Parker had asked her, "Do y'all have colored folks out in California at your school? Are any of them in your class?"

She remembered squirming, having regretted staying inside this long before running outside to play. "Yeah, I think so." But she was actually thinking of the Hispanic kids. Some of them were her friends.

Marli learned later, as an adult, that Yazoo City did not fully desegregate public schools until 1970. By that time, the whites had already moved their children to their own segregated private schools to avoid, according to the Citizens Council, "the mongrelizing of the white race." Some figured the group to be the uptown Ku Klux Klan—a bunch of professional businessmen, leaders of the community. How appalling!

———

Caroline walked out of the elevator with an envelope and handed it to her mother.

"Thank you, dear." She pulled out a couple pictures. "Here they are," she said, pointing to an old, faded black-and-white photograph of a house in the woods. "That's the old house in the country. Wasn't it beautiful?"

The columned front porch shaded the seat swing that hung from the rafters, and a Model-A truck was parked in front.

"It sure was. I'd like to have a copy of that if I could," Marli said.

Aunt Mae smiled. "Sure, I brought a couple with me, figuring you would both want one."

"Great," said Ellie. "Thank you."

They took their time studying the photographs and swapping stories. But mostly it was Aunt Mae who talked, and talked, and talked. Each subject blended effortlessly into another for her. Aunt Mae was a fun, lighthearted person who thoroughly enjoyed life. Her enthusiasm and sense of humor contrasted sharply with their dad's missing footloose and fancy-free attitude. Finally, Marli yawned and realized how tired she was.

"I'm going to bed. We've got a big day tomorrow and I'm falling asleep."

This prompted them all to follow suit and call it a night.

———

There they were in Pickens, months after Dad's death, stepping out of the car onto the lush cemetery grass on that sultry Sunday afternoon. Arriving early had allowed the four women to wander around, read tombstones, and reminisce. Aunt Mae seemed to have known just about everybody laid to rest here. For over an hour, Caroline read the names out loud to her mother, who had by this time leaned against a tall grave marker topped by an angel, perched ready for flight. At least it provided a bit of shade.

"Did you know Jeb Benson, Mom? It says here he was born in 1921."

"Hmm, let's see." Aunt Mae scratched the back of her head. "I think so. He might've been the pastor's nephew."

Marli wandered off toward a quiet, secluded area to be alone with her thoughts.

———

Dad's headstone read:

WILLIAM VERNET
HUSBAND OF VIOLA VERNET
FATHER OF MARY OLA AND ELLIE MAY

Their father had mentioned to his sister what he wanted written on his headstone when she'd come out to visit last summer.

"Why you can't do that, Will. That's just not what you put on headstones," Aunt Mae had told him. "Y'all are divorced."

"Oh, yes I can," Dad argued. "I can put whatever I want on there. It's my grave!" That's just the way he was. Argumentative and stubborn.

———

Jim Cole, the Pickens undertaker, and his wife drove onto the grass and let their German Shepherd out of the car. The canine was a nice diversion. He ran around the perimeter of the closest grave markers before collapsing in a panting heap at Jim's feet. The elderly couple convinced Aunt Mae to sit in the air-conditioned Lincoln to cool off, rest her legs, and talk with Mrs. Cole. The three younger women walked over to the small, freshly dug hole. The headstone sat squarely near the crumbling edge of the wheelbarrow-size hole in the ground. The aroma of loamy soil and freshly mowed grass filled Marli's nostrils. It made her think of gardening and she remembered the Naked Ladies she'd left in the car.

"Just a minute," she told her sister and Caroline. "I'll be right back."

When she returned to the site, carrying the pink bouquet of slightly wilted flowers, Jim said, "Well, aren't those lovely. Your grandmother always had those in her yard, if I'm not mistaken. You know, I really liked her. She was a real sweetheart, but I'm sure glad I never had her as a teacher. I heard she was pretty tough. But after

I grew up I gave a report to the Rotary Club one time, and she told me I got an 'A.'"

Marli looked at Ellie quizzically, wondering how a grown man might still be seeking affirmation from an elementary school teacher.

"That sounds like her," Caroline said.

An elderly lady wearing a tan, stiff-brimmed hat, got out of a car parked along the street. She made her way over to the group using a cane to steady herself.

"Who's that?" Ellie asked.

"Oh. That's Mrs. Bates. I told her about the service yesterday," Jim answered.

"It's BB's wife, Ellie!" Marli said excitedly.

As she approached, Ellie reached out her hand. "Thank you so much for coming. Mrs. Bates, isn't it? And thanks, Jim, for inviting her. Our dad sure talked about BB a lot. He said they were best friends growing up."

"Well, BB thought a lot of your father, too," Mrs. Bates said. "Pickens was a different place back then. A lot like Mayberry was on that old TV show. Now everything's got to be locked up and you hear of folks gettin' held up at gunpoint. It's sure enough changed around here. This town used to be quite a bustling place. Your grandaddy's general store, the post office, the old Chevrolet dealership on the edge of town—"

Jim interrupted. "Ever since they rerouted the highway around Pickens, it just hasn't been the same."

"That's right," Mrs. Bates continued. "The businesses have shut down and all, and now we have to drive all the way over to Canton or Yazoo City for supplies. And don't even get me started on the lack of pride in our little town."

Aunt Mae got out of the car and everyone shuffled over to form a circle in the shade under a nearby tree. Heavy perspiration drenched their clothes and they continuously wiped sweat from their foreheads and out of their eyes. Anything said by anyone immediately sparked a monologue by Aunt Mae, who, Marli felt, had mastered the gift of gab to the highest degree. Marli, who was not an overly wordy person herself, almost admired her aunt's uncanny ability to provide these impromptu speeches.

But she finally interrupted. "What if each of us tells a story or a memory of Dad?" After a brief pause she added, "Something positive," and everyone laughed.

But this again derailed onto Aunt Mae's podium. "I remember Will had been a rather contrary child. He would absolutely refuse to do his homework in a timely fashion and insisted on sitting underneath the dining room table, while Parker and I sat properly, and diligently did our schoolwork. Our poor mother would end up stayin' up late just to help him—"

Marli looked up at the clouds, trying to remain charitable, and thought about the trials of a middle child. She imagined Dad must have felt sandwiched between his perfectionist older brother and his cute little sister who could do no wrong. He wanted attention, too. But his overworked parents had little time or energy to spare.

Grandma was a full-time schoolteacher, and for a while the principal, too, and Grandpa owned the only general store in town. There was probably no way he could outshine either of his siblings—so what other tact could he take for recognition? Of course, he'd seek out his share of attention— no, probably more like ensure it – by his only option: creating a ruckus. He'd wait until Brother and Sis and Pop had all gone to bed and Mother was finished with the dishes. At this point, she'd sit down with him at the table, one-on-one, and help him with his studies. This was probably his only chance of getting her full, undivided attention.

Aunt Mae's voice droned on. Her contributions weren't bad, though—a bit frustrating, but also a little humorous, as nothing formal had been planned for here, since they'd already had his memorial service in the spring, at home. Then Aunt Mae leaned backward a little too far and slowly toppled over onto the grassy knoll behind her. Jim and Caroline helped her up and insisted she go sit in the air-conditioned car again. She looked a little pale. But then again, it was wretchedly hot and muggy. Aunt Mae's topple ended any ceremony that might have been and everyone, except Marli and Ellie, trudged to the car.

Marli pulled the trophy urn from the paper bag and held it up by both handles.

"He really wanted to be buried in a wooden casket back in our canyon. I'd want that for myself, too."

"But it's illegal," Ellie said. "You could bury your ashes there, though."

"Yeah, I know. But it's not the same. You know what one of the things I'll miss about him is?" Marli continued.

"What?"

"His engineering advice. He could figure out how to do anything—whether it was building, fixing, or whatever."

"Mm hmm. He came over one time and fixed our electric gate. We weren't even home," Ellie said.

Marli looked around at the oak, mahogany, cypress, and cedar surrounding the decently maintained cemetery; the same kinds of trees covered the old homestead property. It reminded her of how claustrophobic she might get if she couldn't see far enough to get her bearings within a larger area. She realized then that she needed horizons.

During her childhood, when she was with Dad, Marli felt safe. He was strong, encouraging, and protective. That feeling of being safe was very reassuring to her. She believed he could do anything. Maybe that's why the word "can't" never crossed her mind. As an adult, the main things that would bring her parents, and her own family together were projects. And Lord knows there were always plenty of those to keep them all busy. Their work ethic was never lacking. So, those times were probably when she missed Dad the most—when she needed his advice on how to tackle the latest project. And that's what she had told the congregation at his memorial service at that little Baptist church near his house.

Marli gently placed Dad's urn into the ground and she and her sister got down on their knees and started burying Dad with fistfuls of fresh dirt.

"This is way harder than I thought it would be," Ellie sobbed.

"Tell me about it."

Their eyes filled with tears as they cried, "I love you, Dad" into the humid Southern soup. Marli laid the wilted flowers over the partially filled hole. The reality of losing him, of completing the trip back here and realizing both her parents were dead and gone, hit her like a freight train. Now she was the oldest living member of her family. The heavy atmosphere did nothing but reinforce to her the passing of this bygone era.

6

A SILLY NOTION

Ellie

"What do you think about rebuilding the old house in the country?" Marli asked Ellie over coffee, after Aunt Mae and Caroline left for home.

Ellie looked up and stopped eating her muffin mid-bite.

"You're not serious," she said, chewing slowly, then tipping her mug back as she waited for her sister's response. Not getting one she asked, "Are you?"

"Well—maybe." Marli hesitated. "Why not? It could be an adventure."

"Ha! What for?"

Ellie wondered why her sister would even consider such an outlandish idea. Is she mad? Perhaps she was just trying to entertain her with amusingly ridiculous notions. What purpose could it possibly serve? To rebuild a completely fallen-down house in a severely depressed area, without much hope of recovery anytime soon? Sounds like a pretty hair-brained idea. What on earth was she thinking?

"To honor Dad." Marli laughed. "He used to talk about it, you know."

"Not seriously, though. It was more like a pipe dream."

Marli pulled her fingers through her damp, limp hair. "But really, why not? It might be fun."

"I don't think so," Ellie argued. It's a good thing the relatives had already left. At least they wouldn't have to witness her sister losing her mind.

⸻

Later that morning, the women drove through the historic center of Canton to look for a gas station. Luxuriant, deep-green vines and pungent blossoms hugged the antebellum buildings, adding their fragrance to the humid air. A few pedestrians milled along the sidewalks, carrying on with their business of the day.

"This sure looks different than Yazoo City. At least this town seems to have some life to it," Marli remarked. "I love the old architecture. Let's hang around here for a while. That old Georgian courthouse building is gorgeous."

"It *is* nice. Canton is the county seat of Madison County, after all. Anyway, we need to get gas, and don't you still want to do some exploring?" Ellie asked. "We don't have much free time built into our schedule today." She glanced around. "Don't they have regular services here? Hopefully, there's a gas station at the other end of town."

⸻

They followed the road northward from Canton through French Camp, toward Mantee, and spent the afternoon driving the

Natchez Trace Parkway in their rental. Everything along the roadway was lush and green. Thick woods hid muddy swamps and rivers except when they crossed over bridges or passed by clearings. Huge mowers plowed menacingly beside highways, aggressively chomping branches, grass, and weeds that threatened to take over and reclaim their rightful domain. Kudzu climbed fences and houses, smothering anything in its path. The vine had been introduced from Asia as a hardy garden landscaping wonder, subsequently taking over the South.

Staring out the window at all that kudzu, Marli mumbled, "When will we quit with the assumption that man can do better than nature? More often than not, we seem to be our own worst enemy."

Ellie reminisced. "Hey, I was just thinking about when we used to come back here in the summers, as kids—driving our old station wagon with that big wooden box Dad built fastened to the roof of the car. It's amazing we didn't break down more often than we did."

"Yeah, and how the rear seat was folded down with a double bed mattress taking up the whole back of the car. And we always had to drive straight through to get here, with Mom and Dad taking turns driving."

"Not exactly kid-friendly traveling, huh? God! I'll never forget the torture we went through driving up those desert grades with the heater on so the radiator wouldn't overheat."

"And we'd just be in our underwear, wiping wet washrags over our faces." Marli giggled. "Hey, remember my gigantic doo-doo out in the middle of nowhere?"

"Ha!" Ellie laughed. "Oh yeah!"

"I don't think I'll ever forget that. I guess I complained long enough for Dad to eventually pull over long enough for his daughter not to explode in the car. And then Mom dug out our little potty chair."

The sisters laughed again, looked at each other and started cracking up.

"Dad even said it was the biggest doo-doo he'd ever seen in his whole life!" Ellie busted up.

They drove by a small settlement where a few two- and three-story houses looked as though they had seen better days. A deserted service station and convenience store appeared to have been abandoned years earlier.

"Do you remember those disgusting Stage Plank cookies?" Marli asked.

"Do I ever!" Ellie hadn't thought about those in decades. "We wanted those the most—only because they were the biggest. And then, after we'd already eaten half of it, we saw those worms crawling around in the chocolate? That was so gross!" She squirmed in the driver's seat at the thought.

"They were a nickel each. It was such a treat that we got to go to the store all by ourselves." Marli smiled, shaking her head.

Ellie remembered saving the cookies to savor on the back porch by Grandma's garden. Then Dad came out and saw the infested remains. He'd walked them back to the store to return the evidence for a refund. Dad always did try for fairness and justice.

Ellie asked, "Don't you remember Grandma's house seeming so big?" She paused in thought. "It's probably because we were kids."

"Well, it was huge compared to our house."

Ellie conjured an image of the old Southern house: Grandma and Grandpa's room off the kitchen, the next room their parents slept in, Aunt Iris and Uncle Parker in the front bedroom, Aunt Mae and her family upstairs. And of course, Aunt Daisy's old bedroom where she and Marli would stay.

On the way back to the motel she had an idea. "Let's go see the old Casey Jones Museum and railroad crossing."

"Okay," Marli said. "You know, I still have a box of railroad spikes we'd collected from the tracks outside that museum."

"Really? I don't remember where mine went. Bob probably tossed them out thinking they were just old junk."

Turning onto another dirt road, Ellie slowed to peer through the jungle on each side of the car. Old shanties here and there, and the occasional burned-down, abandoned homesteads dotted the hard-won open fields.

She stopped the car in the middle of the deserted lane. "I think that was a turtle back there! I hope I missed him."

"I'll go check," Marli said, already opening the car door.

Ellie watched her older sister run back through the mud and pictured a fugitive from the movie, *Oh Brother Where Art Thou*. She remembered Dad telling them it was filmed here. Every time they were out on these back roads she'd get a little nervous, aware of the dangers that might exist. Lynchings and chain gangs shadowed her thoughts. The box turtle was wiggling upside down in the road. She watched Marli carry it over to the grass, out of the street. A crushed armadillo, not the first they'd seen on this trip, lay outside her window.

After crossing a creek, Marli pointed to the left. "I think I remember the museum being over there."

Ellie stopped the car and looked in that direction, but couldn't see any structure at all. Dense brambles blocked the view. The sultry, stagnant air, containing the heaviness of melting asphalt, wafted in through the rolled-down windows, as if holding the past roadwork in memory.

"Huh. I'm pretty sure that's where it was."

"Well, it's definitely not there now."

After driving the back roads near Pickens for over an hour, they gave up and headed toward Canton. As they rounded a turn, Ellie saw a middle-aged man wearing a baseball cap picking up trash and throwing it into the back of his truck.

"He looks nice enough," Marli offered.

Ellie cautiously rolled down her window a few inches. "Hi there. We're looking for the old Casey Jones Museum, but can't seem to find it."

"Oh yes," the man said. He removed the cap and wiped his brow with a sleeve. "They moved it from Vaughan a couple years ago. I'm not sure where, though. Are you ladies from around here?"

They told the gentleman why they were here and their connections with family—the kind of conversation that remains very important in small town Mississippi. The sisters then decided they were done exploring for the day.

A few more miles down the road, Marli leaned her face into the air conditioning. "It's so bloody hot. Let's go swimming at the pond. Wouldn't that feel great?"

Ellie agreed. "Okay! One last visit out there before we go home might be nice."

⎯⎯⎯

The sun's rays slanted through the woods surrounding the pond as they parked the car on the gravel driveway.

Shouldering their backpacks down the trail, Ellie glanced around. "It looks like we're alone."

"That's good, because I'm planning to skinny dip."

"You rebel, you! You're such a bad influence." Ellie couldn't help but giggle.

The never-ending drone of the cicada orchestra enveloped them. Marli was the first to ditch the clothes, and piled them haphazardly on top of her satchel. "Last one in's a rotten egg!" She plunged knee deep into the water before performing a shallow dive, ducking her head under to cool off quickly. "It feels wonderful. Hurry up, you're missing out," she called.

"I'm comin', I'm comin'," Ellie said, stepping out of her shoes and leaving them next to her clothes. She waded out slowly, tiptoeing through the pond lilies growing around the edge. The refreshing coolness wrapped around her legs and a yellow butterfly landed on an overhanging branch. The absolutely still air made her a little uneasy.

Most of the numerous lakes, ponds, and swamps in Mississippi are muddy, semi-stagnant bodies of water filled with scum, assorted fish, and water moccasins. But this half-acre pond, on this piece of property the sisters inherited from their father, happened to be spring-fed, with almost crystal-clear water. The constant inflow of fresh water, combined with the continuous emptying of dirty water over the spillway, created a perfect swimming hole for even the faint-of-heart. Even those who wouldn't dream of getting in anything other than a heavily chlorinated, sparkling swimming pool could find respite in this fresh oasis out in the woods.

Marli swam over to the west side of the pond and pulled herself up onto the dock. An old aluminum boat rocked gently, tied to the far side of the wooden deck. She walked to the end, placed her hands at the edge and kicked into a handstand before flipping over into the water. Ellie got out, ran down the dock and canonballed into the pond. They behaved as though they were children again— with wild abandon.

"I wish we had this at home," Ellie panted after coming up for air.

"Yeah, me too." Marli rolled over to float on her back. "I miss him, you know? I remember when the rains came so hard, that winter after the fire, and threatened to take out our new foundation. I'd trenched our side yard to keep the running water from washing away the tiny bit of flat area out there and Richard dug a ditch behind the house to divert the water." She kicked a mosquito off her foot. "Dad came over to help out and he showed me where I should trench and bury drain pipe to save the east side of our foundation. Forever the engineer, you know? I crawled around on my belly, on the muddy ground underneath the porch, and used a metal shovel with no handle to drain the standing water. The ground was so soft. I remember—we both cheered when the water started flowing though the channels I'd made. Aah, the minor successes."

"Yeah, he spent a lot of time at your place."

"Well, he liked coming up. He must've been lonely living by himself for so long."

"He could've come over to see us more often," Ellie snipped. She remembered Dad telling her about fixing Marli's truck taillight the night before they were leaving on a trip. Why hadn't he come by their house more often? They had things that needed fixing, too.

"But you guys are never home. And if you are you're always busy. Besides, he rarely announced when he might show up. Sometimes I'd be busy, but I'd always offer him coffee or a beer. Or, if no one was home, he might just fall asleep in the recliner."

"But he sure did a lot more for you guys than for us," Ellie said.

"And we did more for him. What goes around comes around."

Ellie wanted to get away from her sister. What a self-righteous thing to say. Marli had no idea what her life was like, always trying to please everyone: making sure their social engagements were arranged—as per Bob's expectations, catering to all her real estate clients' demands, and making sure her daughter attended the right cheerleading camps and modeling gigs. She swam under water and came up behind Marli to splash her. "Race you back!"

They free-styled back to the shore and Ellie actually got there first, a rarity considering Marli's level of fitness. But her sister had gotten a delayed start, perhaps still caught up in memories. Anyway, Ellie relished the triumph. They walked through the shallow water breathing heavily.

"God that felt good, didn't it?"

"Yeah," Ellie said, quickly getting dressed. But she was not in the mood for any more talking for a while.

Marli

Riding back to the motel, in the measured silence, Marli felt her sister's disapproval and turned her thoughts inward. She reminisced about a time she and Dad had talked about the old house in the country.

Richard had been doing dishes at the kitchen sink, TJ was playing Legos at his end of the table, and Jasmine and Sage were playing cards. She and Dad were lingering after dinner over glasses of wine.

"Hey, do you remember the layout of the old house? You know, where each room was?" she'd asked.

"Yeah, sure I do."

He started to remind her, but she told him to "hold on" while she got some paper. After sitting back down and brushing crumbs off the table she wrote OLD HOUSE on the top of the page.

"Was it basically a rectangle shape?" she asked.

"Well, I guess it was, sort of. Or squarish," he said.

He tipped back in his chair, the front legs lifting off the floor, and gazed upward at the log house ceiling. As he leaned back down, he rubbed the side of his aging face, more like his right ear, as if it bothered him. He used to do that a lot.

"Well, it was one of those dogtrot houses where most the rooms opened off the wide central hall. In the old days folks would keep their huntin' dogs in the middle where they wouldn't mess up the rest of the house. The kitchen and dining room were kind of one big room. Well, not that big. And there was a small bedroom and a sittin' room—all downstairs," he said. "There was a wraparound porch with cypress columns."

Marli sketched a rectangular box with her stubby pencil and fantasized about those old Southern homes. She took a sip of Merlot. She remembered like it was yesterday.

"Am I drawing the bedrooms right? Kind of like this?" She used the side of a book for a straightedge. "And the kitchen went like so?"

"Well, you know, a long time ago the kitchens were always a separate room—out back behind the house. And a lot of times those kitchens would burn down since they were cookin' on open fires and all. The kitchens in those houses were added on later, like this one was. And they were always in the back part of the house since that's where the help came in. The fireplace was near the middle of the house."

"Oh yeah," she remembered. "A lot of those old houses had the fireplace opening into more than one room, huh?"

"Mm hmm. The staircase was off to the side of the sittin' room." He gestured with his hands. "And there was a breezeway in back, separating the carriage house."

"About what size were the rooms?"

She could almost see the cogs turning in his head as he gave her approximate dimensions, while pointing at the paper, as she sketched his explanations. Marli drew the upstairs bedrooms on a separate piece of paper. They each got their own brand of "charge" from this kind of shared activity. She'd always loved old houses and he seemed happy that she was interested in Pop's old place. She remembered the general layout of the old house, but she wanted to include him. This was just one of the many, many evenings that her dad would stay for dinner and hang out later for conversation and good company before he'd inevitably say, "Well, I'd better head back to town; it's gettin' late."

———

Drifting back into the car ride, moving away from her reverie, Marli watched the trees whip by the side window. Enough time had passed for the sisters to have processed their private thoughts.

Ellie said, "I don't have time to rebuild the old house, but if you really want to then maybe you should just go ahead and do it. But I'm not paying for any of it."

But the thing was, Ellie was kind of joking, and Marli eventually realized that she might not be.

———

The next day they boarded the train in Jackson. Minutes earlier, during a short walk through the area of broken-down brick buildings surrounding the train station, Marli was reminded that things were different now. Change was constant—good or bad, for better or worse.

The locomotive jerked into motion as the steel wheels bumped over the rugged railroad tracks. They left Mississippi in the pouring rain. Marli tried to set her sights on whatever was yet to come. She could almost hear the melody on the rocking of their train: *The City of New Orleans.* Arlo Guthrie so reverently sang, *"Good mornin' America, how are you? Don't you know me? I'm your native son... This train has got the disappearing railroad blues... Through the Mississippi darkness rolling down to the sea..."*

And so began the final leg of their trip, having accomplished what they set out to do. Leaving Dad in his Mississippi homeland and heading back into their own lives, 2,000 miles away, tugged at Marli's heart. She was completing the circle of life, figuratively and physically. They had moved up a generation in their family status. And they were making a loop by train instead of going back the same way they had come. And yes, now boarded on *The City of New Orleans,* they'd "be gone 500 miles when the day was done."

7

FEMALE COMRADERIE

*B*urying her father was hard on Marli that summer, but the long train trip had allowed time for reflection. The railroad had been the right mode of transportation. As rewarding as the trip down South was, she was glad to return home to family and friends. She hadn't known that modern-day trains did not have operational windows and she had suffered headaches from the stale air. They'd gotten off the train at every stop (only a couple per day), claiming to be smokers so they'd be allowed to step out. Yes, it was discrimination to only allow smokers off, but that was the rule when it was only to be a brief halt. Therefore, to her, it felt like a justifiable fib.

Ellie had left her car at the train station in Oceanside. On the way home, Marli insisted they stop to get fresh vegetables so she could resume her mostly vegetarian diet that very same day. Ellie dropped her off and they hugged goodbye. Marli's dog jumped up and licked her hands, greeting her in the driveway. "I'm so glad to see you too, Simon." She sucked in that delicious, healing country air. All the windows in the house were open and the warm, gentle breeze caressed her thankful skin. And it was great to see her family again.

Richard hung up the phone and gave her a hug and a kiss. "I missed you."

"I missed you, too. But I'm real happy we went. I think it was good for Ellie and me."

Their fifteen-year-old son, TJ, came into the log cabin carrying a basketball. "Hi Mom. Did you have a good trip?"

"Yes, I did. But I missed you." She brushed his long hair out of his face and hugged him tightly.

—————

The next weekend, Marli invited her three comrades over for a potluck dinner—she'd thought about them on the trip as well. Tilda brought special ingredients to make leek soup. Rose came in through the kitchen door and uncovered a tray of cut veggies and a raw coconut-mango pie. Carol showed up late, as usual, carrying a brown bag with brie, crackers, and a bottle of wine. Marli's contribution was her old standby: tofu mess and homemade feta cheese from their goat's milk.

"How was the trip with your sister?" Tilda asked.

"It was good. We saw our aunt and cousin. And the train was definitely the way to go."

"I'd like to do that someday," Rose said, sipping her chardonnay. "But I can't see John letting me go anywhere without him—not for very long, anyway."

Marli shrugged to her friend. "You never know."

"Don't you think it's time you made some of your own decisions, Rose? Your kids are grown and he's always at work. Besides, you have a job. You could use your own money," Tilda said.

Rose frowned. "It's complicated."

Marli knew Rose had a rough childhood. Her father had been a domineering, patronizing religious fanatic who'd left his family to preach the gospel to "the primitive heathens in third-world countries." Her mother had been a basket case who threatened suicide on numerous occasions. Rose had married young, after finding a strong, stable husband in John. He loved her and paid for her on-again, off-again horse therapy. She claimed it allowed her to "move on."

Carol cleared her throat. "Sometimes absence makes the heart grow fonder. Tell that to John."

Marli changed the subject. "Everything's so green back there. The jungle takes over everywhere it can. We had to really hunt around to find the remains of the old house. There's not much left anymore."

"I'd like to take a trip, too, one of these days. I've never been to the South," Carol said, dreamily. "And I can't believe school's starting in less than a week!" She was a tenured social studies teacher at the local high school. "My room is *so* not ready. There are stacks of books, piles of art supplies, and chairs and clutter everywhere. It's complete chaos!"

"Well, that's how it always is for you this time of year, isn't it?" Rose asked. "What would you do with yourself if it was any different?" Her smile had a way of lighting up the entire room.

"Yeah, Carol, what would you ever do if things were calm and organized?" Marli teased.

"Well, I'd like to see that someday," Carol answered, grabbing a chip and dipping it into the hummus.

"Uh-huh, you know that's how you function best." Tilda's laugh was loud and unique. She clinked glasses with Rose.

Changing the topic, Carol said, "I've been painting my bedroom again. Oh Tilda, you should see the color I found. I know you'd love it. It's close to the same color you have on that one bathroom wall.

It's this fantastic reddish mauve, very rich-looking, and it almost seems like it has its own texture."

She waved her arms around, demonstrating painting motions and directions of walls. When Carol got stressed, she repainted the walls in her house. She was obsessed with it. Her creativity consumed her. Her latest idea was to collect chairs—from yard sales, thrift stores, and cast-offs from the side of the road—and include them in these painting episodes. Only time would tell what the finished product might look like.

"This is smelling quite wonderful, if I do say so myself." Tilda held her long red hair out of the way to lean over the pot. "Marli, you want to try this?"

"Sure." She opened her mouth around a spoon containing the pale broth, which had a mild onion aroma. She savored it for a moment, furrowed her brow in concentration, and swallowed thoughtfully. "Mmm, that's really tasty. What's in it?"

Tilda stepped back, still stirring, and placed her other hand on her hip. She looked like a movie star. Tall, lean, and sleek. "Well, leeks and garlic, of course. Some mushrooms, garden tomatoes, olive oil—"

"You've got a real knack for creating these yummy concoctions," Marli said. "And you look fabulous, too, by the way."

"Well, thank you. I do clean up pretty good. Don't I?" Without waiting for a reply, Tilda asked, "What's in that pan?"

"It's just my tofu mess again."

"Oh good. You know, we're never disappointed with your tofu mess. Here, let me taste it." She grabbed the spoon and slipped it into her mouth. "Mmm." Preparing to second dip, Marli swiped the spoon from her.

"Oh, no you don't. Wait for dinner."

"Like it would actually kill you to share my germs," Tilda teased. "You know, we could all eat out of the pan when you're out of the room and you'd never know it. Would she?" she asked, addressing the others who were already laughing.

"Give her a break. We all have our issues," Rose defended. She was the smallest and youngest of the group, by a couple years, and always the peacemaker.

Marli did have a thing about germs. Sharing utensils or eating out of the same bowl as someone else bothered her. She maintained she'd catch fewer colds and stay healthier if she didn't ingest others' germs unnecessarily.

Tilda had always made herself at home when she'd come over, opening the refrigerator and eating whatever looked good. She was a grazer, as long as Marli had known her. Her musician friend, who was her roommate back in college, had been a struggling artist and old habits were hard to break.

Rose uncovered her veggies and she and Carol dipped bell pepper wedges and radishes into the zesty homemade jicama sauce.

"What a lovely presentation of colorful beauties. You're so artistic, Rose," Marli said, walking over to sample some herself.

"But I'm not the artist," said Rose. "We all know which one of us that is."

"Hardy-har-har." Tilda often went on about the beautiful music she played on her violin and how she was a "true artist." Whether or not it was because of her Russian descent, she was not shy about tooting her own horn.

"I wonder which glass I should pick tonight," Carol wondered aloud as she lifted each one up to the light to examine the artwork on it. A few years before, they had all gotten together over at her house, and after their usual potluck, had sat around the table painting dishes. They had made six place settings, each containing a goblet, plate, and bowl. There were also a couple of cobalt blue margarita glasses. Rose had a thing for hearts and that was one of her motifs. Tilda had a very detailed, Egyptian theme going on. Marli painted a rendition of her mom's long, brown braid on the glass, while the plate and bowl had her usual doodles of donkeys and Pampas grass. Carol managed to create "salt" on the margarita glasses and Marli convinced her to draw a naked lady, breasts and all, on a wine glass. Carol had bought these dishes for them to decorate and then gave them to Marli after her family had lost everything in that fire. So anytime they all got together at Marli's new house, the special dishes came into use. She displayed them in a lawyer's bookcase in the corner of her dining room.

Marli pushed her plate aside, after eating a little bit of everything. "I'm stuffed."

They all were, but kept sampling anyway. Marli started to tell them about her trip "down South" and "the old house out in the country"—as her dad had liked to refer to it, even though the house had fallen down and been reclaimed by the woods surrounding it.

"Those old Southern houses have a certain charm with their cypress columns and big front porches," Marli said, showing them her drawing of the old house she'd done with her father. Then she pulled a pad of graph paper from the cupboard and put it on the table. No words were needed since they were all visual, hands-on types who loved jumping into creative projects together. They each grabbed paper and pencils and began to sketch.

"Here. I think yours needs a porch right there," Tilda instructed, leaning over to Carol's diagram, adding her own lines.

It was fun—more wine, more drawing, and lots of laughing. Marli drew a claw-footed bathtub into the upstairs bathroom on her sheet of grid paper. How she loved antique furniture and dishes. Rebuilding their house had been all-consuming when she took on the project as owner-builder instead of hiring an expensive contractor. Richard had done his best to step back and let her take over. It was as if she'd become a runaway locomotive, a force to be reckoned with. She needed a house she loved because home was a sanctuary to her, to them. And their new home, like the old 1920s craftsman-style house they lived in before the fire, was beautiful. And welcoming.

And then she said it. It just sort of tumbled out of her mouth. "Why don't we do this? I mean, really do it. We could, you know? Go back there, get some help, and rebuild this puppy. At least the finishing touches. A local crew could build it. Wouldn't it be a great adventure? We could camp out on the land—maybe next summer?"

"Yeah, like I could find the time to do that." Tilda snorted. "Besides, how could you afford it?"

Marli got up to get a drink of water. "I don't know yet."

Rose started to have fun with the idea. "What are we doing here anyway? Aren't we worth finding the time for?" She took a joking stab at Tilda. "What's life for if we don't jump on a raft once in a while and just see where it takes us?"

"Hey, did we change the subject?" Carol asked. "What's this about rafts? I heard there's water moccasins back there!"

"Don't worry, Carol," Marli said. "You'll be on the raft. I'll be the one swimming in the water. Besides, it's beautiful there. It's a spring-fed pond. Not one of those murky, stagnant, green ponds like most of them."

The evening continued with raucous laughter and stimulating conversation until everyone was yawning. Marli walked them out to their cars and opened and closed the gate. She stood outside in the moonlight and gazed at the shining boulders up on the mountainside. The view never got old to her. She could hear frogs down in the creek bed and wondered what their chorus was really about. She gave her Australian Shepherd a pat on the head and meandered back to the house to get ready for bed and snuggle in next to Richard, who'd made himself scarce the last few hours.

8

THE IMPORTANCE OF MONEY

Ellie

*D*uring the two weeks following the train trip, Ellie was in constant motion. Clients had been calling, paperwork was piling up, and she had just managed to clinch a sale on a relatively large estate when she woke up one morning with the phone ringing.

"Hello Ellie. This is Theresa. I just heard that the girls' section of the cheer competition has been moved up a day, to Wednesday. I can still take them, but I wanted to let you know as soon as I found out."

"Oh wow. Thank you so much, Theresa. I don't know what I would do without you. I'll have everything ready for her this evening." Ellie hung up the phone, cancelled her four o'clock showing, and jumped in the shower before cramming her remaining day's obligations into five hours instead of the usual eight to ten.

By five o'clock that night, Ellie was hugging Madison goodbye when her husband walked in the door.

"Bye sweetie," Bob said and gave his daughter a peck on the cheek. "What's for dinner, honey? I'm starving." He set his briefcase on the small, covered table in the foyer and hung his coat on the hook before heading to the refrigerator to peer inside.

"I don't know," she said. "I'm exhausted. How about we order takeout. Chinese?"

"Sure. Sounds fine." Bob poured a glass of a vintage Pinot Noir and asked, "Would you care for some?"

"Yes. I could really use it tonight. I haven't had a break since I got back from Mississippi." Ellie called in their usual order. She sat down to join Bob and took a slow swallow from her glass. "You should have seen the urn Marli put Dad's ashes in. It was a cheap little trophy she'd picked up from a thrift store! She even had the lid fastened on with duct tape. Can you believe it?"

"You're kidding. How disrespectful. You should have bought one at the funeral parlor."

"I know. But she seemed to think he would have somehow appreciated the way she went about it. A tribute to his frugality or some such thing. It's fortunate Aunt Mae and Caroline never saw it. They were already heading to the car when we buried it. Anyway, what's done is done. And, you'll never guess what else—"

"What?" Bob asked, turning the page in *Fortune* magazine.

"She wants to rebuild the old house in the country. Unbelievable!"

"What, really? I hope you told her how impractical that is. Isn't it way out in the sticks?"

"Yes, and of course I told her. But I doubt it made much difference." She pushed a stack of mail over to the side.

Bob poured another glass. "That's why she's always just been a struggling *artist*. A dreamer. Where does she think the money will come from anyway? Has she even thought about that?"

Ellie traced her finger around the rim of her glass. "I don't know. She's a little like Mom, I guess. Always imagining how something *could* be."

Bob left the room to change his clothes and Ellie drifted into thoughts of Grandma's house in town, where they visited when she was a kid.

There had been enough room for all three of Grandma's children plus their families to stay there. The sun parlor was the hub of their Sunday afternoon chats and it shared the three-way fireplace with the living and dining rooms. The kitchen table was large enough for all fourteen of them to share meals together. The carriage house and garage were off to the side, with an old buggy parked in one and a Model A in the other. That house had seemed like a mansion, but it really wasn't.

Aunt Daisy stayed in the added-on studio apartment during the 1960s after living in Belzoni and before moving into a nursing home. She was Grandma's spinster sister. She had enjoyed living by herself, but at a certain point her brothers decided it wasn't safe for her to be alone anymore and insisted she move into their sister's place. Grandma took care of her for years.

Most of Ellie's memories probably came from stories she'd been told, since she was three years Marli's junior, and the family trips back East had stopped when she was still pretty young. She recalled Dad telling her about one time when Grandma was in the bathroom with Aunt Daisy, trying to get her to take a bath. Aunt Daisy, however, wanted no part of it and evidently put up quite a fuss. Grandpa banged on the wall and yelled, "Daisy, if you don't get in that tub right now and quit your hollerin', I'm comin' in to pick you up and throw you in! You understand?" Well, apparently that did the trick and she complied with Grandma after that. Stories like that hung around for decades.

The old place in the country had been left to Dad's Uncle Hank, and then to Uncle Spencer. He later willed it to Uncle Parker, the oldest of Grandma's children. Since he didn't have any kids of his own, he'd then willed it to Dad. He'd had a bad heart, as did both his siblings, but his was by far the worst and it took him out when he was not quite seventy. Dad's didn't quit until he was eighty-seven. His Uncle

Spencer died of a heart attack while mowing his lawn one summer morning. Ellie supposed going quick like that had its advantages. Uncle Spencer enjoyed working in his beautiful green yard. He could have easily afforded to pay someone else to do it. After all, he was a wealthy lawyer. She remembered Dad had always tried to carry a hidden hundred dollar bill in his wallet, whereas Uncle Spencer's mad money was $1,000, even way back then.

Uncle Spencer and Aunt Charlene's house was in Belzoni, not too far from Uncle Parker's. Ellie vaguely remembered having tea with her folks there as a child and how everybody seemed to have help, a housekeeper/cook to almost invisibly keep their households running smoothly. They all were very gracious and hospitable, but there was so much sitting around talking, and talking, and talking.

Both sides of the family had come over as colonists. In French, the name Vernet has something to do with an alder tree by the water. She and Marli each had a family genealogy booklet containing three generations: 1735-1850. This document contained papers relating to the early family history, including copies of old Revolutionary War and War of 1812 company payrolls, pension declarations, land grant deeds, colonial land plats, accounting ledgers, passports—Ellie realized she and Marli really were Daughters of the Revolution. From both sides! But weren't they a stern, conservative group? They probably wouldn't care much for the likes of us liberal women, she thought. Oh well, they can't deny us our birthright.

The doorbell interrupted her daydream and she grabbed her purse to pay the delivery guy for their takeout order. Bob returned from the bedroom, having changed out of his suit and tie into shorts and a Stanford T-shirt. Ellie sat down to divvy up the containers. "At least my sister seems to respect our family's history. So I can sort of understand where she's coming from."

"Wait a minute, Ellie. You're not going soft on me, are you?" Bob asked, dipping chopsticks into his Kung Pao shrimp.

"I don't know," she said, smoothing a napkin over her lap. "Why have *I* always had to be the one to chase the almighty dollar, when I would have much rather been home with our daughter more, and been a teacher or something. You make plenty of money for the both of us." She wondered how things might have been different.

"Because that was our agreement," he said. "You know it takes both our incomes to support our lifestyle. And I, for one, really like where we are. Don't you?"

"Yes, maybe *where* we are, but *who* are we? We hardly ever see each other we're so damned busy. I'm kind of tired of it myself," she said, shifting uneasily in her chair.

"Well, you sure as hell can't use any of *my* money for a cockamamie, hair-brained idea like rebuilding an old collapsed heap of crap out in the backwoods of some swamp!"

The argument grew in intensity and ended with Ellie sleeping in the spare bedroom. Bob left early for work the next morning and she lay in bed tossing and turning.

She remembered Aunt Mae telling them how the old house out in the country had been built by her grandfather, on Grandma's side, when he was only twelve years old! His father had been killed in the Civil War, and as the man of the house, he brought his mother and younger siblings there to homestead. On the Vernet side, Dad's grandparents had owned the brickyard down in Osyka. That house had caught fire and taken his grandma's life with it. When Ellie's sister and Richard rebuilt their house after the fire in 2003, Dad had given her a brick he'd saved from that brickyard. A "V" was inscribed on the face of the brick and was now centered in the stone hearth of their log cabin. How come she hadn't gotten one of those bricks, too, come to think of it? She and Madison, along with Marli's family and Dad, had visited the old place in Osyka and talked to the older folks who owned it. Very few things were the same. But what could one expect? That was in 1998. She recalled the trip fondly. At least Dad got to share his heritage with them in person. And that's worth a lot.

With that thought she rolled out of bed and called Marli.

"Do you still want to go down to Dad's duplex today?"

"Yeah," Marli answered. "I'll pick you up at ten o'clock."

After their father passed away, the sisters had collected any important bank statements they could find. They could've missed some that were covered up by less important papers, piled everywhere in his duplex. Having been raised during the Depression, he tended to save things—most things. Rabbit trails traversed his house, snaking through the living room, bedroom, and kitchen. All areas overflowed with stuff: tools, electronic equipment, boxes, magazines, and more.

The sisters rummaged through boxes from Dad's bedroom closet that morning.

Ellie held up a safety deposit box key and said, "Look what I found hung in the bathroom."

"Well, I'll be darned," Marli drawled.

"Does this mean another adventure to the bank is in order?"

"Yes, I suppose it does." Marli smiled at her sister.

They took the death certificate and a copy of the trust and headed to the bank. Ellie signed in to wait for the next available manager before sitting in an overstuffed chair to read the paperwork. This was the sixth financial institution they'd visited since Dad's death. His affairs could have been in better order.

After examining the documents the women brought with them, the bank manager explained, "There should have been another form here. This doesn't look quite right."

Why was this always so difficult? Everywhere they went, following his trail of assets, obstacles were thrown into their path. This time, though, they were ready. The man disappeared to retrieve yet another form and was gone at least twenty minutes. A teller came over and asked them if they had been helped yet.

"We just want to put something in our safety deposit box," Ellie lied. "We've been waiting quite a while now. Could you take us back there, please?"

"Yes, of course," the teller replied.

Marli leaned over to Ellie and whispered, "Nice one. You sign the ledger. Your initials are closer to his. Just make it sloppy, like he would've."

Ellie was glad her little fib was appreciated.

After committing the "not quite" forgery, they scuttled through the double doors, looking over their shoulders to make sure the coast was clear. The teller unlocked the drawer and showed them to a private stall.

Lifting the lid of the box, Ellie saw two rolls of coins and shoved both into her purse. "He said I get the coins."

Her sister frowned before taking out the only other thing left, a plain white business envelope labeled *MISSISSIPPI*. Marli slipped it into her shirt pocket. They took the box back to the teller and headed toward the exit as the manager came out and waved some papers at them.

"Sorry, we're in a hurry and must be going now. We'll be back another time. Thanks anyway," Ellie said, snatching the forms from him. The sisters hustled to the parking lot and drove off with Marli gunning the engine. Ellie felt like a fugitive in a getaway car.

Once on the freeway, Ellie asked for the envelope. "I want to see what's in it."

Marli took the mystery envelope from her pocket and handed it to her. Ellie broke the seal and pulled out a yellowed page. She carefully unfolded it and written in Dad's shaky scrawl was a note she read out loud.

You probably won't be reading this until I'm gone. As you know, I've thought a lot about rebuilding the old house in the country in

Mississippi, but never got around to doing it. When Mother died, she left me $100K that she inherited from Uncle Spencer. I saved another $100K and put it all in a Franklin Fund. If Marli and Ellie care to build the house back up again, this amount should now be sufficient to do so. I'd like to think there could be something back on the Mississippi property to stay in or rent out. If neither want to take this on, then please think of something you can both agree on that y'all feel I'd approve of. Love, Dad.

"Wow," Marli said. "I didn't expect that. Did you?"

"No. I sure didn't. What should we do?" Ellie asked. "How about we each take half?"

"I'd say—" Marli backed off the accelerator. "How about actually using it to rebuild the old house? Like he wanted."

The other page in the envelope was a Franklin Templeton statement, complete with account number and balance. The market had begun its downward spiral of 2008, but Ellie thought it could still turn around fairly soon. She didn't think selling out now would be such a great idea anyway.

"Let's just leave it for now," she said, looking over the document. "It appears the funds are invested in this bond account. At least here we can keep an eye on how it's doing."

"Really?" Marli said. "Okay. For now, anyway."

———

That evening, Ellie had a lot more to think about besides the rift with her husband. This *find* of today had laid out even more cards onto her already collapsing table. She could really use that money. There were so many things she could do with it: invest it in Madison's college fund, pay down their mortgage, add onto their house, pay off the Mercedes—. Those funds could perhaps save their marriage. Because, as far as Bob was concerned, one could never quite have *enough* money.

9

TO DO OR NOT TO DO

*A*s the days became shorter, the natural light yellowed and grew more intense, with the sun hanging lower in the sky, sending its rays from a more slanted angle. The air was crisper and cleaner, except for the days in which the Santa Ana winds blew warm gusts of dust and debris from the east. Life's pace picked up and left summer behind.

Marli resumed ballet and gymnastics classes for the fall session at her dance studio. For the last twenty-five years, she'd been running her business as "The Home of the Story Ballet" and had created a unique niche for herself. Instead of cutesy recitals and dance competitions, she opted for weaving all the students into a rich tapestry of literature, dance, and tumbling—combining all the levels and ages into a cohesive work of art. Rehearsals would be starting soon for *The Nutcracker*, in which all her students would participate, along with the local belly dancers as the Arabian dancers. Casting parts was always a little tricky, since she had to determine who would be best in each role, taking into consideration which students were graduating seniors, and dealing with how she could cast her own children without causing hurt feelings or having her own kids take heat from jealous parents. This was not a job to be taken lightly. But this year her two older children were grown and gone. TJ, at fifteen, was easily cast as the Nutcracker prince. The other boys were either too young for the role or better suited for different characters.

A month into rehearsals, already mid-October, Katie, the current prima ballerina, arrived late that Saturday morning. She let her heavy canvas ballet bag slide off her shoulder and drop to the floor. Her long blonde hair stuck out in all directions, falling out of her ponytail, and black mascara smeared down from her eyelashes.

"I'm sorry, Miss Marli, but my alarm didn't go off. I'm so tired. I had four tests yesterday including two honors exams, so I've been studying all week." She dug in her bag and pulled out a hairbrush.

"I'll bet you're glad those are over with," Marli said, glancing up from her notes. "When you're ready, come on over here and start your Sugar Plum Fairy dance from stage left."

After tying the ribbons on her *pointe* shoes, Katie scurried over to wipe her feet in the rosin so as not to slip in her leaps. The staccato notes of the piece dictated clarity of movement and the steps would be practiced and perfected. After a quick warm-up, they began.

"Let's turn that one *pas de chat* into a *grand pas de chat* and I'd like to change the *attitude turn* sequence into a *penché arabesque*," Marli said.

Katie was able to make the dance flow a little more smoothly with the adjustments and the little candy cane gymnasts clapped at the end. She gave a quick, little mocking curtsy to them and smiled. Marli sent her over to stage right to practice her part, so she could help the candy canes with their phrasing. Outside, the Mouse King was painting a big box that would be used in Act One to hide Herr Drosselmeyer's life-sized dolls. It was a long Saturday at the studio with different groups coming and going, but a rewarding one. One of the inherent duties for a director is also that of a counselor. Marli was there when a student needed to talk, or vent, about school or home. She felt providing this outlet for someone else also enriched her own life. Once again, she stayed late at the studio to help Katie gain some perspective on her academic life.

She went home to feed the horses and eat dinner with Richard and TJ, followed by a long soak in the tub with Epsom salts. Marli complained at dinner of having "PTLs." Sage had come up with this when she was little, when she wanted to be carried because of her "poor tired legs."

By Monday morning, Marli felt refreshed. The phone rang and she grabbed her cup of coffee and went outside to sit in the sun. She settled into in an Adirondack chair on the porch and talked with her friend, Rose. They discussed their gardens and Rose brought up the Mississippi place.

"Hey, remember when we had dinner at your house and joked about rebuilding that old house? Were you serious?"

"Oh, I don't know," Marli began. "I guess I just wanted to put it out there—maybe to see if I had any takers." She giggled.

"Well—I think it might be fun. I've been kind of wanting to go somewhere, but John's always too busy with work. The kids can take care of themselves now. It might be the answer for me. I've been dying to get out of here. Almost anywhere would do."

Marli wondered. She wasn't sure about mentioning the surprise funds yet. "Hmm. I don't know if Carol and Tilda would be that interested, really, or even be able to get away. We could feel them out, I suppose. It's probably a long shot. Hell, it's a long shot for any of us."

"Yeah, probably so." Rose was quiet for a moment. "Well, I have plenty of work to do. I've got several orders to fill and mail out, two heavily feathered pieces and four with dangling, beaded strands."

She handcrafted delicate hairpieces using feathers, shellacked gourd fragments, small stones, beads, leather, and silver and sold them at the Farmer's Market, craft shows, and through her website.

That evening, Marli was slicing the last of the zucchini from their garden when Richard came in through the kitchen door with an armload of groceries. He kissed her on the cheek and set the sack down beside her.

"So, how was your day?"

"Oh, fine." He took the broccoli out of the Trader Joe's bag and opened the refrigerator door.

"Hey, guess what? Rose says she might be interested in going on the trip to rebuild the old house in the country. Now I'm wondering if this could actually happen."

"Really? Huh. I wouldn't put anything past you, dear. How's your sister feel about it? Has she changed her mind?"

She had already told him about the funds. "No. But I don't even know if *I* really want to do it."

Marli felt confident he would try to be supportive in almost anything she decided to take on. She was a doer with a type A personality. He knew better than to stand in her way. Besides, her being the one to take charge usually worked out pretty well. He usually had to take a backseat during the time they were rebuilding their own house after the fire. Marli figured if something needed to be accomplished, she had to do it herself. She'd learned that at a very young age. Both Mom and Dad had left a stream of unfinished projects in their wake, so she usually opted for the opposite approach.

That week whizzed by for Marli with classes, rehearsals, and getting TJ to and from cross-country practice. During a quick stop at the grocery store one evening, she happened to run into Carol on her way home from school. Her friend was leaning over in the cereal aisle, pulling a box of Grape Nuts off the bottom shelf.

"Hey, Carol! What's for dinner?" Marli asked.

"Oh! Hi, Marli. As usual, I have nothing in the house." She waved her arms around, box still in hand, to demonstrate. "The cupboards are bare. I'm here to find something that's quick to fix. Jack's gone for the week." Her twenty-three-year-old son had graduated from college and moved back home. She was going through a divorce and her younger daughter was currently away at school.

"It sounds like you need a break from it all." She felt she could use one, too. "Remember when we were all joking around that night about going back to Mississippi to build a house? Well, guess who's up for it? Rose." What was she thinking? How could they really do this?

"Yup, she would be." Carol tossed the cereal into her cart. "She's been wanting to travel and get away for a while."

"So—what do *you* think? Would it even be possible for you? Maybe in the summer?" A shiver of excitement, of possibility, shot up Marli's spine. It took her by surprise. Was this thing starting to get out of hand, without enough forethought? Taking on a life of its own?

"Isn't it really hot and muggy back there in the summer? I don't know. I'll have to think about it." Carol ran her fingers through her hair, distracted, and looked up at the top row of jars.

Marli left the store, shaking her head and wondering what on earth she was doing. But it was still a long shot. She decided to try not to think about what might already be set in motion and allow the universe to unfold as it may.

⌣

On Saturday afternoon "The Ladies" as Marli lovingly, and a bit sarcastically, referred to her friends, met at The Naked Bean. Shelves of books created aisles in the back half of the narrow store and small pedestal tables with an eclectic assortment of chairs greeted customers as they walked in. The aroma of freshly ground coffee made Marli salivate, even though she always stuck to her one cup in the morning routine.

Rose walked back from the front counter holding a cup of tea and sat down to join the group. "What ya got there, Tilda?"

"A double espresso. I'm trying to wake up after last night. Our concert ran really late and I'm tired. I had to play extra loud to drown out the fill-in second violin."

Rose adjusted her hummingbird hairpin and again addressed Tilda. "So, what do you think about a Mississippi trip? Would it be possible for you? You know, in between teaching music lessons and rehearsing with the symphony and all that other stuff you find to fill up your time." Rose smiled mischievously.

"Well, that all depends. How serious are you? I'm pretty damned busy." Tilda brushed crumbs off her chest.

"You know how we like creative projects," Marli began. "And we all seem to be interested in old houses and fixing them up. So how about rebuilding one?"

"And I love to paint!" Carol said.

"Yeah, we know." Rose laughed.

"I've got to be bloody insane to even consider it," Tilda said. "But there's something about this that intrigues me."

It was Carol who brought up the bottom line. "So—how, exactly, does something like this get paid for? It sounds like great fun and all, but it's hard enough just getting away, let alone paying for it. What does your sister say about all that?"

They all knew Ellie. Marli included her sister in some of the group's outings, but these women were really her own friends. Sometimes, when Ellie wasn't too tied up with chauffeuring her daughter to cheerleading activities or meeting with clients, Marli would invite her. But not usually to most of the things the group did together, like drumming circles and collaging and other artsy fartsy stuff. Besides, her comrades had nontraditional tastes, unlike her sister.

"Well, that's rather interesting." Marli grinned at her friends. "Our dad had thought about rebuilding the old place, but it just stayed on the back burner of his mind, so to speak. However—" she paused and scanned the room. "Ellie and I found a note in his safety deposit box explaining how we could afford to do it, if we wanted to. Let me just say that he had enough set aside. The trick that I have to figure out, *if* we actually want to do this, is how to convince Ellie to do *this* instead of splitting the money. If you guys are really game, I could try to give it my best shot."

"I'm in!" Rose shouted, pounding her fist on the table like a judge reaching her verdict. Then she covered her mouth, embarrassed, and glanced around the shop.

They all laughed at her thwarted enthusiasm.

Rose regained her composure. "And I can cook for everyone. That's what I do best. I can help with some puttying and painting, but you all have more expertise with building things."

"Carol, didn't you spend some time researching the South when you went to that teacher's conference in Georgia? That had to include some talk about architecture, didn't it?" Marli asked.

"Yeah, some. We did a tour of a historical neighborhood. Those Southern mansions are gorgeous." Carol turned her mug back and forth. "I'd be glad to do some research for ideas. And besides, I'm pretty handy with drywall and fixtures."

"I wouldn't mind getting some more practice, either," Tilda said. "I've laid flooring and bathroom tile in my place. Hey, there's probably a pretty decent symphony in Jackson, wouldn't you think?"

"Maybe there would be a gallery, too, with some original paintings," Carol said.

"You know, we might actually be able to do some of the finish work on the house ourselves. That would save a little money. Tell your sister that," Tilda suggested.

"See how good we are together?" Rose asked. "We could *so* do this. You know what, Carol? After this, you'd be better able to build yourself a house, if you end up having to sell yours in the divorce."

"Yeah. That's true."

"It's not going to be a huge house, is it? I mean, wouldn't we like to be able to make a measurable difference?" Tilda set down her empty mug. "I probably couldn't be gone any longer than a couple weeks."

"No, not at all," said Marli. "I know we couldn't afford that." Was this actually happening? Was she trying too hard to sell the idea? It didn't seem like it. "Wow! I'm starting to get excited, you guys."

A little more discussion and a lot more laughing, along with more muffins and drinks, rounded out the remainder of the afternoon. Marli left, feeling happy, but also a little apprehensive about being able to pull this off, or even *if* it was the right thing to do. But after she and Richard had rebuilt their house after that 2003 fire, she realized how much she enjoyed building. It was a new creative outlet for her.

The next morning, Marli dialed her sister's number. What was she going to say and how would she phrase it? Hopefully, it would just come to her on the fly. That's how she preferred to handle these types of things—to let the spirit guide her, so to speak.

"Top of the morning to you. What are you up to today?"

"Oh, I don't know yet," Ellie answered. "I suppose I should catch up on bills and laundry."

"It's Sunday. How about a hike at the Grasslands?" Marli asked. "We should talk and figure out some of the loose ends with Dad's stuff."

"I guess I could. You want to meet around 10:30?"

Marli hung up the phone and changed into shorts and hiking boots. The trail was dirt, but offered more of a walk than a hike. This conversation was not going to be easy, she feared, but if it was meant to be, things would work themselves out. She just felt she had to give it her best shot to sell the idea and provide enough positive, reinforcing information for Ellie to want to go for it.

When Marli arrived, she gave her sister a quick hug. They seemed to be closer now after their Mississippi trip and burying Dad's ashes together. They walked through the barely green cow pasture and watched a white crane peck the ground around the herd of cattle, enjoying the shade under the oak trees.

"So, what are you thinking now about the money in that Franklin Fund?" Marli asked and let the question hang.

"I don't know. It's a decent chunk of money. The market's not great right now, but it'll probably turn around again. It's not the Depression, you know. We could let it grow a little and then take it out and split it. What do you think?"

Marli thought carefully. "The money that's in there now is plenty to rebuild the old place. You know—it's what he wanted. And then we could rent it out or use it as a family gathering place for all the relatives back there. I don't know." She spoke slowly, not wanting to sound too eager. A red-tailed hawk flew overhead and screeched its familiar call. She looked up and smiled in recognition, silently honoring it.

Ellie responded, "I don't have time for that. How do you propose we do it? I think it's a waste of money."

"But it was important to *him* and it was *his* money," Marli reminded her. She pulled the yellowed drawing out of her pocket she and Dad had worked on together. "Look at this. Dad and I drew this a few years ago." She pointed to the lines on the page that depicted the breezeway, the carriage house, and the fireplace opening to three rooms in the house. "It wouldn't have to be exactly like it was, but it would be fun to play around with it a little." She explained how they could have a small crew back in Mississippi build it and then save money by having an adventure there and doing some of the finishing work themselves.

"I already said I don't have time," Ellie snapped.

"I know. But I do. At least—I want to. Carol, Tilda, and Rose might like to help, too. We could drive back there and be frugal with the funds. You could fly out and check the progress if you want. Besides, it's what he wanted." Marli waited for a response, hoping it would be the one she wanted.

"I'll have to think about it," Ellie finally replied.

"Fair enough."

The conversation drifted into lighter comments about the weather and other innocuous topics.

10

A CHANGE OF HEART

Ellie

Ellie sat in the nail salon enjoying the swirling water massaging her aching feet. She'd been in heels all day, traipsing in and out of six different multi-level houses with a persnickety couple who couldn't even decide which part of the county they wanted to live in. She was happy this day was over, although she still had to go home and endure her husband's moodiness. Lately, they couldn't help bumping into each other's hard places.

After dinner, she got up to clear the dishes and Bob held onto his plate.

"What do you say we leave these 'til later." He patted her hand and raised his eyebrows, smiled, and tilted his head toward the bedroom.

"I'm exhausted, Bob," she said and began telling him about the day she'd had.

"You're always too tired. Or something." He took his hand away. "Don't you care about us anymore?"

"Of course I do, but what about me?" she asked.

"I'm going out," he said. "Don't wait up." He grabbed his jacket and walked out the front door.

She shook her head and groaned. What had happened to them? They used to be so compatible, wanting the same things and enjoying spending time together. She was too tired to cry. She knocked on her daughter's bedroom door, said "goodnight," and flopped down on her own bed. Tomorrow would be a new day.

She phoned Bob during her lunch hour the following day. "Hey honey, I'm sorry about last night."

"I know," he said. "I'm sorry, too. Maybe things will get easier for you after you and your sister finish sorting through your dad's stuff."

"I sure hope so. It feels like we have to hassle over every little thing."

After the phone call she looked online to check the status of the Franklin Fund. "Ugh." She grimaced. It had lost another five grand since last week. This was December and the market reports were getting more and more dismal every day. That's it, she decided. We have to sell!

She reached Marli at home just as she was leaving for the studio. "The Franklin Fund is still going down. We can't afford to wait any longer. I say we bail. Now!"

"That's fine by me," Marli said. "Let's meet at the bank tonight. I think if I leave right after my last class I'll make it before they close."

"Okay. I'll try to get there a little early and start the process. Then we can talk about how to divvy it up." She knew her sister didn't have time for a big discussion right then. That was good. The important thing was to not lose any more money than they already had.

Ellie leaned back in her swivel chair and her thoughts drifted back to her father. He was a born tightwad, having grown up during the Depression. He saved everything because, "you might need it someday." Both Mom and Dad seemed to carry this view with them throughout their lives. Both of their homes and yards were stuffed to the gills with things that might prove useful—someday, down the road.

After their divorce, Dad managed to sock away more money than she'd realized. This Franklin Fund had been quite a surprise. In his later years, he'd loosened up a bit and began spending a little of his savings. He'd been generous with his kids and grandchildren.

She spun around in her chair, enjoying the dizziness it created. It was nice to have enough money to experience the finer things in life. She deserved it. She'd worked hard in her career to get to where she was, but she knew she had to keep working harder and harder to keep up. Real estate was a highly competitive field. But she was beginning to wonder, when was enough going to be enough? Keeping up with the payments on their latest house remodel was stressful. She wondered how much more they could squeeze into each payment to cut down the length of the loan. Life was so complicated.

She thought about Marli and Richard—how they were always there for their three kids, arranging work schedules to spell each other. Of course, it always meant they had to struggle over money, especially early on. They hardly ever went out when the kids were young, at least not like her little family was able to. It all came down to choices. For her and Bob, they wanted newer cars, a nice house in an upscale neighborhood, and the best opportunities for their daughter. They were on the same page. But now Ellie began to wonder about the real cost of it all.

She decided to cancel her afternoon appointments and go out for a walk. She needed time to think. The air had a nip to it, so she buttoned her sweater. Ellie passed her usual coffee shop and bakery before crossing the street to follow the bike trail through the park.

A woman sat on a bench near the pond, talking to an older man in a wheelchair. He reminded her of Dad.

Sometimes it was difficult to be around him near the end. He was so demanding. She and Marli had taken him shopping when he was first moving into the residential care facility, on the independent living side. He insisted he needed a new television, dresser, table, recliner—because he was convinced he'd be moving back home and needed to leave most of his things as they were. This move was only temporary. He agonized over every choice of merchandise. It had driven her crazy.

Almost everything he said came out negatively. He needed to be front and center despite both his daughters having families to care for. He wasn't at his best, being as sick as he was. She remembered feeling frayed and ungracious and almost unable to take it anymore. Those buttons he pushed had become hypersensitized. The years of his "shoulds" and "should nots" would erupt to the surface. One simple comment could come down as a huge cascade containing their entire history. She knew he hadn't meant it that way, but that's the effect it had. She knew it had been similar with Marli. They'd talked about it.

Ellie had walked almost completely around the whole pond as she imagined those poor hospice nurses who came to help Dad shower or to rub his swollen legs. She and Marli had made up excuses and apologized to them for his preaching and moralizing. Because he was truly struggling during that time, she tried to focus on the good stuff. And there really was a whole lot of the good stuff during the span of her whole life.

By 2:00 p.m., she was back in her office, looking to see if there were any more Franklin statements when she came across an old ledger she'd kept concerning her house payments to her father. She thumbed through the pages. "Oh yeah," she whispered. "I'd almost forgotten about that $10K. And the others." Dad had given both her and Marli $10,000 when they'd first bought their homes. It had added appreciably to their down payments. When he got older, he did it twice more, which enabled them to pay their mortgages down sooner. Even though Marli probably needed it far more than her, he made sure to give the same to both of them. Dad had a streak for fairness that permeated his whole life. Being just was paramount. If he gave Marli something, he made darn sure she got something equivalent, and vice versa. Everything needed to be balanced and even in his mind.

———

The sisters met at the bank forty-five minutes before it closed. Ellie had already begun the process over the phone. They set up a joint account for the funds to be transferred into. Ellie took on the finances as her domain, and as long as Marli agreed with the decisions she allowed her to take charge.

"I'll sure feel better once the money is in this account and out of that income fund," Ellie said.

"Me too. Shall we go eat at the Chinese place? I'm starving."

They drove separately to the far end of town, slid into a booth in the dimly lit restaurant, and ordered their food, Dutch treat as usual.

"I still want to consider rebuilding the old house in the country," Marli said. "You know, to honor Dad's wishes."

"But why? Really. Why? I don't think it makes any sense." Ellie stirred the noodles around the plate with her chopsticks.

"Maybe it doesn't. But perhaps that's not the point. To make sense, that is. He wanted us to. I think I'd really like to do it—and it seems that Carol, Tilda, and Rose would enjoy being part of the adventure. You could be, too, if you want."

"But what would we do with it afterward?" Ellie squirmed in her seat at the mention of her sister having close friends who could enjoy such a trip together. She always had too many important things to do, while Marli and her friends got to go to artsy crafty things.

"Once it's finished," Marli began, "we could use it as a vacation place. I think we'd get together more often with our East Coast relatives if there was somewhere to converge. Or we could have a property manager and rent it out. I don't know for sure. What's this *found money* supposed to be for, if not to enable us to do something unexpected? And special."

"Do you need an adventure, Marli? You already had to rebuild your own house four years ago. Do you really have it in you to go through that again? What's wrong with you? You could take half the money and relax."

"I can relax when I'm dead." Marli sighed. "I want to really live now. After losing both Mom and Dad, and most everything we own, you're damn right—I do need an adventure!" She laughed, took a slow drink of water, and then crammed a whole chopstick-load of vegetables into her mouth.

Ellie was silent for a while before signaling the waitress for the checks. Even though the sisters were not on the same page, they hugged in the parking lot before going home that night. Ellie pulled out onto Main Street feeling the power of the BMW's engine. The leather seats and navigation system provided a sense of luxury to her. Why did this kind of lifestyle suit her, but not her sister? She took the curves in the road a little faster just to feel the surge of excitement. Maybe Marli was right. Why not throw up her arms and see what happens. She took her hands off the steering wheel and sang, "Let it Be." Taking her foot off the accelerator and putting her hands back in the ten and two o'clock positions, she took a deep breath and blew it out her lips loudly. Ellie felt exhilarated—for the first time in a long while. Maybe she didn't exactly have the time to build a house from scratch in a Mississippi swamp, but that didn't mean she had to deny her sister the pleasure, or displeasure, of doing it. Did she? Perhaps with some of the money. She'd have to sleep on it.

11

PERSONALITIES AND IDIOSYNCRACIES

The next day Marli got a call.

"I've been thinking," Ellie began. "About the old house—I don't think it's a very sound idea to rebuild it."

Marli's body tensed.

"I don't think we should use all the money. But it *is* far cheaper to build back there. I certainly don't have time, but maybe, if you're willing to only use *your* half of the money, then I might agree." Ellie sighed. "You could collect the rent, but my name would still be on the title. But I'm still not sure."

Marli sat down. She wondered about the prospects. "Do you think you might change your mind at some point, and share the cost?"

"Don't push it," Ellie warned. "We have about $180K in the new account. I think half would be plenty for this project. I just can't commit to anything right now."

"Remember how Dad always said he didn't want his daughters to grow old and destitute and only be able to afford to eat cat food?" Marli laughed. "I think we're a far cry from that."

Ellie laughed, too. "I suppose. Would you be interested in using my architect? The one who designed our remodel?"

"Maybe—" Was this her sister's way of giving the go-ahead on the Mississippi project? "Perhaps." Marli inhaled and exhaled slowly, then changed the subject. Some things were better left alone for a while. She invited her sister to a drumming circle at her house. Mom used to say she wished Ellie could be involved in her drumming or meditation gatherings—she thought it would be good for her. And Marli did occasionally include her sister, but Ellie had her own social circle, which did not include her.

Ellie said, "I'll try. I'll have to check my schedule."

Marli hung up and eased herself onto the dining room chair. She had to. The idea of her sister possibly allowing her to go through with her plan practically knocked her off her feet. Even if it was with only half the money. She hadn't known Ellie had it in her to allow her this folly. It felt as if the rug had been pulled out from under her, but in a good way. Despite this being what she had wanted, she sat there stunned.

She thought of the things Ellie might buy with her share of the money. Half of her house remodel? Landscaping around her pool? Pay down her mortgage? A wave of gratitude washed over her and she smiled at the cat, staring at her from the window sill.

That evening, the sisters talked again, reminiscing about Dad and his generous, albeit emotional, nature.

"It may be the craziest thing we'll ever do," Ellie said, even though she wasn't directly doing any of it. "Maybe I could take a side trip back there next year to check it out. But I doubt it. I hope you guys enjoy yourselves, *if* it ever comes to fruition."

Marli thanked Ellie again for granting her the opportunity for this adventure. Then she headed into the kitchen to make a batch of herbed goat cheese as a gift for her sister.

Tilda wore her usual classic black frock, which accentuated her tall, distinguished frame. She removed her fedora, exposing a tight bun, and flopped down on Marli's couch. She was late again. Marli and her friends had learned to simply accept her the way she was. Tilda was always scrambling to keep up. When waves of creativity struck her she could spontaneously follow her muse in the studio for hours, perfecting those ever so intricate bowings on the violin. This creative side distracted her as she followed some new tune, and then, unprepared, she'd have to frantically search her purse for a piece of paper to scribble the notes onto. That's probably why she lost track of time tonight.

"You know, I was watching a newscast this morning, about the U.S. economy. Man oh man, Obama sure inherited a mess, didn't he?" Tilda commented.

"Well, I just hope he can fix it," Carol responded, setting her bongo drums in front of her chair.

"He's going to need a lot of support to be able to get anything accomplished, but I doubt that'll happen. We've all seen what crybabies the Republicans can be. My country is rolling their eyes at us," Tilda said. She had spent her early childhood in the Soviet Union.

"It's difficult, living in a small, conservative town. Usually we liberals have to keep our mouths shut about our ideas on politics or religion, especially when you earn your living in the same community," Marli explained.

Both she and Tilda, as local artists, had to keep their opinions under wraps most of the time. But occasionally, after taking it and taking it for so long from the vocal, conservative majority, they'd speak out when they couldn't stand it any longer. Tilda tended to have a shorter fuse. She listened to a lot more NPR talk radio and other media, and so was more knowledgeable about current events. Plus, she was a talker. She'd grown up as an only child, hanging out with adults. She thrived on conversation.

Ellie said, "When Marli and I were on the train, we talked to a Canadian couple about their socialized medicine. They said early on, a lot people didn't want it, but now most everyone is glad they have it."

Rose began shaking her rattle rhythmically. Marli knew this was her way of attempting to get them to stop talking and move on to drumming. Both she and Rose could only handle so much outside noise before having to turn it off. Even though the four women would occasionally attend drumming circles and meditations together, it was the two of them who integrated the practice into their daily lives.

Marli grasped the twine in the back of her hoop drum and slowly began a soft pulse. Tilda let out a long breath and fingered the tightly stretched skin on her ceramic, hourglass drum. Soon, Carol joined in with bongos and Ellie ran her finger around the rim of her sister's singing bowl, trying to create a sound. The music took over the room and chased out their banter.

Marli picked up the tempo when she sensed her usual disconnect from the modern world. These days, she was beginning to feel more and more isolated. She wanted real, down-to-earth connections, in true physical and emotional ways, with the community around her. But now it was rare that anybody had time for that. This drumming circle today took a bit of effort to arrange, but nothing compared to the work it took to organize meetings or rehearsals. She'd hear things like, "The only way you can get in touch with me is texting or email" or "Better yet, go on Facebook" or "I never get around to returning phone calls." Everyone seemed more interested in virtual imitations and self-promotion, which were so prevalent online. She believed an important and authentic way of life was getting shortchanged by what the mass media disseminated. Marli felt like she continually bumped up against the modern world.

The rising rhythm of the drums brought her thoughts upward. She recognized the importance of finding common ground with others. Sharing healthy, homemade food with friends; bonding with a liberal-minded book club that appreciated lively, diverse conversation; and teaching others the joys of dance and creative movement—all helped contribute to her sense of belonging. After all, she needed to feel socially connected, in her own style.

The crescendo of the session carried them along. The women beat furiously, amping up the volume into the climax, and Simon howled on the front porch. In her mind's eye, Marli saw herself flying from branch to branch in her heightened state. The group's collaboration subsided and Marli provided the rhythmic heartbeat for the closing meditation. The others sat with eyes closed. After a few minutes, Marli set down her drum and joined the others in silent meditation.

"Boy, I needed that," Carol said when they were finished.

"Me, too. I've been way too busy lately. Thanks for inviting me. Hey—" Ellie began. "Are you guys really considering a trip to Mississippi? Marli tells me you are."

"You told her that?" Tilda asked. "We just talked about it a little. That's all."

Carol added, "We talk about all kinds of things. It doesn't mean we have to act on everything."

"It's too bad we don't, you know, act on more things." Rose took a deep breath. "I wish we did."

"Well, whatever," Marli said, trying to steer the conversation elsewhere for the time being. She wanted to have this next chat alone with her friends, without her sister there.

"Well, as much fun as we're having, I really do have to go." Tilda stood up to gather her things. "I've got a gig later tonight."

They all wandered out to the porch and Simon rubbed on Rose's leg. Marli hugged them goodbye and walked down to open and close the gate as her friends drove out.

———

Marli had just finished her last class at the studio when Carol walked in.

"Hey. You know, one of my classes is putting on a play next week and I'm short on costumes. You don't, by any chance, have two or three of those peasant dresses around, do you?"

"Well, what sizes do you need?"

Carol rubbed her chin. "I have no idea."

Marli dragged the stool over to the back corner, behind the curtain, and stepped up onto it to reach a garment bag full of dresses. She pulled the zipper down and lifted out three different length costumes and handed them to her friend.

"I really don't know which ones would fit," Carol said, shaking her head.

"Just take these and see if any of them will work. They are rentals, you know," Marli reminded her. She knew full well they would probably lay crumpled on the backseat of Carol's car until the last minute before they were needed. "By the way, how are the divorce proceedings coming along?"

"Slowly. I haven't had time to return my attorney's calls. Maybe he's ready for the next step. Who knows?" Carol said, tiredly.

Her strong tendency toward procrastination sometimes bothered Marli. If a free moment presented itself, ahead of the time by which something would need to be accomplished, Carol would fill it with something spur-of-the-moment instead of just getting the thing done. Sitting idle was simply not within her capability. Now that cell phones enabled everyone to fill their time with web browsing and gaming, she no longer had to endure quiet moments. This was Marli's take on it, anyway. At home and even at school there was the continuous presence of email and Facebook. These distractions probably made it especially difficult for her to meet schedules and deadlines. Marli deduced that since her friend was constantly scrambling to catch up, she rarely had time to look within herself and just be. If every waking hour is filled with outside input, there's always the excuse that you have no time for yourself. Perhaps Carol was able to be spontaneous without sweating the details simply because she had no time for them. She could only scramble from one thing to the next. Regardless of whether it was because of, or in spite of, all this, Carol was a fun friend with a fantastic sense of humor.

But for Marli, the world was spinning out of control. She had the feeling that the vast majority of society wished to be connected to everything and everyone, all the time. Marli questioned the meaningfulness of these constant fake connections. She didn't think it was such a good idea to be told what to hear and think so much of the time. It usually took her a while to stop thinking about whatever it was they were discussing on the radio, even after she'd shut it off. She preferred a good deal of quiet time. Without it, she'd probably miss hearing that inner voice of intuition or the revelation of a new idea.

That's why, when Rose called to invite her to go for a ride the next day, she went, even though she had planned to work on the book she'd started writing. It was about the trials and tribulations of a dance studio.

<hr />

They met at the trailhead and after grooming the horses they saddled, bridled, and headed up the mountain.

"My horse is a little sore from having her feet trimmed the other day, so we probably shouldn't go too far," Rose said. "What do you think? Do her feet look alright to you?" She leaned over to the side to look at her horse's hooves, which caused Blaze to sidestep to keep her balance.

"They might be a little short, but that's how Carlos trims them. We'll just take it easy today," Marli said. "Besides, I'd like to get back in time to get something written today." She'd been working on her manuscript off and on for the past year and didn't like too much time to lapse between entries. "It sure is a beautiful day, isn't it?"

"It is." Rose agreed.

The sunshine sparkled off the lake and Marli was glad she wore her sunglasses. She pulled her feet out of the stirrups and rotated her ankles. "You know, last night I was wondering if we'd ever get around to drumming with all the talk about politics." She knew Rose wasn't very interested in *that* topic.

"Yeah, I know what you mean. Tilda and Carol can go on and on sometimes, can't they?"

"Yeah. I can't listen to very much news, either," Marli said. "I feel I can only handle so much noise before I have to turn it off."

"I can't even hear myself think with that racket going on."

"I know, right?"

"Hey, I talked to John last night about the idea of our Mississippi adventure. He's not crazy about it, but he actually left the decision up to me! You know how he worries. I really think I'd like to go. Even if it's just the two of us. Would you be okay with that?"

"Even if Tilda and Carol don't?" Marli asked, pulling on the reins to slow her horse.

"Yes."

"Hmm. Maybe. But we should keep working on them. It probably would be good for them, especially Carol. It might help get her mind off the divorce."

As they approached a stream, Marli took the lead with her Quarter Horse and allowed her friend's Arabian to follow them across. But despite having another horse in front, Rose's mare refused, and after several attempts, finally rabbit-hopped over it, and then ran into the back of Marli's mount. Rose managed to stay on and then shook her head. "You'd think she'd get it by now. But in my sessions they tell us not to force them."

Marli thought about Rose's horse therapy. She said it enabled her to work through a lot of crap. But wanting the conversation to stay light and positive, she countered with, "She is an Arab, after all. They're not exactly known for their love of water. Some habits die hard." Marli laughed. Blaze had made little progress crossing water even though they'd been working on it for years. They stopped to tie the horses to a tree and eat their sandwiches.

Marli sat on a rock. "I wonder if we actually could pull off this trip. It would be an honor, in a way, to rebuild the old house in the country. My dad would've liked that."

Rose adjusted her position on the tree stump and sipped her water. "How about we go to Carol's school play tonight and go out after? I could call Tilda when I get home."

Marli appreciated the initiative her friend displayed. She didn't normally take a lot on. Rose was a quiet, organized, and tidy person. "Everything in its place" was her motto. She wasn't about to force her opinion on anyone else. Her thoughtful, self-deprecating manner kept her family running smoothly. She would often say, "I can't handle too much on my plate at one time. I need to keep things simple." And she did.

Whether in spite of, or because of, her rough childhood, Rose had a real knack for keeping her house and yard looking nice. It helped having a neat-freak husband. For instance, if oil dripped out of a car parked in the garage, he'd be the first to notice and clean it up. They made a good team.

Their family ate a healthy diet of fresh, local food that Rose prepared to perfection. "I love to cook with fresh ingredients and feed the people I care about," she'd say. Her friends enjoyed eating at her house no matter what she fixed: raw, baked, steamed—you name it. If Rose made it, it was wholesome and delicious.

———

That evening, Marli met Tilda and Rose at the Park & Ride by the fire station. They all got in her Subaru and headed up the mountain road.

"Marli, it wouldn't kill you to let one of us drive once in a while, you know. This gets old sitting in the backseat," Tilda complained. "I know you have to sit in front, Rose, since you get carsick. But Marli, why do you always have to be in control?"

Marli's hands tightened on the steering wheel. "I couldn't go at all if I wasn't the one driving up that windy, curvy road. You know that. I'm sorry it bothers you so much."

Tilda periodically took jabs at Marli this way. She never knew when these comments would arise and she was never ready for them. They hurt her feelings, but deep inside she knew it wasn't about her. It was most likely something Tilda was working through, probably subconsciously. Rose just sat quietly.

Tilda dug around in her purse and pulled out a brush. "You know, I've never been to the South. I'm not familiar with any of the music that comes from that region or their way of life. This whole trip idea might be a way I can check it out for myself. Besides, I was thinking about taking a sabbatical from the symphony next summer and let the guy who sits next to me have a taste of being the concertmaster. I could try to figure out a way to do this, if you all are still game."

"That's the spirit!" Marli said.

Rose echoed, "Yeah, I'm in. For sure."

"Wouldn't it be something if we could all go?" Marli knew it was still just talk at this point.

The three women found places to sit in the second-to-last row. The high school students did a decent job performing their roles in *Hamlet*. Carol seemed pleased with opening night and breathed a sigh of relief as they walked out the door to head over to Open Mike Night at The Pizza Station.

"I hope Patrick is singing tonight. He's so good," Carol said.

Marli agreed. "I hope so, too."

They walked in through the saloon doors of the restaurant and found a table near the back. It was dark in the shadows and it took a while for Marli's eyes to adjust. After ordering drinks and a pizza to share, their favorite small town singer, Patrick, stepped up onto the stage. He started picking his guitar and sang "Waltzing Matilda." He finished his set with a seventies' hit from The Doobie Brothers—*"Old black water, keep on rollin'. Mississippi moon, won't you keep on shinin' on me?"*

After the applause died down Tilda razzed Carol. "So, don't you want to feel that Mississippi moon shinin' on you?"

"Well, that depends," Carol responded. "Do I have to go there to feel it or can I just watch it from here?"

"I think you know the answer to that," Rose said. "You'd love to study Southern architecture, wouldn't you?"

"Up close and personal," Marli added. "And besides, it could help take your mind off the divorce."

"Yeah, I suppose it would do that." She was the last holdout. They all figured at this point it was a go for each of them. Their yellow light had just turned green. The project was on! And Marli knew then that it was actually possible. Hell, maybe even probable.

———

Over the next couple of months, Marli toiled over the plans with Carol, using ideas from authentic historical homes of the South.

She showed them to her sister, for her input, and worked with the architect. The women stayed in touch through phone calls or showing up at each other's events—dance performances, craft fairs, or symphony concerts. Each of them stayed busy with their own families and endeavors while dreaming about their upcoming adventure.

12

BITS AND PIECES

Ellie

*T*he New Year rang in new challenges for Ellie. The real estate market continued to decline, making previously "easy sells" into "unloading nightmares." People were losing their homes, unable to keep up their mortgage payments, either from unemployment or variable rate loans with spiking interest. Families too financially strapped simply walked out from under their huge debt to become renters again. It was not a pretty picture.

Bob still hung onto his corporate job while others fell by the wayside. Luckily, his income mostly carried them. They cut back on a few extra expenditures, such as some of their social engagements at the country club, and Ellie almost completely ceased wining and dining her clients. This ultimately proved to be an unnecessary indulgence, anyway. She hadn't realized how demanding all that had been. She was good without it for a while.

Bob and Ellie were doing okay. Not great. She had informed him of her decision to let Marli use half the "discovered money" to rebuild the old homestead. He had not been thrilled. They were having a rare, quiet dinner at home with their daughter.

"I think it's stupid," he said. "I thought you had more sense than that."

Ellie passed the salad bowl to Madison. "Well, half of the money is hers. And it's *my* inheritance, not yours."

Madison asked, "Are you going back there with them, Mom?"

"No honey. Probably not," she said, after shooting Bob a 'Don't you dare start anything' look. "It appears we finally got the title of the place squared away. I got the document from the attorney in Mississippi today. What a relief. I guess the signature from that one witness to the will, who I tracked down, managed to do the trick. *And* the fact that we pestered him enough to want to get rid of us."

"Well, at least something went right. I guess the squeaky wheel really does get the grease." Bob got up to get more barbecued ribs off the counter and dropped one onto Ellie's plate. "That oughta do ya."

"Thanks." Ellie exhaled. "This economic recession, or whatever it is, is hard."

"This wasn't supposed to happen to us," Bob said, lowering his weight into the chair. "We're educated and work hard. We operate in the upper circles. We deserve better."

"You know what Marli says? She doesn't think that it's a totally bad thing. That this is forcing people to finally live within their means and simplify their lives. She says it's helping to 'foster creativity.'" Ellie used two hands to quote the last two words.

"Whatever—I'm just glad it's only affecting our lifestyle a little. It's inconvenient, but we'll get through it," he said, and ripped off a hunk of meat with his teeth.

Ellie thought about the differences between herself and Marli. How she had always kept up with what was popular. Marli seemed to somehow embrace the idea of *not* fitting in. And she looked rather comfortable doing it. Ellie didn't think she could ever be like that. Her sister would make comments like, "I don't deserve anything. Entitlement isn't really a part of my existence." She wondered how they could end up with such different outlooks on life, having been raised together in the same household. Ellie remembered back when Mom had encouraged her to enter that Miss Teen competition.

Her parents had splurged, buying her some new outfits and taking her to a salon in the city to get her hair and nails done. Mom had told her she was the pretty one in the family, so she ought to give it a try. She'd practiced her speech in the car while Marli rolled her eyes and stuck her head out the window. But on the evening of the competition, her sister surprised her by wearing a nice dress and taking her hair out of the usual braids for the occasion. She was amazed she could remember that, since she'd been so preoccupied with her own nervousness at the time, and was concentrating on her speech. Then she remembered carefully walking up those stairs in her new high heels, on the side of the stage.

"My name is Ellie Vernet and I'd like to be Miss Teen because I feel that I can represent our community well."

She giggled with the memory of standing in the photo lineup, next to her nemesis, Sarah Hatcher. That girl had a wicked streak all the other girls despised. It had been no surprise when she wasn't in the placing. Ellie was voted runner-up. Not too bad.

After graduating from college, she got her real estate license and moved up through the ranks quickly. Marli had dawdled through college and spent her free time dancing and working part time. Their parents had at least paid for her university tuition, but since Marli had done community college first and settled on a degree in the arts, she had to pay part of her own way. Those were their parents' rules.

And now she wants to write a book? Who does she think she is, anyway? Twyla Tharp? Although her sister did write a column in a local dance newsletter, it was small potatoes. A book? Why? It seemed like a waste of time. She'd never get anything from it, that's for sure.

Perhaps their previous paths had led them both to where they were today. She wondered where her daughter might end up. Or Marli's children, for that matter. Or was it all just a roll of the dice? Maybe her sister's more carefree attitude, since losing everything in the fire, was the way to go. She could almost sense her own bolts begin to loosen.

Ellie thought ahead to next Sunday, when she and Marli would be sorting through more of Dad's things. She recalled the previous year, when he still lived in his own duplex. She and Marli had gone with their kids to help him sort through his stuff.

"That's all I want for Christmas is help to clean up my place. I don't want to leave this whole mess for you guys when I'm dead and gone," *he'd said. So they obliged, or at least they tried. She knew it wouldn't be easy, but they all had higher hopes for that day than what ensued. He had them begin on the other side of the duplex, the part he didn't live in.*

Ellie had Madison sort papers, making piles "To Keep," "To Recycle," and "Don't Know." The sisters decided to focus on the living room, which the front door opened into. That way, they could at least clear a path to the rest of the house. Dad went over on the other side to take a nap in his recliner. The idea of moving his stuff around had evidently already exhausted him. She looked around and felt overwhelmed by the massive amount of "junk" they had to deal with. Why on earth would anyone in their right mind want all this old crap?

Ellie directed the kids as to which items to carry outside and where to put them. Marli hauled out more questionable things and tried to separate them accordingly. In a couple hours, the front yard resembled a patchwork quilt. Like items were grouped together. The tools were spread out on a tarp with piles of hammers, wrenches, screwdrivers, power tools, and such. Nuts, bolts, and screws were nearby. Old televisions, radios, and oscilloscopes were stacked beside the old Ford Taurus. Books and magazines took another square. They practically had the whole living room cleared out except for the pounds of dirt and debris that covered the carpet. The place probably hadn't been vacuumed in twenty years.

Dad teetered out onto the porch and down the front steps. "Get me a chair, will you please?"

Marli dragged a lawn chair under the tree and ushered Dad over to it. "Here you go. We've got the whole living room cleared out."

Ellie said, "We figured we could make an area on the porch for the stuff to get rid of, and then we can organize the rest inside."

Dad looked distressed. "Hand me that box."

Marli gave him the shoe-sized wooden box. He slowly began pulling one thing out at a time, telling them what it was. "This was my mother's silver spoon when she was a baby. Give me that bag," he said.

Marli handed him the brown paper sack. He needed help to pull out a hacksaw that was wrapped with fishing line. She broke the string using the blade and lifted the rest of the contents out, which were all tangled together. Ellie glanced at her sister, picked up a pocket knife, and asked him where it had come from while Marli directed the kids to start a trash pile.

"Wait a minute. Just hold on!" Dad yelled, holding up his hands. "I'll say what goes and what doesn't and I haven't looked at that stuff yet," he barked. He was beginning to sweat.

"We'll never make any headway at this rate," Ellie warned, beginning to get irritated with the thought of their time being wasted. "This will literally take twenty years if you have to pick up each piece of paper, analyze it, set it down, and then re-visit it after you've put it in the 'I Don't Know Yet' pile. We can't do this. We have jobs and we've taken today to help you. There aren't that many times we can spend a whole day doing this."

Dad shook his head. "Well, it's gonna take a while." He went back inside and the kids walked down the road to get burritos for lunch.

"We're fooling ourselves, Marli. It will probably actually kill him if we do this while he's still alive."

"I agree."

Ellie thought they must have come across as rude and insensitive that day by just giving up—the very same day they had begun. The two of them started hauling everything back inside and dumped it all onto the living room floor, trash and all. Their attempt at helping their father had been completely futile.

———

But Dad was gone now and when Sunday morning rolled around Ellie began to feel a sense of dread come over her. All that stuff. But maybe they'd find something valuable. You never know. She got out of the BMW and gave Marli a cursory hug. They'd need their energy today to make any headway whatsoever.

"I've already cleared an area to collect all the tools," Marli said.

"I think I'll start with the boxes in his bedroom." Ellie turned her body sideways to make it through the cluttered hallway. She dusted off the top of a metal case, unlatched the clasp, and opened the rusted lid. Hundreds of haphazard black and white photographs filled the trunk. She pinched a torn corner of a 3" x 4" print and lifted it toward the window to get a better view. It was Mom. She had on a green, A-line dress and stood holding a baby. Her, since three-year-old Marli was playing in the sand in front of them. A larger picture showcased her in that Miss Teen lineup she'd thought about earlier in the week. Youth, she thought, why can't we all just stay young and beautiful? She continued rummaging through the assortment, but only found a few more images of interest. Most of them were probably Mississippi relatives who she didn't recognize, in their younger days.

An hour later, she went out to the garage to check on Marli's progress. Hammers, drills, wrenches, and screwdrivers were lined up on the workbench.

"Aren't they beautiful?" Marli asked, presenting them with a flourish of her hand like a salesperson. "He sure has a lot of them. I especially like this one." She picked up an antique cranking drill and moved the handle around in circles. "I'd like to take it home. "

"We could probably sell it, and most of these others, too, and at least get some money for our efforts," Ellie countered.

"No way! He would want us to keep them. If we wanted to. And I'd be able to use quite a few of these. They're part of our history."

"Well, just don't take very many. I want to sell them. But don't take any home today. I want to see all of them first," Ellie insisted. "You can take the boxes of photos, though. They're mostly old ones of people I don't know. Maybe we should just throw them away."

"No, don't just toss them. I'd like to look through the boxes."

"There's so much to sort here. I think we should always come down here together, so we can decide jointly. There're probably some things that are quite valuable. Let's make it worth our while."

And so it went that afternoon—opening boxes, arranging tools, looking at pictures, questioning the usefulness of particular items. It seemed as though Marli had a different idea on the value of things than she did. Anything she wanted, Marli wanted, too. She was trying to be as fair as she could, but Marli was being stubborn. Marli seemed to be more sentimental about certain things, but then she'd relent a little. Ellie needed to go through everything herself, she knew, but what an undertaking. They had fought over Mom's things and had barely begun divvying up that stuff before the fire came and took it all. At least Mom was gone and hadn't had to experience the total loss. But now they needed to get this duplex cleaned and ready to rent. The market was too ugly to even consider selling right then. She wondered how many years this could possibly take. The lost income would cost them far too much. She knew she could manage it and get a decent rent. But time was money. They needed to get a move on.

13

REVERIES AND DETAILS

Sorting through Dad's things was challenging and exhausting. Marli didn't want much, she didn't think, but she wished her sister would just let go of some of the old tools. *She* would actually use them. She'd even keep them in the little shed Dad had built on her property. They belonged there. Marli didn't understand why these mattered to her sister. Ellie didn't need any of them. But then again, Ellie tended to accumulate things and hold onto them more than she did. Marli hated clutter. She was a lot like her friend, Rose, in that regard. However, she wanted to keep a decent representation of Dad's belongings—at least the ones that served a purpose or held meaning for her. It felt like Ellie simply wanted to be in control.

That evening, the sisters locked the duplex, and the garage with the all the tools laid out on the workbench, and walked out to their cars. Marli reached for Ellie's arm.

"Hey. Do you remember when we took that last trip with Dad and stayed in Atlanta? I'd gone into Joy's barn with him and he got real upset about Grandma's piano being out there. He'd wanted to bring it back to California, but Aunt Mae had insisted Joy needed it."

"Yeah, he never got over that, did he?"

"No. He sure didn't. But what got me was when he said, very seriously, 'There's no way my place is as cluttered as Joy's. Is it?' It took me a second to respond. I wondered if he was joking, but he wasn't! I stared at him and said that yes, it was. And that his place was actually way worse than hers. He was shocked! He really had no idea what his house looked like to other people," Marli explained.

"It's like he had blinders on," Ellie said and opened her car door to get in.

Marli looked up at the top of the palm tree in the front yard. The breeze lifted her bangs to one side of her face and she shook her head in amazement. "Well, let's not end up like him. Okay, sis?"

"You got that right," said Ellie, shutting her door.

On the drive home, Marli pictured her dad sitting in his recliner, surrounded by piles of magazines and large cereal boxes crammed with metal parts of gadgets that didn't work anymore. After his passing, the cleanup job was daunting, to put it mildly. He had lived there for thirty years, collecting, storing, and not cleaning. When Marli went in, she felt overwhelmed. Where to begin? And how could she decide what she wanted and what she didn't? She was working on letting go of things, and at least now, she was having an easier time of it since the fire. After you've lost everything, you just sort of figure that it could happen again, so why cling to things so tightly? It was rather freeing, but she still felt conflicted. Her sister tended to want the same things she did. It was the same after Mom died, too. They hadn't divided much of anything because of it. The fire came along and had taken that battle away from them.

Simon met Marli at the gate, wagging his tail and licking her hand.

"Thanks for greeting me, pup dog. I'm so lucky to have such a loyal friend."

She went in the house and set her bag down in the wide windowsill before going to the kitchen. Richard was frying onions and greens from the garden and a bowl of cubed tofu sat ready on the counter.

Marli filled her glass with filtered water. "Can I help?"

"No thanks, I think I've got it," he said and emptied the tofu into the pan. It sizzled nicely.

Marli stepped in anyway. She was starving, and quickly set the table and got out the Bragg's Liquid Aminos as a condiment. TJ was at a friend's for the night and they had the house to themselves.

"You look tired. Is everything all right?" Richard asked.

"I'm just frustrated. I don't know how we're ever going to get Dad's place cleaned up. We can't seem to agree on anything. Every time I express an interest in something, of course, she wants it more. This could ruin our relationship. I don't know."

He dished up plates of the vegetarian fare. "Well, that's nothing new. I remember what you guys went through when you tried to sort your mom's stuff. It was hopeless. It's not your fault, or hers. It's just the way you guys are with each other."

Duh, she thought. Of course he's right. But what should they do about it?

When they finished eating, she stood and carried her plate to the counter. "I'm going to take a bath. Maybe that'll help."

Later that night, lying in bed, Richard snuggled close and spooned her. He kissed the back of her neck. "I have an idea," he whispered. "Just hear me out and don't say anything until I'm finished, all right?"

"O-k-a-y," Marli said hesitantly, slowly turning her head so his voice wouldn't be so loud in her ear.

"What if you just let your sister have it all?"

"What? Are you serious?" she said and pulled away to face him.

"Wait a minute. Let me finish."

"O-k-a-y." Her heart started beating faster.

"Why not let Ellie take everything she wants home with her. You wouldn't even see it. After she's gone through everything, you could go look to see if there's anything left you want."

She lay quietly and listened thoughtfully, but a little defensively.

He continued. "I'm sure she'll give up after a while. There's so much there. When she's finished taking stuff, then I'll clean up the place. I'll treat it as a job, pack my lunches and have at it. I'll have the time this summer. I won't be teaching any classes at the university and could start by the end of May. What do you say?"

Marli contemplated, weighing the pros and cons of the proposal. "Why on earth would you want to take that on?"

Richard propped himself up on his elbow and faced her. "Because how can it possibly get done with you and Ellie wrestling it out? It would tear you guys apart. Just when your relationship has improved since the train trip. We're going to need your half of that rent money and I'll have the time then," he said.

Marli sat up. She was intrigued with the proposition. She'd have to really practice the Zen of letting go—*if* she agreed. "Hmm, it might actually be a good idea. It'll be hard, but I could try not to get involved. That's awfully big of you, Richard. You're a real sweetie, you know that? I'll give it some thought." She leaned over and kissed him.

———

She called her sister the next morning. "I've been thinking," she began. "I don't want to fight over Dad's stuff."

"Me neither. But I didn't know we were."

"Well, kind of. I don't want this to undermine our relationship. Richard and I were talking about it last night and he had an interesting idea."

"What's that?" Ellie asked.

Marli could sense an edge to her voice. "What if you take whatever you want?" She took a shaky breath and waited.

"What do you mean?"

"Just what I said. I'm willing to let it *all* go. As much fun as it all is," she joked, "playing tug-of-war and wanting the same things—it's not worth the damage it might cause us. That's all."

"Huh." Ellie got real quiet for what felt like a long time. "I'll think it over."

———

Of course Ellie ended up agreeing. But she didn't sound convinced that they would have fought about it. How could she not recognize the obvious? Marli knew better. She accepted the challenge to move out of the way. She was removing herself from the potential battle. Ellie had even told her to go ahead with her "Mississippi adventure." Again. She actually encouraged it this time by saying if the project went over the $90,000 budget, perhaps she'd toss in another $10,000. It didn't sound all that generous, but this was the first money offered that was actually her sister's to give.

Marli thought maybe that was why Ellie finally and truly gave in about rebuilding the old homestead. She might even be willing to let some money come out of her own pocket! Perhaps she had finally realized just how much Marli was giving up to keep the peace. Dad's valuables were hard to let go of, but they weren't worth losing a sister over. And Ellie could get whatever she wanted.

———

In February, Marli invited Ellie over to show her the plans the architect had drawn up. She removed the rubber band and unrolled the multi-stapled blueprints onto the dining room table.

"These are just the preliminary plans, so check them out to see if we should change anything now, before it's too late." She was still a little nervous that her sister might put the kibosh on her dream.

"How fun—" Ellie said, tracing her index finger over the lines representing the future house. "Look—if we make the kitchen three feet shorter here, the living room gains enough space for the hearth right there." She pointed to the blue lines.

"Yeah, okay. That's a good idea." Marli calculated the changes this would mean for the whole house. "I gotta say, your architect sure works fast."

"He does. I kind of wish I could go, too, but I just don't have the time. Madison's got a big cheer camp this summer and I'll have to work a lot, as well as finish going through Dad's stuff."

Marli couldn't help but say, "We all have the same amount of time. And we make our own choices. *We* just have different priorities."

Ellie took it well. They were in a good spell with each other, now that Marli had agreed to let her sister have first choice on *all* Dad's things. Sibling issues came up now and then for them, as they did for everyone. Perhaps it was better that each of them was taking on a different endeavor. The sorting *or* the building.

One late afternoon in April, after feeding and watering the horses, goats, and chickens, Marli lay down on the grass in the side yard. She stared up at the clouds as they drifted through the blue sky. Simon rolled nearby, scratching his back and groaning in pleasure. She chuckled, continuing to watch the white turtle transform into a jumping horse. Before long she was lost in a reverie.

She remembered a time when she was perhaps seven or eight years old, and they had just finished dinner and baths.

"It's almost time for Cimarron Strip!" Dad called from the other room.

"Okay, I'm coming," she'd answered.

Dad was already lying on the couch with his head propped on a pillow and his left arm stretched out to the side. Marli nestled in beside him, resting her head on his arm and feeling the warmth of his body next to hers. He felt strong and protective while at the same time loving and caring. She thought she could lie there forever. But now, looking back as an adult, she figured his arm must've gotten pretty sore or fallen asleep, but she couldn't recall him ever complaining about it. They just lay there watching that handsome Stuart Whitman ride his slick, shiny horse and smile his way into her heart. She also remembered watching The Rifleman and thinking that Chuck Connors' television son, Mark, was kind of good looking and closer to her own age. And then there was Gunsmoke starring Matt Dylan, Miss Kitty, and Festus; and of course, Bonanza. The two of them shared the world of westerns and Marli loved that special time with Dad while Mom and Ellie did other things—like brushing hair, reading, and getting ready for bed.

Later, as an adult, Marli felt like a part of her belonged "back in the olden days" as they called it. She often preferred the idea of horses and buggies and Model-As to modern conveniences such as cars with automatic windows and navigation systems. The endless mind-numbing, self-promoting, virtual living these days held little interest for her. She simply felt out of sync with the current culture.

Her parents also liked to retrieve things from a previous era. In the 1960s, they chose autos from the 1930s. She remembered Dad driving the old Model-A truck and Mom drove that Model-A coup, which lacked the rumble seat but sported the traditional "a-ooga" horn. She got to sit on their laps and learned to drive while tootling around the canyon.

She smiled wistfully, coming back into the present day, and looked up at the changing sky again through moist eyes. She missed Dad so much. What a waste, the way we learn and work so hard to become something in our lives. And for what? To just revert back to nothingness in the end? What's it all for anyway? Oh hell, there's so much we don't understand. She rolled over onto her side to face Simon and he licked her face, offering his condolences.

⌒

By the middle of May, the sisters were each proceeding with their own plans and agreements. Both were involved in a flurry of activity, including performances, conversations with Mississippi workers concerning ongoing construction, sorting through mountains of items in the duplex, and paperwork. With the spring dance concerts behind her, and only the one county fair production remaining, Marli began to feel the letdown from a long, ambitious performance season. The phone rang and she answered, holding the receiver with a raised shoulder while stirring the feta cheese chunks swimming in whey in the stainless steel kettle.

"What's going on out there?" Marli asked. The Mississippi contractor they hired to rebuild the old house in the country was calling about the gas line easement on the property. Aunt Mae had known this guy's family and recommended him for the job.

"As long as you keep inside the edge of the woods I think we're all right," she said.

The crew had cleared out the underbrush and left the big, old beautiful trees around the house site. The foundation had been marked out, formed, and poured, and the subfloor was laid. The exterior walls were up and the roof trusses were almost complete. They were still making minor changes in the plans as they went, but Marli was impressed by how relatively easy it had all been. *After* getting her sister on board, that is.

Ellie tried to stay ahead of Richard, sorting and taking, while he carted things to Goodwill and the recycling center, and lined up a dumpster service. He was now immersed in his summer job, albeit unpaid, but not unappreciated by his wife. He was holding an ongoing garage sale in the front yard, with a sign advertising "Free Stuff. Take All." A Craigslist account was set up and altered weekly. He made many trips to the metal and toxic waste recyclers, doing his best to throw as little into the landfill as possible. Marli was sure of that. Richard liked leaving as small an impact on the environment as possible. Each morning, he'd drive the truck down to Lakeview and sort like a demon.

"You know, Marli. I spent a couple hours reading old letters from your grandma in Mississippi. I hope that's okay. It's amazing how many there are," he said. They were eating dinner out on the porch on a warm June evening.

"It's fine. In fact, I'm glad you're reading them." It was touching that he took an interest in such things. "Would you please set them aside so I can read them too—when I have time?"

Each day, Richard would drive up the little hill nearby and park at the top to eat lunch in the fresh air. He talked about hacking the crud from his lungs. Marli pictured him coughing out the decades of dust this job was stirring up.

In the afternoons, he'd haul stuff to places like Amvets and second-hand electronic stores, or make phone calls to organize pickup times for the Salvation Army or responders from Craigslist. It was an enormous job, one that would take the entire summer. For better or worse, this would be the process in California while Marli and her comrades would pursue their building adventure in Mississippi.

———

"The Ladies" came over for dinner and a planning session one Friday evening. A few Naked Ladies presented themselves in the front yard. The beautiful pink tubular clusters poked up out of the earth, welcoming anyone who came to the canyon.

"These flowers don't usually bloom quite this early, do they?" Rose asked.

"No," Marli answered. "I don't know what's going on. It's really weird. My dad had brought some bulbs back from his folks' place. This must be his way of letting us know it's time to 'commence to begin' as he would say. The time is right." She shook her head and began picking a small bouquet of her lovely, pink Mississippi friends and arranged them in a vase after they all walked in together.

By this time, the old/new house in the country was really taking shape. Marli dug out the most recent photographs the contractor had sent, and showed her friends the progress they'd made.

"I can't believe we're actually doing this," Tilda said, dancing around the table like a teenager. Marli hadn't seen her friend this excited about anything since college.

"Yeah, and we're leaving in less than a week. For more than two weeks!" Rose shouted enthusiastically.

Marli placed a bowl of salad in the center of the table and tried to focus on the task ahead. "Our rental camping trailer is supposed to get there tomorrow. I hope we'll all fit," she said. This whole endeavor needed to fit together like a puzzle and she was beginning to feel the pressure.

"It'll be fine. At least it's June, not the middle of summer, and there's space outside," Carol said.

"Well, here's to our grand adventure." Marli held up her glass to toast everyone.

"And away from school and divorce lawyers," Carol added.

"To making my own decisions." Rose raised her glass.

Tilda sang, "And may we all hear the songs of the South."

14

ON TO MISSISSIPPI

"*M*an, this state is huge! It feels like we've been traveling forever," Carol complained.

"Yup, that's what I remember about Texas—coming this way every summer to see Grandma and Grandpa and all the cousins." Marli pulled the blue Subaru into the Stuckey's parking lot. The restaurant/store had been advertised miles in advance along this desolate stretch of highway. Sandy, bare land was broken up only by the occasional low-lying creosote bush or barrel cactus, and heat waves radiated from the pavement. A gas station stood adjacent to their destination. As Marli gassed up the car, the others went inside to peruse the aisles and search for cold drinks.

Marli found her friends sitting at the soda fountain studying the menu on the wall and watching the waitress with big hair and too much makeup flirt with an old guy at the end of the counter, all the while operating a noisy blender.

"Wow, they still have malts here! That's what I want. I can't even remember the last time I had one. It was probably with my dad. I'll get a small chocolate malt, with lots of malt please."

"Hell, I want a large," said Tilda, digging into her oversized, black bag.

"Medium for me," Carol added.

Rose took hers without the malt. The women sat, perched on stools, and quietly drank their treats while eavesdropping on the conversation at the end of the counter.

"You shoulda seen that bass George caught. I'll bet he weighed ten pounds, Suzie."

"Get outta here. I can't believe that. You gotta be pullin' my leg," the waitress answered.

"Oh nah," he said. "You know I wouldn't do a thing like that to such a purdy lady such as yourself, Suzie."

Tilda rolled her eyes at Marli.

The waitress tipped her head back, forcing out a chuckle, and turned on the blender again. Then she raised her eyebrows toward the four out-of-towners.

Small town America—the simple life and courteous pleasantries. It reminded Marli of her own simple pleasures, or Little Happies as she called them.

Just a few short years ago, she and Dad had gone for a ride on his quad. He straddled the seat while she leaned against the old milk crate bracketed on the back. It was a warm spring evening. Suddenly, a cock quail, sprouting a beautiful top plume, skittered over the small boulder they were parked beside and jumped off the edge into the bushes. A plump, gray hen followed over the rock, and then hopped into the brush. And then a baby quail, with its quick little running steps, ran across the granite. She held her breath, wondering what might happen when it got to the edge. It jumped off! Then it scurried through the leaves below, catching up with the parents. They smiled at each other, she and Dad, as another wee one appeared on the rock and did just what the first had done. And then another and another and another. They kept very still, breathing lightly, so as not to disturb the family's journey. Marli felt lucky to be there, so close to them and to her father. This was surely one of those Little Happies.

After they used the restroom and picked up supplies, Rose arranged the snacks in the car. Pretzels, peaches, and almonds were within easy reach for future munching.

Tilda claimed the front passenger seat and buckled herself in. "If I have to listen to much more of that hillbilly kind of talk, I'm not going to last. What a bunch of senseless chatter."

"This, coming from a talk-a-saurus?" Carol teased.

"Touché," Marli said, while slowly pulling out onto the highway and turning up the air conditioning.

"I'm no worse than the rest of you," Tilda insisted. "We all talk a lot. You're one to talk, Carol. You go on rants all the time."

"Okay you guys. Be nice to Carol. Remember, she's going through a lot right now," Rose said.

"Yeah." Carol rolled up her sleeves and put her cell phone back in her purse. "I just got a text from my lawyer. It looks like Shithead is stalling again." She ran her fingers through her light brown, shoulder-length hair in frustration. "I don't know what he thinks he's accomplishing with this."

"I'm sorry, Carol," Rose said. "Is there anything we can do?"

"No. You're already doing it. You guys had to rescue me before, too, from my groupie days. I hadn't even realized how abusive *that* guy was, being a rock star and all. I just thought he was cute and creative and a free-loving hippie—not somebody who lost his temper and took it out on the closest one around: me. No. I owe you guys big time for getting me out of there."

"That's what friends are for," Tilda said. "He *was* good looking, but really Carol, you deserve better."

Marli rolled her window down a crack to test the temperature of the outside air. She remembered when Carol started going to see

The Rockers on Friday nights. Eventually, she ran away with the band when they left to go on tour. The only contacts they had with her over the next year were birthday or Christmas cards. It was as if their friend had left them forever. But that all changed when Carol called Marli and asked her to come pick her up at the airport.

"All I did was come get you," Marli said.

"You did way more than that. You stayed with me all that night and talked some sense into me. That's what you did."

"Yeah. It's what she does best, isn't it?" said Tilda, and winked at Marli teasingly.

"It's what we all love about her," Rose crooned.

Tilda shook her head. "Even when it's unwanted."

"No. Really. If it weren't for all you guys, I probably never would have gone back to school and become a teacher." Carol leaned her head back into the neck rest where the breeze coming in through the open window could dry her tears. "Wow. I didn't feel this coming. I'm such a mess."

"No, you're not," said Tilda. "Look at me. I've never even been married. I can't stand staying with the same guy for longer than six months. One year tops." She waved her hand toward the vacant landscape. "And I'm as barren as this Texas highway."

"Well, you have a good excuse," Marli reminded her. "That series of *winning stepdads* wasn't all that helpful for you. But still, you do all right. You're happy on your own anyway, aren't you?"

Tilda rolled her window down partway, which created a percussive, thumpity-thump air flow throughout the car. "For the most part, I guess. It's just—sometimes I wonder what it would have been like if I'd chosen to have kids." She pressed the button and the window closed. "What would it have been like to have a family?"

Eventually, they made it out of the Lone Star State and into Louisiana. While driving along the bayou, Tilda yelled, "I see an alligator!"

"Where?" Rose shrieked.

"Down there on the bank. Right next to the water!"

Marli pulled over to the side of the road. They all got out of the car for a closer look.

"Sure enough. That's a gator all right," Marli concurred.

"How exciting!" Rose clapped her hands together. The dark gray reptile ducked into the muddy water and was gone.

Carol admitted, "I think I'm liking this adventure of ours." A trickle of sweat ran down her forehead. "Except for this darn mugginess." A heavy dank odor rose up from the bayou. "Okay. Next adventure?"

They cackled together and clamored back into the car.

The women hauled their suitcases in through the New Orleans motel room's door and Rose called dibs on the shower. Carol and Tilda plopped down on the queen beds and turned on the TV to watch the news. Rose headed for the bathroom and Marli climbed up on the counter in the dressing area and took off her socks. She pulled her feet up into the stained, off-white sink under the running water. After unwrapping the soap, she began to lather and rub her hands together.

"What do you think you're doing, dirtying up our lavatory like that?" Carol asked.

"I'm sorry, I just couldn't wait to get my socks off and soak my feet. It feels great! You oughta try it. You know, Jesus knew the importance of a good foot washing." She grinned slyly.

"Well, I think Jesus had something entirely different in mind with his washing of the feet thing, but we'll let that be for now.

Leave it to the dancer to do those kinds of body contortions on top of the counter," said Tilda, before taking the remote from Carol and changing channels.

"Okay, who's next?" Rose asked. She continued to dry her long black hair. "Do we really have to have the TV on?"

"I'm starving. Let's go eat." Tilda got up with a groan and turned off the boob tube. She lifted her large purse off the tan carpet and opened the door. "Shall we?"

"Good idea. I'll shower later." Carol stood up from the bed.

Marli hung her towel on a rack by the sink. "At least my feet are clean. I'm ready."

They headed down toward Bourbon Street and found a little French café. Ruffled, green curtains hung decoratively in the front window. After a five-minute wait, they were seated at a table that looked out onto the street. Waiters and busboys almost ran into each other, trying to keep up with the pace of this busy establishment, while delicious aromas made Marli salivate. Seafood had always been her weakness.

After perusing the menu, Tilda began her usual habit of ordering several different things to share, including turtle soup, crawfish, oysters on the half-shell, and seafood gumbo. "We may as well experience the local cuisine," she said.

Rose looked quietly at her menu.

"Can you find anything you might like?" Marli asked her. Rose wasn't quite as adventurous as the others.

"Maybe—I think I'll try the salad with broiled chicken."

After gorging themselves on the local fare, they waddled out the front door and turned right to enjoy an evening walk.

"Window shopping and people watching are enjoyable entertainments, especially here in this artsy, exotic city, don't you agree?" Tilda took charge of the direction they took.

"Indeed it is." Marli took note of the familiar surroundings.

A man on stilts, in clown garb and heavy makeup, juggled tennis balls in the middle of the road. Two teenage boys tap danced on a corner and a cross-dresser blew kisses to the men standing in front of a bar across the street. Music from one place blared loudly, mixing with sounds from another doorway. The noises blended until they got closer to the next establishment, where the dominant melody would change. An old black man was playing a trumpet in the park. Marli wondered if it was the same guy she, Dad, and Ellie had seen the last time they were here together, ten years ago.

Tilda sat down on a bench to listen. "He's amazing. It's like he's truly one with his instrument. Such soul and artistry."

"Yeah, he's something else." Marli sat down beside her and sensed Dad's presence as the sultry air wrapped around her. Less than a day's drive northward would take them to his hometown.

Carol and Rose walked over to the edge of Jackson Square, where Marli could see a three-man band playing harmonica, banjo, and twelve-string guitar. Reds, greens, and oranges reflected off a brass trombone mounted on a stand. The assortment of traffic, melodies, and voices bounced around, creating a dizzying head rush for Marli. Incredibly still air weighed heavily on her sweaty body and her eyes welled up with tears. She couldn't believe she'd never be able to share this place with Dad, ever again. Even though it had only been once, it had meant so much to him. The thought slapped her across the chest, stinging her already throbbing heart.

"I miss him so much."

Tilda patted Marli's knee. "I know, honey."

They sat together in silence while Marli processed her thoughts. A few minutes later, they joined the others in the appreciative crowd gathered to listen to the band. The irresistible rhythm instigated stomping feet and bobbing heads.

"This is fun." Rose began two-stepping toward the river.

As daylight began to fade, Tilda put her arm over Marli's shoulder and the foursome strolled over to sit on a bench and watch the sun set. A big, old-fashioned steamboat paddled by, churning the muddy water of the great Mississippi River. The dark brown liquid poured off the paddles as each one lifted above the surface. Marli listened to the cascading waterfalls above the drone of the engine. A faint hint of fish, mixed with sweat, hung heavily around the women. She smiled, feeling the old familiarity of her Southern heritage. It awakened all her senses. This had been a beautiful day. The red and blue haze in the sky now faded into twilight. The music and ruckus continued, muffled in the background.

"This is really nice," Rose said. She sat tall and took a deep appreciative breath, but then started coughing.

They all laughed and Marli said, "The air here is a little muggier and thicker than at home, huh Rose?"

"Uh huh," she responded, still attempting to clear her throat as they continued their light-hearted razzing.

Marli closed her mouth and took a deep breath of the sultry air herself and thought about her sister. And Richard. What they might be doing right then. It was two hours earlier in California. Perhaps they had worked at the duplex today. She was glad she had made the decision to let go of all the things they were sorting through. She was happy to be here on this trip with her friends. It felt right. It was what she was supposed to do.

———

The next morning, they left New Orleans and headed northward. Marli had been telling her friends about the Lake Pontchartrain Causeway. "We'll be crossing a twenty-four-mile-long bridge over this huge lake. Within eight miles from either shore, you can't see any land and it can be a little unnerving." She felt the hairs rise on the back of her neck just thinking about it. She glanced over at Carol, who sat beside her in the passenger seat, and noticed her wiggle uncomfortably.

"You know, I don't much care for heights," Carol said as they approached the bridge. "How high is it?"

"I don't know." Marli was already clutching the steering wheel tighter than necessary.

Rose pointed ahead. "Those clouds look really dark. I hope it doesn't rain while we're out there."

"Why not?" Tilda asked. "Wouldn't that just add to our exciting adventure?" She leaned over to peer between the front seats, heckling the others with her familiar, mischievous laugh.

About two miles onto the thin, spaghetti-like road, it started to sprinkle. Then the drops got bigger and bigger and it began to pour out of the sky by the bucketful. The pounding on the metal roof of the car made it impossible for any conversation—just fierce concentration on the part of the driver and hopeful thoughts by the passengers. Visibility lessened as they progressed. Marli turned on the headlights, and the windshield wipers beat about as fast as her heart rate.

"It's raining cats and dogs out there," Tilda shouted.

"I'd say more like falling elephants, myself," Carol yelled through clenched teeth.

"Can we all just be quiet for a while?" Rose begged.

"How are we all liking this adventure now?" Tilda threw her head back and laughed defiantly.

Cars spewed waves of water from the road as they whizzed past and Marli slowed down substantially. Were those drivers insane? Finally, there in the distance, she could make out the outline of a hill. Land was imminent. A lifetime later, she carefully maneuvered the Outback onto solid ground.

There were noticeable sighs of relief and a return to normal breathing once they were off that bridge and on firm, albeit not dry, soil. The rain slowed down to a sprinkle by the time they crossed the border into Mississippi. They drove up Highway 55, passing exits to small rural towns before eventually reaching Jackson. They took time to drive by the courthouse and federal buildings and then continued on to their destination near Pickens.

An hour up the road brought greener, more heavily forested surroundings. Marli rolled her window down to take it all in and sample the air. It blew in warm and humid against her face. "It's amazing how quickly it can heat up right after a rain, isn't it?"

Rose lifted her hand into the breeze. "It doesn't do this in California."

"How about some air conditioning?" said Carol. "It's too muggy for me, that's for sure."

"Well, y'all best get used to it," Marli teased. "It's here with us to stay. We'll be arriving momentarily, humidity and all." She exited the county road and turned left to go over the bridge. Then, there it was. The familiar gravel road that would carry them to their home away from home.

"Well, here we are," Marli announced. She drove the car up the dirt road and stopped in front of the camping trailer parked about a hundred feet from the side of the developing house. "Wow." She opened her door slowly and let the vision register. This was really happening. It seemed so quick for a house to spring up from the jungle. The late afternoon sun filtered through the woodland canopy and she swatted at a mosquito buzzing around her ear. She smiled at the others as they got out, but paused, crossed her arms, and leaned against the car to let it all sink in.

A well-built, middle-aged man walked toward her. He smiled and held out his hand. "Hi, I'm Jody. Are you Marli?"

She allowed him to take her hand in his and offered a return shake. "Yes. I'm Marli. And these are my friends, who were just crazy enough to join me on this trip. This is Rose, that's Tilda, and Carol's the one with the funny hat."

"It's good to meet you ladies. Did y'all have a good trip back?" he asked. "Let me introduce you to the boys." They walked over toward the house as the other men converged. "This here's Jake and that's Travis and over yonder is Joe. This thing's gone up pretty fast."

"Boy, I'll say," Marli could hardly believe it. "It looks great. Oh, this is so exciting."

"You gals must be plum tuckered out from your trip," Jody said. "Here are the keys to your palace. They brought it over last week and we hooked it up for ya." He was referring to the camping trailer the women would be calling home for the next ten days. The white hulk sat under a tree, making the place look like a campground.

"I think we'd like to check out the house first. At least I would."

"Yeah, me too," said Rose, already moving in that direction. She turned around. "Can we?"

"Of course." Jody led them up the steps to the front porch and through the doorless entry.

"This must be the living room. I love these big windows. What a great view of the meadow and those trees," Carol said as she looked out one of the windows and stared up at the lush green canopy.

They followed Jody up the staircase to check out the two small bedrooms and bath.

Tilda peered into one of them. "This one would make a nice music room. Oh, the pond is right over there. It's lovely in the setting sun."

"Oh! I was hoping this might be the view from here," Marli said. "It's so hard to be sure ahead of time, when you're planning it. You know, how it will turn out? It's wonderful!"

Loud banging and footsteps came from the men working on the roof. When the racket subsided, Carol added, "I could see a window seat there. Wouldn't that be nice?"

"Yeah, that's a fun idea." Rose agreed. "And maybe one in the other bedroom to catch the morning light."

More thudding from overhead took over the moment and Jody motioned for them to follow. "We'll leave that decorating stuff up to y'all. That's not our expertise."

Once downstairs, they walked past a small bathroom and then back through the kitchen. Wainscoting was already being installed. Pine boards lined the entire ceiling.

Marli fantasized about what these future rooms would look like. She could tell her comrades were doing the same. The men were in the process of roofing the house quickly in case one of those Southern summer showers descended upon them. Then they could finish sheet-rocking the interior walls so the women could work their magic.

"I'm glad you were able to salvage so much of that slate from the old roof. It looks good." Marli remembered how she and Ellie had seen the giant slabs of gray rock lying in the weeds.

"Yeah, it was an adventure, to say the least, digging up all those shingles out of the grass. But it was worth it." Jody grinned and dimples formed on each side of his mouth.

Marli followed him out to his truck to work out some remaining construction details before joining her friends to start unpacking.

"Sure is hot here," Tilda complained, fanning her damp blouse away from her stomach.

"And muggy, too," Carol attested.

Rose walked between them and quietly said, "Let's not be complainers now, girls."

Marli overheard snippets of the conversation and was grateful for her shy friend, gracefully keeping the others in line. She knew Rose didn't want her to feel bad about dragging them all the way across the country just to satisfy some debt to her father. They each had made the choice to join her, but Marli might well feel hurt if they acted like ungrateful guests. Rose's quiet nature sometimes allowed her to observe a situation without planting herself smack dab in the middle of it, as Tilda tended to do. This perspective enabled her to act with diplomacy, rather than just react. Marli admired that skill.

That evening, after the workers left and the ladies figured out their designated spaces, they heated up cans of tomato soup and munched on crackers. Tomorrow, they would head into town for some real groceries. The trailer was a little cramped with all four of their bedrolls and suitcases occupying most surfaces and compartments. Marli and Rose shared the double bed in the back, while Tilda took the top and Carol the bottom bunk bed. There was a picnic table out front where they could eat and hang out.

Marli assessed their living arrangements. "This works out pretty well, doesn't it? It's like we have an outside dining room."

"Yeah, I agree." Rose gathered the bowls and took them in to the small kitchen sink to wash. "But I'm exhausted. Do you guys think you'll want to go to bed soon? I feel ready now."

"Mm hmm, I am." Marli stood up to help. "Let's tidy up and hit the hay."

After they'd all gone to bed, Marli found she couldn't sleep. She left the trailer quietly and walked over to the house in the subtle light of a half moon. She sat on an old wooden chair on the porch, leaned back and started rocking. The chair creaked and groaned and she wondered which one of the fellows had thought to put it out here. It was a nice touch. She heard a splash and figured it was a fish flipping in the pond behind the thick curtain of trees. She noticed the crickets were out in full force and the summer night air hung like a heavy veil around her, almost smothering with its cloying weight. But at the same time a welcoming sensation of déjà vu embraced her.

Dad would've liked this. She wished he could be here to enjoy it. She remembered him taking her and Ellie out on the pond in a boat when they were kids. They'd fished and caught enough for Grandma to add to their supper. Dad had always spoken so reverently about this place. She was glad to be taking on this project, as much for her, really, as for him. It was good to just be back here to stay for a while and get to know the place better. She stood up to stretch and the rocker continued its motion without her. She decided to call it a night and moseyed back to the trailer, hoping for sleep.

15

GRUNT WORK

Ellie

A neighborhood dog ran across the street as Ellie turned the BMW into the small front yard of the duplex and parked under the towering pine tree. Dust-filled cobwebs stretched between the rafters of the porch ceiling, catching unfortunate flies and moths. The dark brown netting had almost become part of the architecture for lack of any recent cleaning. At least the filthy stacks of magazines and newspapers were gone now. She cradled a Starbucks coffee in the crook of her elbow and turned the key in the lock. When she opened the front door, semi-organized stacks on the living room carpet greeted her, like sentinels from the past. She wondered what decisions might lay ahead. After finishing the last dregs, she put the empty cup in a trash bag and decided to start in the bedroom.

The rolling stool pulled out easily once it bounced clear of the crescent wrench embedded in the rug underneath the desk. Ellie grabbed a washcloth from one of the piles on the rumpled green bedspread and wiped the dusty seat. After opening the torn, sun-bleached curtains and turning on the ceiling fan, she sat on the stool and began with the drawer she'd left off with the day before. Her focus was to assess anything of value that might add to the revenue of this undertaking. Sure, there were photographs and notes they'd written as kids that she'd have to save, but for the most part it was just junk. Perhaps she might find some nugget worth something, buried in the thirty-some years of sedimentary layers that lay stratified in her father's house.

From an old yellowed envelope, she pulled out a picture of her mother. She must've been in her late twenties. Mom's long brown braid hung over her shoulder and she held a baby—her. Little, blonde ragamuffin Marli stood beside them, clutching a toy rifle with a scowl on her face. Mom was grinning slightly, but seemed reserved. Dad probably took the photo. Were they already having problems?

Ellie ran her finger over the scalloped edges of the picture and remembered a similar one on the fireplace mantle, in the sun parlor in Mississippi. She could sense the crowdedness in the room on those long Sunday afternoons in the summer, after church and dinner (lunch), when everyone would sit together and talk. And talk and talk and talk. Except Mom. She never said much, Ellie vaguely remembered, but that was mostly from stories her family told. She didn't know if these were actual memories or recollections of things she'd heard.

But Mom didn't seem very happy in Mississippi. Her lack of the gift-of-gab showed starkly against the nonstop gossip. The sisters grew up unable to tolerate rehashing the same old crap, simply for the sake of discussion.

Another photograph from the drawer showed her and Marli in red Christmas dresses. Marli had a wild look in her eyes as if ready to bolt at any second. Ellie was younger and hugged Mom's leg. She still felt insecure in a way, and missed Mom so much. They had been very close. She longed for their nightly phone conversations. She didn't remember much about her parents' happy days. Marli said she did. But now Ellie just wanted to get through this sorting phase and be done with it. Why did Marli want to expand this into an unnecessary project 2,000 miles away? She leaned over a stack of boxes and cranked open the window to let fresh air into the room.

She lifted a large, ripped, dirty box out of the closet and opened the flaps. Dust billowed out onto her T-shirt and white jeans. "For cryin' out loud." She coughed and dusted off the top contents in the box. Electronic manuals, technical instructions, and bank statements had all taken up residence together in this cardboard condo. Why on earth couldn't this be more organized? Why did *she* have to be the one stuck with all this anyway, while Marli got to just go off and play with her friends? Ellie felt abandoned. It wasn't fair. She started to cry and blew her nose on a napkin she picked up off the dresser.

But then again, her sister did tell her she could have whatever she wanted. And Richard would clean it all up afterward. Why was going through all Dad's stuff so important to her? Well, it was important! There could be tremendous value in something she might miss. Like that Franklin Fund money. How was Marli able to let it all go? Let her have anything and everything. Did Marli really believe they could not have done this together? Her sister had indeed changed after losing it all in that fire. But some things didn't make any sense.

In another box, Ellie came across some old china. It must have been from Mississippi. She recalled the big family meals with Grandma and Grandpa and all the uncles, aunts, and cousins. On Sundays, after church, they'd all gather around the huge oval kitchen table for "dinnah" and say grace before passing around the "budda beans, paeys, hayam, cream cown cassrol, and slast tuhmayduhs." She shook her head, recalling the accent.

"You chillun eat like birds," Grandma would tell her and Marli with a warm smile. "How 'bout anuthah helpin?" Ellie would just chew some more and try to swallow what was already getting stale in her mouth. The cousins, however, seemed to have no trouble finishing what was on their plates, along with what they piled on for seconds. They were more used to eating Southern fare. After all, their mother, the cook in the family, was a born Southerner regardless of where they happened to live.

And then, after the midday meal, when the adults would head for the sun parlor to sit and talk, the kids would sometimes escape to the backyard. They'd wander between the corn stalks in the garden and make mud pies and play restaurant by the back steps amid the ever-present drone of the cicadas. She loved Grandma's beautiful pink amaryllises surrounding the house. They'd always called them Naked Ladies—their common name. Dad had brought some of the bulbs back to California. Marli now had them growing in her own yard and had even carried some in her wedding bouquet.

Ellie could still picture those trips back to Mississippi. By the time she was an early teen, the family vacations had stopped. However, she guessed most of her memories of Mississippi were probably colored by Marli's or Dad's reports of the family's history.

She looked out the window when a motorcycle sputtered by. Dad didn't live in the nicest neighborhood; the duplex was only a block off Main Street. Who knows, maybe someday the city would want to buy these places for urban redevelopment; certainly not right away, with the market tanking the way it was. But hopefully, the area will turn around eventually. For now, though, they needed to get it ready to rent out, so at least it wouldn't be a money drain— or get vandalized.

After using the bathroom, she opened the top drawer in the file cabinet next to the toilet. She flipped through the folders and took one out that read *OIL*. Taking it back to the bedroom and sitting on the bed, Ellie thumbed through the papers. There were lease agreements, royalty check stubs, and miscellaneous documents. She dug her phone out of her Gucci bag and punched in the number at the bottom of a notarized oil agreement. A man answered in a thick Southern drawl.

"This is Mitch with Watero. How can I help you?"

Amazing. An actual person answered the phone. "Hello, I'm calling for my late father about his oil lease. His name was Will Vernet. Do I have the right number?" Ellie asked.

"You said the last name was Vernet, ma'am? Oh yes," he said. She could hear papers shuffling in the background. "I see it now. I'm so sorry for your loss. What can I help you with?"

"Well, I was wondering about what kind of deal you have or had with my dad. Could you give me any information?"

"Well, unfortunately, I'll need a copy of the death certificate and proof you're his daughter," he said. "But I can say that we were about to contact him anyway about a new lease on a different site on his property."

Ellie was intrigued and agreed to fax him the information that night; he promised to call her the following day. She knew there were small royalty payments on other leases, but wondered how lucrative this mystery deal could end up being. She thought she knew her dad, but he kept on surprising her.

Richard drove into the yard and got out of the truck. She decided not to say anything about it for now. After all, Marli was gone so she'd have to deal with it anyway. But she liked it that way. In matters of finances, she wanted to be in control.

"Where should I start today?" he asked, poking his head in the door. He held a peanut butter jar half-full of his morning smoothie.

Ellie carried one of the boxes into the living room. "There's a few more in there, too." She motioned toward the bedroom with a tilt of her head.

Richard had already finished clearing out the garage last week and the other side of the duplex was almost done. It was this side, the part Dad had lived in, that was bogging her down and allowing Richard to catch up. They didn't usually work together. She'd go through things of relevance and stay ahead of him, and then he'd finish with the cleanup. He sorted and categorized mountains of Dad's accumulations, taking trips to the dump, toxic recyclers, and thrift stores—and had a continuous giveaway out front marked by a handwritten sign stating, *FREE STUFF.*

He took the box from her and headed out to the porch. "Marli called and said they made it to Mississippi. It sounds like the house is going up pretty quickly."

"Yeah, she called me, too. It must be nice." She felt a wave of jealousy sweep over her. Going through Dad's belongings was no picnic.

Richard carried the other boxes outside and got to work. Ellie looked out the window. Why would he volunteer for such drudgery? Her husband never would have done that. He's too busy, anyway. He'd probably want to hire someone to do it *for* him. She wondered again how she got suckered into this.

The ringing of her phone startled her away from the window. "Hello?"

It was her assistant, informing her of a house showing that had been rescheduled for this afternoon.

"Great. I'm a mess."

After a couple more hours toiling in the crowded, dreary rooms, she cleaned herself up as much as possible and took off, cell phone pressed to her ear. She waved to Richard, who had his leg in a large garbage bag tamping down the trash, and drove out of the yard. *She* had to go to work.

16

INVITED TO SUPPER

Marli woke early the next morning and walked over to the pond just as the sun was beginning to come up. Reddish clouds streaked the sky. Tall trees surrounding the water, clumped densely together, buffered sounds and obscured their sources. Birds twittered eerily in the overgrown canopy. The woods tended to be mysterious and haunting places partly because of this. She hiked up her jeans to the knees and squatted at the shore for a closer look. Little minnows scurried by and a dragonfly landed on a floating leaf. She admired the intricate grid pattern on the transparent wings. How beautiful and natural everything felt here.

The men arrived early to continue making the roof rain-worthy. The radio forecasted showers by the weekend, if not before. Marli and Carol wandered through the house to get the feel of each room and what color schemes might work.

"I think this wall begs for a big, bold color. What do you think?" Carol asked as she presented the unfinished two-by-six studded framework of the future living room wall with a flair of her right arm.

"Perhaps. The possibilities are endless, aren't they?" Marli pictured a loud, popping shade of red, and was caught off guard. This nature girl generally preferred earth tones and shades of blue. But perhaps she should, at least, consider some other ideas.

Their absorption in the creative process was interrupted by harsh words coming from above.

"Get on outta here! Ya hear? We don't need ya. Now, go on. Skidaddle!"

"What the hell?" Marli questioned.

They quickly walked outside and down the front steps in time to see a black man hurrying away and then ducking from a Coke can that had been hurled in his direction. He held up his hands protectively in front of his face and lurched backward.

Tilda and Rose came out of the air-conditioned trailer carrying cups of coffee.

Jody's voice boomed down from above. "That's enough, Jake! You can't treat people like that. In fact, you need to leave. Now! You're off the job!"

Marli moved to the front yard so she could look up to see the men standing on the partially slated roof. Jody's baseball cap was pulled down over his forehead and she watched his scowl deepen.

"That's fine with me!" Jake yelled back. He threw down his nail gun, sending it sliding down the front pitch.

"Look out, Marli!" Jody shouted.

She jumped sideways just in time to avoid a serious knock on the head. What was going on?

"I don't want to be around no nigger lovers anyhow. Yer just askin' for trouble. I was just doin' y'all a favor, but you're just too dumb to see it." Jake was down the ladder by then and storming off toward his old, beat-up, tan Buick. He tipped his dirty white cap to the ladies as he stomped toward the driveway grumbling. "Goddamn motherfuckers." He spun around and kicked the half-empty Coke can before he sped off down the dirt road, spinning up a cloud of fresh dust.

Marli stood there with a sick feeling registering in her gut and looked up at Jody, who now stood on the edge of the roof. "I hope he doesn't hit that guy. I didn't see where he went. What was that all about?" she asked.

Jody took off his hat and wiped his sweaty brow with the back of his sleeve. He seemed to need the time to cool off, emotionally. Marli wondered if *he* might blow now. The other two men had set down their tools and were watching him expectantly.

He took a deep breath and scanned the horizon. "Jake's bigoted and stubborn. I thought he'd changed. We needed the help so I hired him. My mistake. But he's gone now." He threw his arms up in surrender.

"I guess I didn't realize there were still people out there who were that racist. At least that loudly," Marli said.

"Oh, there are plenty of them." Travis walked over to Jody and handed him a water bottle. "That poor guy was just lookin' for a job. Jake didn't have to be so mean."

"No kidding." Marli used her hand to shade her eyes. "Do you know that man? The one that got chased off, I mean? We should apologize to him."

"Yeah, I'll do it on my way home," Jody assured her. "I go right by his place. Okay, let's get back to work."

The men picked up where they had left off and Marli walked toward the trailer to join her friends in the shade.

"That was uncomfortable." Rose sunk down onto the bench at the picnic table. She looked shaken. "I didn't know anyone felt that way anymore."

"I'm sorry, Rose. But I'm afraid this is one of the places it's still at its worst. Believe it or not, it has gotten a little better than when I was a kid, but obviously not enough." Marli shook her head and took a swig from her water bottle.

Carol stood up and walked around the table. "I remember one time Leon told me his band played at a club near Atlanta. For a while, they had an African American drummer and this one guy in the audience stood up and started yelling, 'Get that nigger off the stage.' He said he hadn't paid good money to listen to that. Anyway, it escalated into a big fight and the band had to take a long break. It was ugly."

"Racist bigotry." Tilda frowned. "Lack of education and no exposure to the arts. Mind you, I'm not saying that solves everything, but it helps." She picked up a paper plate and began fanning herself. The stagnant, mugginess hung heavily around them.

"You know, one of my ballet mentors was touring with the New York City Ballet, under Balanchine, sometime during the late sixties or early seventies. One of their performances was in Jackson, Mississippi. She was a principal and was partnering with a black man. She told us there were riots in the street over it." Marli paused, shaking her head. "Unbelievable."

———

Around midday, a small, white car pulled into the yard. A woman wearing a baseball cap got out and carried an ice chest over to the porch. She walked with a determined gate, sure of where she was going.

"Hi. I'm Fran, Jody's wife," she said and reached out to shake Marli's hand.

Marli returned the gesture and couldn't help but notice how short the woman's auburn hair was cut—like a man's, and she barely cleared five feet in height.

"Well, I just brought the fellahs some lunch." She stepped back and looked up at the house. "They're doing a nice job, don't you think?"

"Yeah, I think they are." Marli batted at a mosquito. "You must live near here to bring them lunch like this."

"It's not far. But I don't do this every day. We just had a bunch of leftovers from last night so I told Jody I'd swing by. Oh, that reminds me. I'd like to invite you ladies to supper tomorrow night. Y'all must be tired from your trip."

"A little, not too bad. And thanks, that would be nice."

Tilda had ambled over from the campsite. "That sounds wonderful. I sure hope you have air-conditioning."

Fran laughed. "Yes, of course we do. All right then. Jody can tell you how to get there. I'll see you tomorrow. See you tonight, Jody! Hey Travis! You and Joe make sure and join us, too."

Travis smiled down at her. "Yes ma'am."

"Thanks, honey. I'll pick up some corn on the way home," Jody said from the edge of the roof and tipped his cap like a gentleman.

As Fran backed out of the driveway, Rose and Carol came out of the trailer with a pitcher of iced tea and some glasses. Tilda and Marli joined them in the folding chairs out front. They all continued to fan themselves with paper plates.

"How did you talk us into this anyway? It's miserable here," Tilda huffed.

Carol added, "You don't say. I sure hope I can adjust to this heat and humidity. Throwing this on top of menopause is rough."

"Hey, it's not just you, you know," Marli interjected. "We're all in this steamy boat together."

———

That afternoon, the women found the local market and stocked up on the groceries they would need for the next few days. Rose picked out her healthy favorites, at least the few she could find there—like green beans, lima beans, and the loaf of bread with the shortest list of ingredients.

Marli grabbed a bunch of okra. "Might as well sample the local fare."

Carol and Tilda added pasta, rice, various bags of chips, boxes of crackers, and jars of salsa. Marli handed the cashier her credit card.

"Where you gals from? Your accents sound like y'all are from California. Are ya?"

Tilda told her she had guessed right and to have a nice day before the woman could hold them up and extract more personal information.

The following evening, the four travelers walked up the brick steps and rang the doorbell. Marli counted seven chimes ring before Jody opened the door and welcomed them in.

"It sure feels good in here," Tilda said. "I don't know if I'll ever get used to this muggy heat."

"Something smells wonderful. What is it?" Marli looked around the small living room to the mantle over the fireplace, where an antique clock sat, ticking away the seconds.

"Oh, Travis has some bass on the grill in the backyard and I'm making a lemon-caper sauce to go on top." Fran quickly stepped behind them to close the door and then led the women into the kitchen.

"We brought a bottle of wine. Is that all right?" Rose asked.

"Why sure it is. Well, it's all just about ready. Jody, could you get the door? I think Joe just pulled up."

Travis came in with a steaming platter of fish and set it down on the oval dining room table. It reminded Marli of Grandma's kitchen table except smaller. Jody and Fran's ten-year-old son, Eddie, skipped in behind him carrying the salt and pepper shakers. He was a cute kid, freckles and all, and obviously enamored with Travis.

When they all sat down, Joe shyly introduced his girlfriend, Mary. He was the youngest of the men, only twenty-four, and Mary, with her long, straight blonde hair, looked even younger. Fran's mother, a small stern-looking woman, had joined them for supper. She brought mashed potatoes and insisted on saying the blessing. She shut her eyes tightly and bowed her head.

"Lord, give us the grace to receive this food, in all its bounty, with your blessing. In Jesus' name, amen."

"Amen," they all repeated.

"Red or white, Marli?" Jody asked with a warm smile.

"I believe I'll have white tonight, to go with the fish."

The wine and food were passed around. Marli remembered her grandparents' meals served like this—dishing up from a platter and then passing it to the next person before taking the next course.

"I love those little blue feathers. It's beautifully made, isn't it, Mary?" Fran asked, leaning closer to get a better look at the delicate, handmade hairpiece in Rose's long black hair.

"Yes, it is," Mary said after taking a sip of ice water.

Rose touched the beads hanging from the clip. "Mostly I just make them for fun. Nobody really taught me how."

Marli elaborated. "And she actually sells them, too. She's got her own little cottage industry going."

"It's true," Carol attested. "We all just dabble in projects without having a clue what we're doing." She smiled smugly and giggled.

"Now, wait a minute." Tilda shot her a glance. "You've got a natural eye for what works and what doesn't, Carol. Don't sell yourself short."

"You know," Fran began. "A few years ago a friend of mine took a class down in Jackson. She said it was called Artist's Way or something like that."

"Yes, that is what it's called," said Tilda. "Julia Cameron wrote the book and now classes are offered all over the place, teaching people how to get in touch with their creativity. Anyone can take those classes. But I sometimes wish there were some offered to working artists and musicians, for when we need a little boost."

"Real artists, right?" Rose teased.

"You know what I mean. Those of us trying to make a living at it."

"Yes, yes," Carol said. "The *real* artists."

Eddie wiggled in his seat impatiently. "Can I have dessert yet?"

"Yes, you may, Eddie." Fran smiled at her rambunctious little boy. "Would you like to cut the cake for us? It's in the fridge."

Eddie bounded to the granite counter and grabbed a knife, eager to begin carving the Mississippi Mud Cake into large, sumptuous squares.

"You're cutting the biggest one for me, right, son?" Jody asked, turning to give him a pleading look.

"No, silly. That one's for me." Eddie giggled and licked his lips.

Travis said, "I'll slip you a tip if you give it to me." The men vied for the boy's attention.

"That would come from you," Jody said. "You're pretty sly there, mister."

Fran stood to start clearing the dishes and ruffled Travis' hair. "Yup, that's why he's the perpetual bachelor. This one knows how to have a good time." She smiled and raised her eyebrows at the visitors.

"And I want to keep it that way." Travis laughed good-naturedly and winked at the women sitting across the table. Joe and Mary grinned at each other.

"So, how long are you ladies going to be with us?" Fran asked. "Do y'all have any plans while you're here?"

"Probably ten days or so," Marli answered. "Do you have any recommendations for us?"

"Jackson's worth checking out," she said. "They have museums and concerts, and of course, the Capitol building has tours. There are other historical things of interest there, too."

Marli pushed her chair away from the table and started to help Fran clean up. "Hey Jody, did you stop by and talk to that guy about yesterday?"

"Yeah, I did. I talked to his mother and she told me he was out fishing. She appreciated the apology, but also apologized for Jed coming over and bothering us. I told her he's no bother, that Jake was the obnoxious one. You see, Jed's a little slow. He never finished school and he still lives at home with his mother. She takes care of him." He paused and rubbed his chin. "He must be in his forties by now."

"Oh. Well, thanks for doing that," Marli said. "I really do appreciate it. I don't want anybody getting the wrong idea about us."

Eddie served each guest insanely large pieces of cake before sitting down to begin devouring his own biggest square of heaven.

"Wow! This is really good," Carol raved. "I'd like the recipe."

"I used to make Mississippi Mud Cake for my dad's birthdays," Marli said. "He always requested it. This is sinfully delicious, I must say."

Joe got up and took a bucket of ice cream out of the freezer and put it on the table. He looked at Mary, who smiled back at him sheepishly.

"Thanks, Joe," Fran said, and put a scoop on top of her piece of cake. "I'll have to start dieting again tomorrow."

"Me too. Or maybe when I get back to California. We'll see." Carol laughed and the others joined in.

After supper, the women thanked their hosts for the lovely evening and Jody walked them out to the car.

"We'll see y'all bright and early Monday morning."

Driving back to the homestead, Marli smiled with contentment. "They sure are nice folks, aren't they? We lucked out getting these guys, I think."

"Except that one Jake guy," Rose reminded them.

"That's for sure." Tilda agreed. "He's bad news."

"I'm glad my aunt happened to know Jody's folks, way back when, and recommended him, since I had no clue who to hire. What a stroke of luck."

17

THE FISHIN' HOLE

A few days had passed since the women's arrival in Pickens. It had rained the day before, which left the air thick and gummy. The sun's heat penetrated the atmosphere in a much more oppressive way than in Southern California. Along with the drone of cicadas and buzzing of mosquitoes, the counterpoint effect of hammering and drilling filled out the backwoods symphony. From sunup to sundown, the assault on the ears was unrelenting. Since they were down one man after the ugly racial incident, Marli had climbed up on the roof to help the men finish before the rain came. Tilda and Rose focused on cooking the meals, while Carol helped Travis pound nails into the siding. The air conditioner in the camping trailer ran non-stop, providing a cool refuge when one or more of them needed a break.

By the time Sunday rolled around, everyone was ready for a change of routine. Marli had asked Jody about fishing in the pond and he offered to bring the gear so they could all have a go at it. And, of course, sample the catch of the day. She pushed her bothersome bangs out of her face with the back of her hand while stirring the noodles in boiling water for macaroni salad. Rose chopped onions and tomatoes from the neighbor's garden, while Tilda and Carol sat right outside snapping beans for a side dish. The main course of the barbecue was to be whatever they managed to catch in the pond that day. Having risen at the crack of dawn, the morning air felt wonderfully crisp.

"I hope the guys remember to bring extra fishing poles. I want to see what I can catch," Carol said. "Hey Marli, didn't you say there were catfish in the pond?"

"Yeah. You know, I can't believe you guys haven't wanted to go swimming yet. You'll see. It's great down there." She carried the pot of steaming noodles over to the sink and poured them into the colander.

Tilda stood up after tossing her last green bean into the bowl. "We've been busy, *you know*, acclimating to this Southern humidity. Besides, we had to help out before the rain started."

"All right. I'll give you that."

Jody drove up in his old red pickup, tires crunching on the gravel. Eddie jumped down out of the passenger seat and ran around to the back of the truck. Marli looked out the doorway, noticed the boy's excitement, and smiled. A minute later, Travis and Joe pulled up in a dusty little white Ford Ranger. Jody lowered the tailgate and hopped up athletically. Marli noticed how his T-shirt hugged his lean, muscular torso as he unloaded tackle, fishing gear, and bait.

Looking over toward the trailer he called, "Don't worry. I brought enough stuff for y'all, too!"

By 7:30 a.m., the group was heading down to the pond, each with an armload of gear, while Travis and Joe carried the aluminum boat they'd brought. After laying out everything, Jody and Travis attached hooks, lines, and sinkers to the poles.

"Do you want to help Rose and Carol, Joe? Travis is gonna go out with them," Jody said as he handed Carol a rod and showed her how to reel in the line. Joe nodded. Travis put a pole in the boat and then helped Carol and Rose climb in. He and Joe slid the vessel into the water and then Travis hopped in. The boat rocked, making loud slapping sounds against the water.

"Whoa!" Carol shrieked and grabbed onto the sides. Rose laughed and held on, too.

Tilda and Marli climbed in the other boat, while Jody and Eddie detangled it from the reeds and untied it from the dock before getting in. All was a hush across the water once they were settled into the crafts. Travis cast the first line in with a whir followed by a plop. Then the rest followed his lead. Relative silence descended on the expectant bunch as the first half-hour of fishing passed. *Plop... whir... splish... splash... plop, plop...*

Marli enjoyed the cool droplets of water on her face and arms. She put her hand down alongside the boat and scooped a handful of the refreshing water before releasing it onto her hair. "I love this."

Tilda smiled and nodded in agreement. Carol was having trouble hooking a worm and Travis leaned over her shoulder to assist.

"Here." Travis held the worm between his thumb and forefinger and pierced its mid-section.

"Ugh." Carol grimaced. "The poor worm."

Marli noticed Carol breathe in Travis's scent. His aftershave drifted over the water. Dark blond hair fell onto his chiseled face, which was close, just a short hair's length, behind Carol. Travis put his hands over hers and slowly let out some line from her reel. They leaned over the edge of the boat and watched the long, slender creature wiggle. Marli could see it, too, through the beautiful clear water.

"It's a whole different world down there, isn't it?" Travis whispered. He and Carol remained transfixed with what was happening below the pond's surface, as well as above. Rose turned away and cast her line off the back of the boat and Tilda raised her eyebrows at Marli.

Jody pulled a medium-sized catfish off his hook and slipped it into a bucket.

"I think I got one, Dad!" Eddie whispered loudly.

Jody grinned and helped him reel it in and release it from the hook. "Boy oh boy. This is the life, isn't it? That's a nice little catfish you got there, son."

"Well, I must say, this sure beats sitting in front of a computer—any day. At least here I can physically *do* something and understand the consequences. And it's so peaceful." A slight breeze rustled through the nearby trees and through Marli's hair.

Tilda dragged her pole back and forth. "Technology has its perks, too. I don't know what I'd do without my laptop."

"I don't know," Marli began. "It's supposed to simplify things, but I personally don't see it. I think it generates more paperwork, not less."

"Now everybody just passes the buck. No one understands the whole picture anymore." Jody slowly reeled in his line. "Like how you can't even talk to a real person on the phone, at a business. It's always some recording."

Tilda jerked her line absentmindedly. "Facebook's pretty cool, though. If you don't spend too much time on it."

Marli rolled her eyes and watched Jody help Eddie untangle his fishing line. Again, she felt like she continually clashed with the modern world. Writing skills had gone out the window since nobody needed to write more than a text, a tweet, or an email. Instructions for devices were now so poorly written, you could hardly figure out the directions. Sometimes, what the printed words actually said had nothing to do with what the writer had intended. She felt she needed to keep connecting with people the old fashioned way—personally.

About forty minutes later, Rose cranked in her line with a wiggling bluegill on the end of it. "I can't believe I got one!" Travis grabbed the slippery fish, pulled the hook out of its mouth, and dropped it into the bucket.

Tilda caught one shortly thereafter. Joe had been fishing from the bank and had several small ones. The morning was warming up and the insect noises escalated, adding to the human chatter.

"Hey! Stop rocking the boat, Travis!" Rose laughed.

"Woo hoo!" Travis bellowed from his standing position in the middle of the vessel. "There must be a serpent under our boat." He held onto his hat and looked like some trick rider on a rodeo horse.

"Yeah, and if you keep this up he's going to eat us alive!" Carol gripped the side of the boat.

"Whoa! Did you see that Marli?" Jody asked.

"What? Where?" Eddie asked, turning away from his rod.

Jody peered down over the edge of their boat. "That. Right down there. Is that a water moccasin?"

"Where? I don't see it," Marli said and leaned farther over for a better view.

"Right there!" Jody yelled and he gently pushed her into the water. Then he dove in after her.

Eddie squealed with laughter and hopped out of the boat, too, clothes and all, followed by everyone except Carol. They all splashed each other and carried on.

Travis grabbed the bow of her boat. "What's the matter, Carol? You afraid?"

"No," she said. "I'm just not that fond of swimming."

Joe called, "I'm hungry. Can we eat yet?"

"All right. All right," Travis answered. He turned the boat around and began pulling it to shore using a modified sidestroke.

The rest of them swam in while Jody pushed his boat in front of him. They pulled the boats onto the shore and unloaded their loot. They wound up with quite a few fish to barbeque in spite of their impromptu shenanigans. Each of them gathered as much as they could carry and trudged up the hill toward the trailer and house.

It was only a short walk, but Marli could already feel the sweat under her bangs. "I grabbed your pole for you," she said as she caught up with Tilda.

"Why do you always have to do that?" Tilda snapped.

"Do what?" Marli wondered what had set her off this time. Everything seemed to be going so well. Tilda was the unpredictable loose cannon of the group.

"Say stuff like that. Remind me you did me a favor."

"Sorry. I didn't want you to think you had to go back and get it, that's all." She knew better than to take these things personally. Tilda would just have to work through her own crap. It always seemed to happen like this—out of the blue. She walked ahead, shaking her head. It still got to her, though. Things like this sometimes made Marli feel like an outcast—like she didn't belong.

Joe started digging a shallow pit while Jody and his son gathered firewood. Travis pulled a grate and some chairs from the truck, along with a cooler full of beer. "Now this is how Sundays are meant to be spent," he said.

Carol carried out some chips and salsa along with a spray bottle of water and set them down on the picnic table in front of the trailer. There was an ant on one of the chairs and she flicked it off at Travis, before sitting down.

"You better watch it, lady," he said and quickly picked up the spray bottle and squirted her.

Rose followed Marli into the trailer. "Are you okay?"

"Yeah. It's just that Tilda seems to be in one of her moods again. I've got to learn to see those dark clouds coming sooner and dodge the bullet. But thanks for asking. I appreciate it."

"I got your back, Jack." Rose chuckled and opened the refrigerator. She handed one of the big bowls to Marli.

Jody and Joe deboned and filleted the fish, while Eddie helped Travis light the fire in the pit before setting the grate over it. Tilda was tossing twigs into the fire. Before long, the aroma of wood smoke and sizzling fish filled the woods. Marli noticed how the sounds of laughter and chatter wound their way through the trees and created an almost otherworldly effect.

"Wow, will you look at that beautiful macaroni salad," Jody crooned when Marli carried the large wooden bowl out of the trailer. He swung his legs over the bench to sit at the table.

"It was my mom's specialty," she said and couldn't help but notice his warm, inviting smile and bright blue eyes. He had a sort of rustic, John Walton look about him.

The group descended on the home-cooked meal laid out before them on the picnic table, and each person helped themselves to the delicious fish, green beans, macaroni salad, and green onions. The spray bottle was passed around periodically to cool off with. Even with the humidity as high as it was, sometimes a quick little spritz could actually help.

"This catfish is amazing, Jody," Tilda said, closing her eyes into the ecstatic tasting experience she was evidently having. "How did you get the pond flavor out of it?"

"Well, if you soak the fish in milk for a while and then roll it in cornmeal, it helps a lot."

"This is really good food," Rose said. "It probably wouldn't have anything to do with how hungry I am, though." She lifted her chin and squirted water on her sweaty neck.

The giggling started from Eddie when he pulled a long strand of fish sinew from the chunk of flesh he held between his teeth. His right arm extended all the way out from his face, stretching a single thread of the disgusting material.

Carol managed an, "Oh gross!" before spewing a mouthful of beer onto the ground in front of her.

"Who's being gross now?" Travis asked with a chuckle. Then he politely handed her a napkin to mop up with.

Tilda set her plate on the table, and, laughing hysterically, fell sideways onto Joe's lap. Her mood had obviously improved immensely.

"Here, I think you need some more of this," he said and held his bottle of beer over her mouth.

Marli stood up and snapped the seat cushion out from under Tilda and started dancing around with it, fanning the smoky area. "You'd think something else was burnin' in this campfire besides wood cuttings," she mused.

Rose got up and started swaying around, holding her plate of food, moving to the country and western music coming from Joe's open cab door. She went over, turned it up, climbed in back, and started dancing. It seemed obvious they were all feeling the effects of the alcohol. Except Eddie, the adolescent who had started this tomfoolery. He hopped up to join her and clashed a couple of beer cans together like cymbals, and strutted around Rose like a marching band.

The lighthearted ruckus continued into the late afternoon before the men decided it was time they "best be gettin' back home to do their chores." They thanked their new summer friends and drove off down the dirt road.

18

THE LOCALS

"What on earth are you doing, Marli?" asked Carol the following morning.

"What does it look like? I'm trimming my bangs. I couldn't stand them anymore." Marli sat cross-legged on the floor in front of the mirrored closet door in the bedroom of the trailer. She held the scissors just shy of vertical and snipped little bits of hair, catching them onto a magazine resting in her lap.

"Are you guys almost ready?" Rose called from outside.

"Yeah, we're coming," Carol answered. "As soon as Marli is done butchering her locks."

Marli finished her task by dumping the remnants of hair into the trash and blowing on the magazine for good measure. It was as if part of her past had been held at the bottom of those bangs. She sensed this simple act just might help clear her view and stay ahead, mentally, of what needed to be done as the building continued. Besides, with the humidity as oppressive as it was, this would allow her forehead to be cooler and perhaps her mind less bothered. Lately, her thoughts of Jody's amiable character and pleasing physique occupied more of her thoughts than she was comfortable with. They were both married people, after all.

She wiped her face with a wet paper towel to remove any remaining cuttings before grabbing her purse and heading out the door. The four of them piled into the Outback and made their way down the dirt road before turning right onto the paved street that took them into town. Rose lowered the passenger side window and fresh air blew through the vehicle.

"I sure hope they have some interesting colors to choose from," Tilda said as they parked in front of the local hardware store. A corrugated, multi-colored awning stretched across the entrance, shading the welcome mat at the door.

"Well, I hope they have all the stuff on our list," Marli added. "I really don't want to spend any more time shopping than is absolutely necessary." The florescent lights and intrusive marketing devices in retail stores typically made her feel ill and agitated. She was a born homebody/homesteader—at least in some ways. With the exterior walls of the house wrapped up, the roof dried in, and most of the downstairs drywall and wainscoting completed, the women needed to have the supplies on hand to begin painting and start on the finishing work. They couldn't wait to dig in.

Tilda and Carol headed for the paint aisle, while Rose and Marli checked out hinges, doorknobs, and wallpaper. The musty interior of the business reeked of mothballs and new plastic. Marli knew a headache would come on soon if she didn't make this quick. She wanted at least one bedroom and bathroom to have an old-fashioned look, complete with wainscoting and flowered wallpaper—true to the old house. Luckily, they found some black filigreed hinges and antique-looking fixtures.

Rose ran her finger over the textured surface. "Aren't these pretty?"

"Yes. I think these will work just fine." Marli paused to count how many they might need. Fortunately, there were enough, barely, and they scooped the remainder of them into the cart.

"Ooohs" and "aahhs" and laughter came from the paint section. They walked toward the commotion and around a corner.

Tilda held up color cards against the wall. "How's this?" and "What about this with that?"

Carol stood back to get a better perspective and snatched a crimson red card off the rack. "Here, hand me that pale green one."

Tilda stood back, crossed her arms and squinted. "Oohh, I like it."

"I do, too." Rose moved in to get a closer look.

"What do you think, Marli?" Tilda asked.

She stared at the cards. "It's all right. Yeah, I think so." The paint fumes were beginning to get to her. This place had absolutely no ventilation. She personally wouldn't choose such a bold color, but she had invited her friends along and couldn't really deny them basic decision-making freedom. She knew they had good taste. And this was supposed to be an adventure. She decided that stretching the imagination here would be a good thing.

"This is so much fun." Carol giggled like a schoolgirl. "I get to choose colors and paint and not have to pay for them."

"Yup, that's pretty special, isn't it?" Rose grinned at the group.

"You're right. This *is* fun. I'm so glad we all got to do this together," Marli said, putting her arms around the gang in a group hug.

Rose pulled away and pointed toward the back wall. Hanging above the stacked shelves were window trim samples of varying shapes and lengths. "Look at those. The one on the far right is beautiful, isn't it?"

Marli led the way through the aisles to the lumber section, with the others following. She gave a cursory glance at the passing bins before stopping and looking up at the displays. Rose had recognized a true find. The wide, sculpted one on the far right really was gorgeous.

"I'm glad you saw that, Rose. I think it's perfect for all the trim. In the whole house! What do you guys think?"

"It's fabulous!" Carol agreed.

"Let's do it then!" Tilda said and Rose went to find help and get a bigger cart.

Marli called Jody for the approximate linear length of all the trim and then ordered enough for their entire job. Jody said he'd pick it all up later. The women laughed and danced down the lumber aisle, getting a few sideways glances, and picked out the rest of what they had come in for. An elderly clerk at the checkout counter insisted on helping them out to the car with their purchases.

"What are you ladies gonna do with all this paint and stuff?" he asked.

"We're rebuilding the old James homestead, just off the highway. My dad owned it, but he passed away and we decided it would be a nice tribute to him."

"Well, I think that's a great idea. Good luck with it. Y'all come back now, ya hear?" He tipped his cap and Marli watched him as he walked inside and looked back at them once more, before reaching the counter.

———

Travis climbed down the ladder when the women drove into the yard. "Here, let me help y'all with some of that stuff."

"Well, thank you, sir," Carol replied, and pointed out the five-gallon bucket of paint in the back of the car.

Marli went upstairs to where Jody was working.

"Look here, Marli," he began as he scored a sheet of drywall with an Exacto knife. "Do you know how to do this?"

"I've done it before, but I'm really slow. I could probably use a refresher course," she said and walked over to stand next to him, by the sawhorses.

"Here." He handed her the knife. "You try this one. Right on the line now."

He grabbed the metal straightedge and leaned over next to her, carefully nudging it just to the left of the blue chalk line. Marli began scoring while they both held the metal edge down. When she remembered to breathe, she became aware of his masculine scent. He was so precise and gentle with those skilled hands. She noticed a Band-Aid wrapped around his left thumb and immediately moved her own hand out of the way of the cut. She stepped aside as he picked up the four-by-eight sheet and broke it along the line.

"Just like that," he said, smiling.

She grinned back. "Perfect."

Tilda walked up the stairs as Jody was finishing his calculations concerning how many sheets it would take and where best to put each one for the least amount of waste. He asked Marli to show Tilda how to score the drywall to get a clean break.

"If y'all want to finish this upstairs room, Travis and I can get back to work downstairs. Joe's gonna try to finish the taping and mudding everywhere else."

"Okay, sounds good to me." Marli went out to the top of the stairs. "Come on up here, Carol! We've got work to do. Hey Tilda, bring me that bag of drywall screws, will you?"

Tilda grabbed the paper sack and one of the power drills. She was handy and unafraid to tackle almost any project. Despite her on-again, off-again, surly attitude, her sense of humor and "can do" attitude made her fun to be around. The two of them did have a long history together. Tilda pulled the measuring tape along the edge of the board and penciled marks accordingly.

Marli said, "I'll snap the chalk line."

Tilda helped hold the straightedge down and Marli scored. Together they snapped the board in two. Marli carried the smaller rectangle over to the corner and held it in place.

"How about that?" she said, raising her eyebrows at Tilda.

"Pretty damned good for two rookies, huh?" After that, Tilda measured, drew the lines, and cut; then Carol held the large sheet up against the wall while Tilda screwed it into place with the power drill. Marli moved over to the other wall and worked on her own. She got a kick out of watching her friends gain mastery over the tasks at hand.

"Nothing to it!" Tilda aimed her loud voice down the stairs toward Jody, and then chuckled, self-assured.

Slowly and meticulously the covering went up. It took a while for the women to do this, but they became better at it and faster as the day went on.

Jody studied their work. "Not too bad. I must be a pretty good teacher."

"You're giving yourself an awful lot of credit, don't you think? You know, this isn't my first time doing this. But yes, I suppose you did all right." Marli gave him a little light-hearted push.

Each of the four walls was a patchwork of cracks. It resembled a puzzle whose pieces had shrunk.

Jody ran his hand over the rough wallboard. "We can fix these gaps with tape and mud later."

By evening they were all famished.

"I sure hope Rose has dinner ready soon. I'm starving." Marli had been hearing her stomach growl for the past hour.

"Me, too," Tilda and Carol said, almost in unison. The men had already gone home.

"Then let's call it quits for today." Marli took off her tool belt. "Boy, am I dirty." When she dusted off her pants white, chalky dust billowed around her. "Whew! Let's get out of here," and they headed downstairs.

———

A day later, the men were finishing up the last touches on the roof while the women prepped and painted. Marli had gone to get some iced tea from the trailer and was coming out the door when a tan Oldsmobile pulled into the yard. An overweight, middle-aged man got out of the car and walked over toward her, leaving the car door open.

He removed his straw hat. "Hello, my name's Jim Wordsworth. My family owns the property with the cotton field over on the other side of town. You wouldn't be Will's daughter, now would ya?"

"Yes. That would be me. I'm Marli," she said and offered out her right hand, brushing the blonde hair out of her face with the other. "How'd you know my dad?"

"Well, you see, my uncle went to school with him. He had lots of stories to tell. My Uncle Reed came to live with us when I was a child, after his wife died. I heard many things about the old days," he said. "I heard y'all were fixin' up the old place. Harold, down at the hardware store, told me about it. I think that's terrific."

"Would you like some iced tea, Jim?" Marli asked. As she waited for a response she dusted off her plaster-covered jeans. As the white powder floated to the ground she was aware of his eyes on her. She was wearing a tank top and she figured that he, like other men, was intrigued by her muscular arms.

"I'd love some," he said.

They sat in the chairs out front of the trailer while Marli listened to Jim's recollection of the "good ole days."

"Uncle Reed said he used to go over to your grandfather's general store after school to sweep the front porch so he could get a free piece of candy. He'd leave after that, but Will would have to stay longer to repackage stuff or dust shelves. Sometimes my uncle would wait around for him so they could go fishin' down at the river. You know, they'd take their old homemade poles and dig some worms out of the muddy bank and sit there for hours talkin' about the girls in their class. From the sound of it there were only a handful of kids in each grade back then."

"Yeah, I guess it wasn't much more than a one-room schoolhouse during that time," Marli said. "My grandma, my dad's mother, taught school. Later, she was the principal. My dad told me he didn't have much free time. I guess he must have felt a bit of pressure from his mother at school and his dad, too, owning the Pickens General Store and all. I heard he spent a lot of his Saturdays making deliveries in the ice wagon, pulled by an old mule."

"I think they used to tinker around with cars sometimes, too," Jim said, taking a sip from his glass.

"Yeah. Dad said his little sister would always tag along with him and watch him work on his Model A and hold things for him when he needed help. He was always busy fixing this or building that. He became an engineer, you know? He worked as an aeronautical, electrical, mechanical, and civil engineer out in California." Marli set her empty glass down on the ground beside her.

Jim finished his iced tea and looked around at the woods surrounding them. His mass spilled over the tiny camping chair, which made it look like he was sitting uncomfortably on four sticks. Marli chuckled at the image, but quickly turned her gaze toward the trailer as if something there had made her laugh.

"You know, Uncle Reed told me the James place out here was one of the prettiest around these parts."

"Yes, I heard that. I gather it was also a good-sized cotton plantation back in the day, too. I just want to rebuild it to some semblance of the old place. For my dad. He really loved it out here."

After Jim left, Marli took a walk down by the pond. She needed some time alone to try to make sense of some of her dad's perspectives on things. Ducking under an old oak limb, she wondered how he would've approached this project. Certainly not the same way as her. He would have come back here and worked right alongside the crew, doing all the electrical himself—as cheaply as possible. No time to party. Just get it done. She looked upward into the woodland canopy. High above, a thousand diamonds sparkled, even if they were only sunlit leaves acting as mirrors. Here was the time and space needed to resurrect her childhood memories, and the three life-changing events: first losing her mom; then everything they owned in the fire; and last, but not least, her father. These had been hard knocks, ones she wanted to learn from somehow. And now she needed to take the time to really smell the roses and enjoy the process of things as much as the goal. Being so goal-oriented had its downfalls. That's one of the reasons she'd decided to invite her friends on this trip. Wouldn't it be good medicine for them, as well as her? Besides, mixing business with pleasure might actually be a good thing, in this case.

But really, why on earth would she take on this rebuilding endeavor in such a severely depressed area? During a recession! She had to be nuts. She reached up to part some leaves hanging in front of her, but they tickled her nose and made her laugh. Her steps were almost imperceptible, muffled with silence as she walked along the mulched forest floor. A splash in the pond, most likely a fish, brought her back. The sense of achievement and satisfaction from following through on this creative work of art, while honoring Dad's wishes, might be reason enough for this journey. A bit frivolous? Absolutely. But life is short. So perhaps it's justifiable, after all.

19

COLLAGE

*T*he house was really beginning to take shape. The dark grey slate roof was finished and blended nicely into the thick woods surrounding the structure. The wraparound porch looked almost complete, with its cypress columns and wide plank flooring. Covering the exterior walls were horizontal, overlapping slats, a kind of clapboard style, typical of houses in the Deep South. The color was yet to be determined—plans were for a hue that wouldn't stand out too boldly. Marli would make sure of that.

The men were now concentrating on the inside trim: baseboards, window trim, and wainscoting. Marli and Rose were focusing on the bedrooms upstairs, the ones Marli especially wanted to be similar to the original 1880's house. Tilda and Carol were busy painting the downstairs bedroom, experimenting with wonderful colors and figuring out which worked best.

That Friday evening, after the men left for the weekend, the women discussed how the house was shaping up.

"Hey, Marli," Carol began. "Did you decide which color you like best?" Each wall of the downstairs bathroom was painted a different color to be able to see a big enough area to make an informed decision.

"I think I'd like you guys to decide. I trust your judgment. It's just the upstairs I especially want the antique white and wallpaper."

———

Tilda and Rose stood at the kitchen counter in the trailer, unpacking the local takeout they'd picked up. Marli had wanted her friends to experience fried catfish, hush puppies, and coleslaw, so she had called in the order earlier.

"This is definitely going to destroy my figure," Carol said as she uncorked an inexpensive bottle of Merlot. "Hey, I think it might be time for us to make collages again. What do you think?"

"I agree. It might help give us some more ideas about colors and the direction our decorating is going," Tilda answered.

Carol smiled. "And guess what. I just happened to grab some old magazines from the barber shop next door to the café when we picked up our dinner. They were just sitting out front with a sign that said, *FREE*."

This "collaging" activity was something they did together as a group at least once a year, to help them recognize trends in their lives. Their rule was to take fifteen minutes (with a timer) to rip out pictures that affected them personally from the magazines. This was not to be a well-thought-out process, but one of quick, intuitive judgment. If it spoke to you, rip it out. After the fifteen minutes were up, the magazines would be put aside and they'd each cut out their own special pictures or words—to create an unforeseen statement about themselves. During this phase, excitement and possibility would fill the room as they tried out possible areas on their pieces of cardboard for the placement of each cut or torn out illustration. After gluing them all down, the finished collages got a once-over by the group—mildly influenced by the potluck dinner, a little wine, and the female camaraderie.

The next morning happened to be Saturday and the guys would not be around. Tilda, Carol, and Rose took a walk down the dirt road while Marli went over to a neighbor's house to take up an earlier offer to pick some fresh garden produce. The women came back together for a bite of lunch, referred to as "dinner" in the South, before preparing for their afternoon project. Tomato, lettuce, and cheese sandwiches, with fresh sliced watermelon, provided a tasty, nutritious meal in fairly short order. Marli pulled a small brown paper bag out of her satchel and set it on the table.

"What's in there?" Tilda asked, pointing to the sack.

"Why don't you open it and take a look for yourself?" As Marli bit into a large wedge of watermelon, juicy red liquid ran down her chin and she used the back of her hand to wipe it off.

Tilda pulled a balled-up baggie out of the sack and started to unroll it. "Is this what I think it is?" She opened it and sniffed the contents.

"Well, is it what you think it is?" Marli asked, smiling. She had to work hard to keep from cracking up.

Tilda grinned back. "Yup, I believe it is. Where the hell did you get it?"

By now, Carol and Rose had stopped eating and came over to smell the pungent contents.

"The lady who has the place across the road has been watching our progress. She assumed, I guess since we're from California, that we might enjoy some of her special herbs. I was shocked, but tried not to show it, because the little voice in my head said, 'This might be fun!' Isn't it about time? I figure it's something that might have been in each of our younger days, but why not now? Here?"

Their nervous giggles turned into howling laughter.

Rose frowned. "Do we have to smoke it? I don't think I want that stuff in my lungs."

"We could eat it, I suppose," Carol suggested.

"I know what we could do!" Tilda announced. "Let's make cookies! I actually saw a YouTube video about it. It showed how you can melt butter with the leaves and make some kind of infusion. They say you can't even taste it then."

"What do you say we give it a try?" Marli asked. "Are we all in?"

"We sure are!" Tilda bellowed. "Let's start baking!" She grabbed the handy spray bottle and squirted her friends, even though the air conditioner was keeping the humid heat at bay.

After lunch, they all crammed into the tiny trailer kitchen and melted butter with the *special herb*, and mixed flour, cinnamon, and sugar—giggling like naughty children as they worked. Once the cookies were in the oven, they checked on them, often, to make sure they didn't burn. When their little darlings were ready, and only slightly cooled, each friend took a cookie.

"All right. Everybody takes a bite on the count of three." Tilda scanned the room. "Okay?"

On the count of three, each of them took their first tentative bite. Marli knew they all had at least tried weed before, but they had never done it together, except for her and Tilda back in college.

"Mmm. Not bad." Carol studied the remaining portion in her hand. She was the tallest and largest of the group and had just come off a diet. Unfortunately, the weight was slowly creeping back on.

"Not bad indeed," Marli said.

After finishing their special cookies, they hauled the magazines, scissors, glue, cardboard, and water bottles over to the house. Each sat on a cushion, which they had taken from the trailer, and Tilda passed out the magazines in the newly forming living room. Carol began flipping madly through a *Sports Illustrated* and tore out a page, shrieking with delight.

"Wait a minute!" Rose shouted with a wide grin. "Are we supposed to start yet?"

"Why the *hale* not?" Tilda drawled, opening her *Reader's Digest*. "We're on Mississippi time. Isn't that sort of like Hawaiian time?"

Marli slowly opened her periodical, which already had the cover ripped off. She gazed at a parrot flying outside someone's jungle boudoir. It somehow reminded her of when she and her sister, as young adults, had been here with Dad and stayed at Grandma's house.

"Did you see that?" Marli had screamed to Ellie late one night. She was sure she'd seen a huge, silent, bird-like creature fly through the wall and they had both screamed. They must have looked ridiculous to Dad: two grown women fleeing into his room. "This house is haunted!" they'd insisted.

"That's absurd!" he'd said, shaking his sleepy head. "Go back to bed. There's nothin' there."

That old house really did feel like it housed some out-of-the-ordinary energy, or did it have something to do with the fact that both of them were reading those Carlos Castaneda books at the time? This energy had kept Marli up half the night, during which she sat at Grandma's old living room piano and composed a piece, trying to harness that alternate reality. She didn't have any staff paper, so she had made her own on notebook paper. She started humming the tune now.

"I still don't feel anything," said Rose. "Do any of you?"

Carol sat up straight, got real serious, and turned her head back and forth—rather bird-like. "No, I don't, either."

The women continued flipping through the magazines, stopping occasionally to rip out a page and toss it into their collage piles. Marli glanced up the stairs and thought she saw a dark figure.

"Do you guys see that?" she whispered.

"What?" Rose looked upward from Marli's pointed finger.

"Up there. At the top of the stairs. I could have sworn I saw something. Or someone."

"I think she's feeling it now," Tilda said and laughter erupted. She volunteered to go fetch more cookies, while Marli and Rose tossed their magazine remnants into the center of the circle.

"Hey, wait! I'm not done yet!" Carol wailed.

"You're never done when we are. It's nothing new," Tilda reminded her. "You just finish up by the time I get back. Ya hear?" She groaned and pushed herself up off the floor.

They all laughed as Carol frantically flipped more pages and yelled, "I just need a couple more!"

Tilda exited the room as the others began cutting out their pictures. Marli's thoughts returned inward. Somehow she sensed her vision might be her mother's presence. It had a dark feel, but then she remembered how Mom had not felt at home here. Was she trying to now? For Marli's sake? But she was dead and gone. She was probably reading *way* too much into it. Even so, the house still felt *occupied*. Sort of.

Marli remembered how sometimes those Sunday afternoon gab sessions in Grandma's sun parlor would veer into discussions like, "The schools have gotten so bad, since integration is now required. We simply have to send our children to private schools." Mom got uncomfortable when the conversations took this turn and would utter things under her breath like, "Why don't you girls go play on the other side of the tracks?"

"Oh, you betta' not do that. It's not safe ova theya." These folks did their level best to put the fear of God in you, with stories of scary fights and shootings on "the other side of the tracks." But Mom couldn't help injecting her snide little remarks.

When it was time to start fixing supper, the women would get up and head into the kitchen. Mom didn't make it easy on herself, or for Dad, either, when she'd just wander off alone instead. It was clear these divided roles were not something she was going to go along with.

Marli jolted back into the present when the kitchen door banged shut. Tilda entered, munching on another cookie, and passed the plate around. Snapping scissors, ripping, crinkling of papers, and chewing echoed through the mostly empty room. How long had it been? It seemed like forever since Tilda had left the room. And why did she go? Marli couldn't remember. Oh yeah, that's what getting stoned felt like.

A little while later, Marli started giggling—over an illustration of a woman with a tree growing out the top of her head. In fact, it looked like a pot plant. It wasn't really all that funny, but she couldn't help it. She laughed harder and harder.

"Someone's feeling the magic cookies." Tilda snickered.

That's all it took. That's what brought it on. They all started losing it—one right after the other. Tears streamed down their faces. Rose tried to say something, but it didn't come out right and nobody could understand her. And that was *really* funny.

Carol flipped a page and hollered, "This one's for you, Marli!" She turned it around so they could all see it. It was a picture of a frog turning a backflip into a cup of tea, as a ballerina was about to take a sip.

"I love it!" Marli grabbed the magazine from Carol and tore out the page.

As the women cut and glued images onto their cardboard, the collages began to look like avant-garde creations. Marli glued the little frog and ballerina into the center and placed the cannabis-headed woman in the upper left corner. Trains, flowers, and animals filled in the spaces. Butterflies flew around a backyard fountain in Rose's piece. Tilda walked around the circle spraying water on her friends. This method of cooling off had become second nature and hardly slowed them down.

"I'll bet we'll see something entirely different when we look at these later." Rose massaged her tiny stomach. "All I can think of right now is eating. I'm so hungry."

Rose and Marli took a break to go retrieve some food from the trailer to bring back to the party.

When they returned, Tilda crooned, "Oh good! Ice cream! Y'all did bring *ass tea*, too, didn't ya? What is it with these Southerners? They just love their *ass tea*."

"*Ass tea* you say? Are you makin' fun of our *ass tea*, woman?" Marli teased.

"Oh no, but I've never heard of people anywhere else who enjoy that beverage as much as they do here. That's all," said Tilda. "*Ass tea.*"

Still giggling, Rose sang, "Look, we brought chocolate sauce and pickles and leftover corn-on-the-cob."

"Yum," Carol said.

After devouring the weird combination of food, Rose suggested they look at their finished works. Two pictures that happened to be side-by-side in Carol's unfinished collage, since she never seemed to be capable of actually ever finishing one, showed interior walls: one painted mud red and the other a deep forest green.

Tilda yelped, "Look at this! These colors look amazing together. How about using something like this in the downstairs bedroom?"

"I like it," Marli said, and Carol and Rose agreed.

"I guess I'll just have to finish this later," Carol groaned as Marli collected the fragmented magazines while Rose and Tilda began putting the food away.

"Well, if you chose a smaller piece of cardboard you might be able to finish alongside the rest of us," offered Rose.

"Yeah, yeah. Same old, same old." Carol said.

"Is that a train right there?" Rose asked, pointing at Marli's collage.

"Yeah, and it looks like the train is heading straight for that tunnel," Carol offered. "Boy, does this one have sexual undertones."

"Hah! I'd call it more like overtones myself," Tilda shouted. "Especially with that beautiful open flower presiding over everything from that top corner."

"And that Siamese puss in the bottom right—" Carol said, "gazing at that vessel near the center."

"Oh, you guys are terrible! You're all really misinterpreting this," Marli said in mock defensiveness.

Their art critique was cut short when Marli dropped the magazines on the floor in hysterics. She slipped on one of the loose pages and fell onto her rear end and then rolled around clutching her stomach.

"I hope I don't pee my pants."

Rose, obviously trying to catch her breath, wiped her eyes. Carol stood at the entry, opening and closing the door, trying to create a breeze. And Tilda turned around in circles, gesturing "craziness" with her hands.

"I think we all needed this." Marli carefully got up from the floor.

"Yeah, I'd say so. But what a mess." Tilda nodded at the littered floor.

They began, once again, to clean up the new living room and give themselves, and the men, a clean slate to continue the work where they'd left off. Marli felt, with a renewed sense of gratitude, how fortunate she was to have the friends she did. And that they, evidently, thought enough of her to join in this Mississippi adventure.

The evening came and brought with it a light rain. Marli loved the refreshing smell and walked outside to take it all in. She wandered down to the pond and watched the drops hit the surface of the water. "Good night, Dad," she whispered, and breathed in that sultry Southern air.

20

SORTING OUT

Ellie

Ellie spun her chair around to face the computer in her office. Horizontal lines of sunlight came in through the blinds, dividing her desk into warped, fragmented sections. This was a common morning distraction she occasionally took the time to notice.

She scrolled down the list of sites her dad's oil royalties came from. There were three. All were in Mississippi, on or near the old place in the country. And now, they had an opportunity for a fourth. These oil leases were a bit confusing, since two were located on parcels they did not own. A long time ago, the property had been much larger and when parts of it were sold off—the mineral rights had been retained.

The first lease had petered out years ago. The second was producing marginally. And the third was with the same company she had recently contacted. If they went deeper on this well, it would save drilling costs—*if* the new area was opened up at the same time. There was a catch, though. The proposed site was right next to the new house. The oil company had decided on this location over a year ago, before any plans for the house rebuild were considered. But the sisters had known nothing about it.

She'd tossed and turned all night, wrangling over the paperwork she'd received from Watero, via email, just yesterday. After reading through it, she'd forwarded it to her sister—along with a pleading letter. She knew this would *not* go over well with Marli. But somehow, they would just *have* to agree. The oil man had promised a check for $20,000 upon signing the deal. She did not want to lose this opportunity. She had that same feeling she'd get just prior to closing escrow with a client.

Ellie walked out into the lobby, past the water cooler and over to the counter. She stared out the window at the busy street below while stirring a packet of sugar into her coffee. The microwave clock read 10:30 a.m. Now was as good a time as any to send Marli another nice prompt, right before going out to meet a client at 11:00.

After a business lunch with a colleague at the mall, Ellie strode semi-confidently down the walkway, her high heels clacking with each step as she pressed her cell phone to her ear. She was heading toward her 2:00 p.m. hair appointment and had just punched in Marli's number.

"Hey, I got your email," Marli answered.

"Well—hi to you, too."

"Yeah. Hi," Marli backtracked. "You know we can't have some giant, smelly environmental hazard right outside the front door. What are you thinking? There's got to be another option."

"Not if we want that twenty grand in our pocket," Ellie stated, matter-of-factly.

"I don't think it's nearly enough," Marli argued. "The cost is too high. We've moved forward now on this family project and I, for one, don't want it wrecked. The place is beautiful, Ellie. You really ought to come check it out."

Ellie was silent.

"Are you still there?"

"Yes." Ellie thought about the alternative, which the oil company had reluctantly mentioned, but decided against telling her sister— yet. They'd said they could drill on the neighbor's property and pipe it underground through theirs. They'd still get *some* money, a smaller royalty since their family had less mineral rights there, but the neighbor would get the lion's share. Plus, they'd get a little from the pipeline lease through their property. She figured Marli would want to bring the neighbor in on it, making it a win/win—for everybody.

Why did her sister have to be so broadminded? *Just spread the wealth* and all that crap. But that way, nobody would get much. They ended their conversation with pleasantries. Best to let it be for now. Besides, Marli might wake up and smell the coffee after a good night's sleep. Ellie deposited her phone in her purse and walked into the mini spa for her massage, haircut, and pedicure.

———

At 7:00 p.m., Ellie met her husband at their favorite seafood restaurant. The waiter took their drink orders: a whiskey sour for him and a margarita for her.

"I sure hope Marli goes for this oil deal. That twenty grand would sure be a nice bonus," Ellie said.

"She'd be stupid not to. Her half could help fund that silly project she's doing. It's beyond me how anyone in their right mind would actually build anything new back there." He shook his head in annoyance.

"Well, there's more to it than that. There always is. I'm sure she's weighing the profit versus the environmental impact, and God knows what else. It'd sure be easier if it was just mine to deal with."

"Having money just makes life easier. And a hell of a lot more fun, don't you think? But your sister wouldn't know about that." Bob took his glass from the waiter and tipped back several swallows.

Ellie sipped her drink. "I remember when we were kids—all our summer vacations were uncomfortable road trips. Sleeping in the car, driving all night, breaking down, being hot and sweaty with no air conditioning. Dad tried to put money aside, but we always struggled. Life was hard and really, he didn't save a huge amount, at least until we were grown and out of the house."

"That's probably why you don't want to live like that now. I'm glad. I don't think we'd be married otherwise. We work hard and put in long hours. We deserve better."

They both ordered the halibut and she impulsively picked up her phone.

"Still no word from Marli. I guess I was just hoping to get a move on this thing."

The waiter arrived with their food and opened a bottle of Chardonnay.

While the wine was poured, Bob asked, "How's your dad's duplex coming along? Is Richard almost done cleaning up? I still can't believe he's willing to do that."

"I know it, right? We are getting closer. There's so much stuff." Ellie motioned with her arms wide.

"This fish is a little dry," Bob said. "How's yours?" Not waiting for an answer, he signaled the waiter and asked for a rarer fillet. She continued to eat hers. "You've got to rent out that duplex, Ellie. Every month you guys continue to sort is another month with no income."

"I know. I know. It's just a lot of purging."

"Hey, I looked online this morning and at least *some* of my investments are starting to bounce back. I have to keep reallocating, though," Bob said as he poured another glass of wine.

Ellie sipped her chardonnay and noticed a pang of nervousness. "Why do we always have to stay on our toes—concerning money? We have to be so vigilant all the time to just keep what we have. Don't you think it's draining? Aren't there better things to do in life?"

"What's better than *this*? It allows us to live *this* lifestyle," he said as he gestured toward their well-laid table.

Driving home, she felt slightly anxious. Or agitated. She didn't exactly know what it was. Maybe it came from all that rifling through Dad's stuff. Ellie hoped Marli would see the light and get with the program. All of a sudden she recalled an ugly incident between her parents. She really couldn't remember much good between them, but this was pretty bad.

They'd had yet another argument and Mom waited until he had gone out to his shop to cool off. Then she went out and shoveled horse manure into his Pinto hatchback. Mom had actually told her and Marli what she'd done. They'd thought it was funny—until he came back. Dad hollered until he was hoarse. Marli grabbed Ellie's hand and they hightailed it to their grandparent's house down the dirt road.

———

It was afternoon by the time Ellie arrived at the duplex in Lakeview. Nobody was there, so she figured Richard had taken the truck to the top of the hill and was having lunch. He pulled up right after she'd let herself in.

"How's it going?" he asked, carrying in an empty box.

"I'm exhausted. How about you?"

"Oh, I'm doin' all right," he said, setting the box down on the Formica table in the kitchen.

"Do you think Marli's going to go for the drilling at the old place?" Ellie was careful not to mention the proximity to the house, unsure about how much they had discussed.

"I don't know. I kind of doubt it. But it's between the two of you, not me. You guys are going to have to work it out." He dropped nuts and bolts into empty soup cans he'd found in the garage.

She thought about how refreshing his attitude was. Leaving things up to Marli and helping out with the dirty job of cleaning out this place. She longed to be able to really talk to someone about her relationship with Bob. Richard would probably truly listen. Not just give lip service. But she felt if she started opening up, then the floodgates would burst and she'd completely fall apart. No, she couldn't do that. There was too much to do. Too much to hold together.

21

MIDNIGHT MEANDERINGS

*T*he muggy summer weather forced every living organism to move and breathe at a nearly imperceptible pace. The blades of grass in the lush front yards of the houses in town retained warm moisture even at high noon. The ever-present clouds hung steady in the hazy blue sky, trapping any and all evaporated drops and pushing the heavy vapor back down toward the ground. Perspiration kept clothes draped or wrapped around the body, adding weight as the day wore on. No wonder these folks were so fond of drinking iced tea while sitting in air-conditioned sun parlors.

Marli poured a glass of the refreshing beverage in the nearly completed kitchen late one night when she couldn't sleep. This insomnia must be yet another gift of menopause. She thought of Tilda calling it *ass tea*. She was right, folks around here did pronounce it like that. She shook her head, amused.

She looked around the room, soaking in the warm quiet, and ran her hand over the smooth, butcher block counter that capped the antique-white cabinets below. A faint whiff of paint fumes hung in the air, even with all the windows wide open. A train whistled in the distance. Glass knobs sat in a paper sack, waiting to be screwed into their future homes, and an iron pot rack hung over the off-white porcelain-enameled sink. She put the pitcher of iced tea back in the refrigerator and sat down on a work bench. It was the only seat available.

Thoughts of Grandma's sun parlor came to her often these days. When she'd come back in the summers, everyone gathered there on Sunday afternoons after church. Here, you were called by both your first and middle names, together. Her sister was always Ellie May and she, Mary Ola. That Southern drawl was a kind of music—mesmerizing and relaxing. As kids, they would try to be seen and not heard—up to a point. This was the expected behavior. But then they'd hightail it through the kitchen, then the pantry, which reeked of rotting fruit (or something), and out the squeaky screen door into the backyard to make mud pies. Or wander through the corn stalks and okra growing in the garden. Or sit on the front porch swing and share stories with the cousins.

Marli was pleased the kitchen was now finished enough to use. She liked the enameled sink—it felt more permanent and earthy compared to stainless steel. The tea even tasted better in here than in the camping trailer.

She thought back to Grandma's house and pictured her grandparents' bedroom off the kitchen with a dark little bathroom in the back corner. Grandpa used to sit in a recliner, between the bed and the dresser, and Marli would comb his hair for a nickel. He used to love that. She did it for the money, but he enjoyed the head rub. Dad liked it, too. Marli had come to love it as well—a good scalp massage was hard to beat.

A large insect hit the window and jarred Marli from her trance. She knew her sister would want to move forward with that oil deal. The money would be great. However, an eyesore and health hazard sitting right outside the front door would not be great at all. This evolving house was becoming like a friend to her, developing a life of its own. It was blossoming under the loving hands of the women. And the men. She could almost sense gratitude emanating from its walls and felt obliged to protect it. How could she get her sister to understand, when she was only just beginning to realize it herself? Pondering these thoughts, she shuffled off to bed. The screen door shut behind her and the crickets welcomed her into the night.

———

"What should I wear?" asked Carol the following morning, while rummaging through her suitcase and the side of the closet allotted to her. "I'm tired of these clothes and none of them fit right." A heap of rumpled laundry littered the floor.

"That's it. We're going shopping," Tilda stated. "Let's find you something fun *and* comfortable."

They were getting ready to head over to Canton to window shop, have lunch, and get away for the day. Hammering and painting were all great fun, but after working three days straight, with plaster-dusted hair and grimy fingernails, the ladies were more than ready for an outing. Marli rinsed her coffee cup and looked forward to having a little space that day.

Rose called in through the trailer door from outside, "Aren't you two ready yet?"

"We're comin', we're comin'," Tilda answered.

Rose started the car and waited as Marli walked over.

"You guys have fun. I think I'll go over to the neighbor lady's house to thank her for the 'happy herbs' she gave us. Maybe I'll learn a little more local history while I'm there."

Tilda and Carol finally came out and got in the car and they pulled out of the driveway. Marli waved back at them and wandered over to her beloved house. It looked like the guys were doing fine, working on the many details that remained as they neared the end of construction. Jody was nailing trim onto the front porch ceiling while Joe cleaned out the air compressor. Travis had just left on a supply run to pick up trim boards for the upstairs bedrooms, and finishing nails.

Marli headed over to the trailer when she heard a car horn. A portly fellow got out of a big white Cadillac.

"Hi, my name's Wes and I'm with the oil company," he said. "How do you do, ma'am?"

"Hello, I'm Marli Vernet. I'm probably the one you want to talk to." She wondered what her sister had gone and done now.

"Yes, in fact you are. The company I work for has the oil lease here and we want to start drilling in the next month or so. We're also lookin' to pipe in CO2 to facilitate more oil production," he explained. "Yours is the last signature I need. Your sister faxed hers back last week."

"All right," Marli said slowly. "Is this visit also about the new drilling site here? By the house?"

"Well, yes it is ma'am. Is there a place we could sit for a spell and look over the forms?"

"Yes, of course." A sick feeling crept into her gut. "Let's use the picnic table here. I'll get us some ass tea." Oops. She hadn't meant for it to come out like that. Hopefully, it just sounded like a Southern accent.

The first group of papers dealt with the existing lease. Hers was the last signature needed on a long list of names. She picked up his ballpoint pen and signed the renewal form. "Just please try to minimize the impact on this beautiful property, okay?"

Marli wasn't crazy about the whole oil drilling thing, but she was only one, of many, who owned mineral rights here and there wasn't much she could do about it. She got less than a sixth of one percent of the profits, which was usually nothing, since the wells had been in existence for decades, and completely shut down for the last few years.

Wes opened a manila folder and pulled out a thickly stapled document. He turned it around and handed it to her.

"I believe you've seen this before. If we can drill here, then you and your sister will get a check for $20,000, payable immediately upon signing. Ellie's all ready to fax hers back today, if you agree."

Marli took a deep breath and pretended to read, trying to formulate her thoughts. "Look over there, Wes," she said and pointed toward the new house. "Isn't it beautiful? She's almost finished." Marli paused, for good measure, and hoped he'd notice the pretty flowers in the yard.

"Yes," he said. "It's a nice house."

"Tell me if I'm wrong, Wes. But don't you think large, smelly oil equipment right beside the house might kind of ruin the ambiance of the place?" She paused again. "We've all worked so hard rebuilding this old homestead."

"Yeah, I s'pose I can see your point," he said, and looked again over toward the pastoral scene.

Marli studied the man's face. "And, it most likely would affect resale value. Am I right, Wes?"

"Hm." He scratched his chin. "Well, there is one other way we could do this. You won't get that twenty grand upfront, but you could still get some royalties plus a bit more from the pipeline running through your property already."

"Really? How's that?" Marli sipped her tea and noticed him shift uncomfortably.

He pointed across the road. "If you could talk that colored woman over yonder into drilling the well on her property, then we'd pipe the oil underground through yours." He turned back to face her. "Not too far from the gas line that's already there. It'd be a lot more complicated and not as lucrative for you. But it would still be a little boost for you and your sister. You'd get some of the royalties from this new one, since you own some of the mineral rights there."

Well, this was a turn of events! She knew *that colored woman*. It was Rachel. That nice neighbor across the road. Why hadn't her sister told her about this other option? She had to have known about it. Ellie would have found out if any other options existed, knowing how Marli would feel about tearing up the front yard. Was she really that greedy?

Marli smoldered beneath the surface, but figured she ought to maintain a sense of reason. She managed a smile for Wes and politely told him she'd go over and have a chat with the neighbor.

Wes handed her another manila folder and got back into his car. "This one's for Mizz Barlow," he drawled. The driver's side dipped down with his weight and the tires crunched over the gravel as he drove down the driveway.

Marli finished her *ass tea* and took a cold shower. After eating some vanilla yogurt with granola she felt, just barely, calm enough for a visit. But she was still fuming about her sister's underhanded methods. She walked down the dirt road. The neighbor was sitting on the front porch with an old brown hound dog lying beside her. He picked his head up when Marli climbed the stairs.

"Hello, Rachel." Marli greeted her with a smile. "I want to thank you for that little care package you gave us. We had a lot of fun." The dog came over and sniffed her feet, so she petted him.

"Oh splendid," Rachel responded. "I thought y'all might. You remember Marli, don't you, Rusty?" She set her bowl of snap beans on a side table and dusted off her lap. Green stems fell from her apron.

The two women sat out on the porch and started in on what Marli figured was one of the South's biggest pastimes: rocking and talking. The dog seemed content and lay back down.

"I remember your grandma," said Rachel. "She was a sweet woman and such a frail-looking little thing."

"Yeah, she was pretty skinny, wasn't she? I remember her being so concerned about having good posture that she always leaned way back, to make sure of it." Marli pulled her own shoulders back self-consciously. "I thought she might actually tip over backward one day."

"Yes, she did have extremely good posture," Rachel agreed. "And it seems to me there was some expression she always used to say. Hmm..."

"Oh my goodness alive!" Marli said, laughing.

"Oh yes. That was it. It always made me laugh, too, when she said it. I was sorry I didn't keep up with her. I was just so busy back then. You know how that goes, with children and all, I'm sure." A soft, welcome breeze fluttered the sheets that hung from a clothesline next to the house.

Do you have a minute?" Marli asked, a little nervously. "There's something I'd like to talk over with you. If you don't mind."

"Yes. Of course, Marli," the neighbor said, removing her glasses and giving her full attention.

"Well," Marli began hesitantly. "I had a visitor come over this morning. He's from an oil company that's interested in drilling more around here." She carefully explained how the deal had been presented to her, what she understood it to be, and then handed over the folder. "I'm not that crazy about the whole thing," Marli said as she straightened out her legs. "But it might work in the best of both our interests."

Rachel scanned the pages and asked, "Why wasn't I consulted on this by the oil company?"

"I have no idea," Marli replied. "Other than that they seem to much prefer the simpler approach of just impacting our property. But now we've rebuilt this house and I don't want it right outside the front door."

"Is that where they want to put it?" She gasped and covered her mouth.

"Yup. And my sister, too, evidently." She went on to explain to Rachel the uncomfortable situation she had on her hands.

A grey tabby walked up the front steps and started to rub on Rachel's legs. She bent down to stroke the cat's head. "I don't blame you for not wanting that. I'm not sure how these oil companies work and why it would have to be right there." She flipped a few more pages of the heavy document, moving her lips as her index finger traced along the lines of print. "It looks like it could be over in the northwest corner of my land."

The cat meowed and brushed along the railings on his way over to Marli. "Hello, pretty kitty." She scratched his back a little before looking at Rachel. "Well, read it over and see what you think. No pressure. Really. I'll respect your decision. That's your copy."

Marli had visited for over an hour, rocking and talking. When she got back to the house, she fixed herself a quick snack and went out to the porch. She needed to try to forget about all this oil business until tomorrow. She had decided not to talk with her sister before then. Better for the dust to settle first. Sometimes things would work out better by themselves if you just let them go for a while and try not to fret. She opened her book and eventually was transported to another place and time.

Later, just as Marli closed her book, the ladies returned from Canton. "How was the shopping?" she asked.

"Oh, not bad," Tilda said, trudging up the steps. "We got Carol a great new outfit so she won't have any more reason to complain."

"Well, I'm glad to hear it."

Carol carried several large shopping bags and drawled, "I really must have a glass of *ass tea* right away. My throat is parched as an alligator in a drought."

"Well, don't that paint an interestin' picture," Tilda drawled back. They all went cackling into the house to start making supper, as they all referred to dinner, now that they were becoming "Southernized."

22

AN ART OUTING

Rose

O ver a week had passed since the four friends had arrived in Pickens. Rose was amazed at the oppressive humidity this place possessed. Marli had warned her, but she had no idea it would be this bad. She'd never experienced anything like this—day in and day out. At least in Southern California, when there was humidity it was temporary. But not here. It assaulted her senses as she tried to adjust to it. This was Mississippi, after all.

Rose was on her morning walk; after the dirt road stretch, she circumnavigated the pond, ducking under low-lying branches as she went. She'd risen early as usual, had her coffee, and headed out at the same time Marli took off for a run. The hazy sun was barely up in the sky, but the cicadas were already beginning their relentless chorus. The boards creaked as she walked out on the dock. The boat sat quietly in the dark water, moored with an old rope wrapped around a post. She was glad to be out here despite the mosquitoes. Early morning was the only time even close to comfortable.

Her cell phone rang and she saw John's number on the screen. She knew he'd try to convince her into coming back early. Truth be told, he hadn't wanted her to go in the first place. But being around her three strong, independent friends had bolstered her and she'd become more assertive, at least more sure of herself than she used to be. Thank goodness for that. She took a deep breath and answered. Sometimes he'd call from work, during a break, to check in with her. He, of course, knew she'd be up. She always was by this hour. And with a two-hour time difference, it worked out pretty well. He always got up very early.

"What's up, honey?" she asked, dangling her bare feet in the cool, refreshing water.

"I'm just wondering when you're coming back."

"You know. We talked about it," she said, annoyed, but a little intimidated by his insistence on a shorter trip. "We've got, oh I don't know, maybe another week or so here. And then the drive home." It was only slightly easier to stand up to him from a distance like this. God, what was she doing? Why was she such a wimp? It was a little scary though—what if he left her? She didn't think she'd be able to manage on her own.

To start with, she'd never be able to earn enough. She hadn't had much education. Just a few community college classes after high school, and then they got married. But honestly, it sometimes felt like she had to take care of him. She knew he'd never eat right. He didn't have time. His blood pressure would skyrocket. It was probably going too high right now, as they spoke. Maybe she should just get on a plane and go home now. But instead, she gritted her teeth and quickly changed the subject. "How are the kids? Have you talked to them lately?"

He told her he'd had dinner with them at a friend's house. Both boys were living on their own and checked in with them every couple weeks or so. Rose then cut the conversation short by claiming she had to get back, and hung up. She felt a little surge of pride for having stood up to her husband. It was a small step, she knew. But, by golly, she didn't want to lose the little ground she'd gained by giving him the chance to talk her into coming home early. She watched a dragonfly hover over a water lily and admired its iridescent colors before heading back to the house.

———

Tilda announced it was high time for a visit to an art gallery. She had done some research at the local library. "I found a place in Jackson that has a special showing of soldier art. It has to do with the Civil War in the South. There's only a few more days left before they take it down and I'd like to go see it. Anybody wanna go with me?"

Rose was glad they'd all agreed to do some fun outings, besides just working on the house. After all, it was supposed to be a vacation.

"Do you think we could find a plantation tour the same day? You know, as long as we're in Jackson?" Carol asked. "I'd still like to see more old-style architecture. More than what we've seen cruising through neighborhoods."

Rose recalled that during the first few days after arriving, they'd driven around neighboring towns to look at houses and front yards and acclimate themselves to the area and its merits. They all enjoyed doing this no matter where they were. It was a great way to get ideas for landscaping and yard art. She knew Marli liked to do this with her family when they'd go on vacation. Rose also enjoyed walking along side streets of different neighborhoods, since it provided easy exercise with nice views, and the benefit of collecting visual images for later retrieval.

A two-day trip was planned to fit in everything the four of them wanted to do. Besides the art gallery and a plantation tour, Marli wanted to see a ballet.

"Hopefully, there won't be any riots this time," she said, referencing the mixed race pas de deux she'd told them about before.

Carol shook her head. "This part of the country was not ready for that type of partnership."

"I wonder if they are, even now?" Marli questioned.

Rose was not well acquainted with racial attitudes in the South, since she was a native Californian who'd barely ever been out of the state, and not a big consumer of news. She relied on her husband to keep her informed and that probably resulted in her being somewhat sheltered.

The women packed their suitcases and drove an hour south to Jackson. Traffic was much lighter here than at home; there were no congested freeways. It was a relaxing drive along the two-lane roads that connected the small towns and cities. The heat waves that rose from the asphalt highway had a hypnotic effect, and Rose soon began to feel drowsy. She was thankful Marli was driving. When the others drove, she sometimes got queasy with their quick braking and swerving turns.

The soldier art exhibit at the museum was interesting and informative. There were sketches and an occasional watercolor depicting the war from a soldier's point of view, intended for his family or sweetheart back home. These men portrayed their daily lives and preserved memories amid the chaos of war. Professional artists' work was also featured here. Among them was Conrad Wise Chapman, whose oil paintings of Charleston Harbor offered a glimpse into wartime scenes. After the war, many Northern artists produced works that glorified and memorialized the valor and bravery of Confederate soldiers.

Tilda said, "Man, look at these minute details here. I can almost imagine what military life must have been like."

"Yeah. It's like the artists were looking from the outside in and seeing how the soldiers might have seen themselves." Carol leaned forward to scrutinize the next framed work of art.

"Some of these are absolutely incredible," Marli whispered.

"But what a horrible thing to have to live through." Rose was beginning to understand more as she looked on.

She learned that during the Civil War, families at home insisted on knowing the particulars of the lives of their sons who were fighting in the war. Of course they would. Never before had there been such a demand for news. Many journalists were wounded, captured, or killed in the field or incapacitated by disease. By the early 1860s, a new feature of the press was the illustrated weekly newspaper. All of these, such as *Harper's Weekly* and the *New York City Illustrated News*, were published in New York City. Unfortunately, their circulation in the South was cancelled in 1861 due to the war.

Carol read aloud, "During the process of the Union armies taking over the South, much was lost to fire and looting. Some works survived, such as Henry Lovie's. He had gone to Europe to work from there." As she walked ahead, she read another placard. "*The Southern Illustrated News* was established after a year and a half of war, but unfortunately the dire economic situation of the South did not allow this publication to have many illustrations. They could not afford an artist in the field, and only occasional pictures and cartoons were included."

Tilda and Carol seemed especially interested in the historical significance of all this. Rose was self-conscious about her lack of academic background. She often felt a little insecure since all three of her friends were well-educated women. After spending two hours in the gallery, they walked through the double doors and out onto the sidewalk.

"I'm hungry," Rose said.

"What's new?" Marli asked. "Just teasing. I'm hungry, too."

They had booked rooms in an old plantation mansion that included supper. Luckily, it was to be served early, which would give them time to catch the ballet at 8:00 p.m. They drove out of the downtown area to the outskirts of town and then up a long, narrow driveway lined with very old pecan trees. After they pulled into a designated parking space, the lady tourists toted their suitcases up the steps onto the soaring, columned front porch. Roses bloomed in profusion.

"Wow, this is impressive." Carol gazed around her. "Will you look at those beautiful French windows."

Marli opened the large, glass-paned door and let her friends go in ahead of her. Dark wooden shutters, which were swung inward, let in breezes and soft light. She walked up to the front desk to check in. Their rooms were on the second floor.

"This is gorgeous, but I sure wouldn't want to have to clean this place." Rose slid her hand along the smooth banister, checking for dust.

"I'm sure they have lots of help to do that. Look at all those ornate spirals." Carol pointed out the scrolled stair railings.

Rose found it difficult to walk up the stairs while dragging her suitcase—she hardly watched where she was going since her eyes kept drifting to the elaborate details of the place. This brick antebellum mansion stood strong; it had survived floods and urban sprawl. Obviously, great care and lots of money kept this relic a beautiful, functional masterpiece. It was an absolutely grand, gorgeous work of art. She couldn't help contrasting it to her own small, manufactured home. This was unbelievable. Like a castle in a fairy tale.

Rose and Marli would share a corner room. Tilda and Carol had a suite that looked out over back lawns surrounded by roses and lush magnolia trees. Rose flopped down on one of the beds, grabbed a pillow, and poofed it up to rest her head on.

She breathed out a contented sigh. "I could get used to this."

"Me, too." Marli pulled a lace curtain aside to get a better view of the side gardens and carriage house. "It's too bad this place is so far away from home. I think I'd come back here regularly if it were closer."

"I know it, huh?"

At 5:00 p.m., they all headed downstairs to a large dining room. Halfway down, Tilda stopped to point out an oil painting of a Southern belle, complete with the typical stern expression.

Carol asked Rose, "Does your room have a fireplace in it?"

"Yes, it does."

"I think most rooms do in these big, fancy mansions," Marli said.

They sat at a square table set for four next to a large picture window. An African American woman, wearing a black and white uniform, served platters of Southern fare, including fried chicken and okra, mashed potatoes and gravy, and rolls. They passed the dishes around and helped themselves, in a hurry to leave soon for the ballet.

"Oh good," Carol said. "More fried food. Just what I need."

"We'll all have to go on diets when we get back home." Marli was getting fuller by the bite.

"Are you all right, Tilda?" Rose asked. "You're awfully quiet."

"Yeah," Tilda replied. "I'm just thinking about those Confederate illustrations. They showed so much detail."

Rose noticed the effect the museum tour had had on Tilda. Usually, she was such a talkative person, always wanting to have her say. But tonight she seemed different. Every so often, Tilda would get into a mood. Sometimes you'd get the silent treatment and sometimes a verbal swipe. Hopefully, this would pass soon.

Later, at the ballet, the lights dimmed and the curtains parted. The symphony began to play and Rose watched Tilda close her eyes and smile slightly. She noticed Marli and Carol gently sway to the music. Halfway through the ballet, Carol rifled through her purse to retrieve a breath mint.

Rose asked Marli, "Has Giselle come back to life or is she a ghost like those others?"

"Well, she died of a broken heart and now she's joined the Wilis in the afterlife. All those fair maidens also died from unrequited love. Que sera, sera," Marli whispered.

Rose watched as the story unfolded through the dancing. The tale of *Giselle* was bittersweet and heart-wrenching like so many ballets, she'd heard. Giselle falls in love with Albrecht, a duke disguised as a peasant. Albrecht, however, is engaged to a noblewoman he does not love. Giselle eventually learns the truth and dies of a broken heart. She becomes a Wili, a ghost who seeks nighttime revenge on unsuspecting men. In this particular rendition, Albrecht visits Giselle's grave, where he is forced to dance to his death by the sister Wilis.

The storyline is fleshed out with more characters and Marli told her the ending can vary. "The musical score was composed by Adolphe Adam and first performed in France in 1841. This ballet, mostly because of the beautiful music, is one of my absolute favorites. I choreographed and directed a version of it for my own company, remember?"

Rose did remember. All the soloists, as well as the corps de ballet, had danced well tonight, and reminded her why her friend was so passionate about ballet.

It was late by the time the final curtain came down and the foursome ventured back to their lodging.

On the drive back, Tilda said, "All those love-sick tales look the same to me. But the orchestra played beautifully."

"Yes it did." Marli turned right at a light. "Those stories can be quite similar. I find it rather amusing that most of the men seem a little stupid and completely at the mercy of the women. I think it's a good lesson, sometimes, for the teenage girls. Every time I tell one of these story ballet plots to my students, it somehow comes across that way to them, too."

"Good lesson indeed," Carol affirmed.

Rose laughed with the others, relieved that Tilda now seemed back to normal. It had been a long day of sightseeing and she was looking forward to bed.

———

The next morning, they got up early for the first plantation tour of the day. They joined a group of ten and followed a young woman who narrated little historical tidbits as they walked through the house. The place was immaculate. Carol stopped and ran her fingers over the filigree on the edge of a desk next to a window.

Once outside, Rose said, "I can't believe how green and beautiful everything is here. I wish I could grow gardens like these."

They would have been happy to stay longer, but they wanted to get back to Pickens before dark. So, after a leisurely lunch, they left Jackson and headed up the 55 once again.

23

WHAT COLOR IS THAT?

*T*he large, drooping canopy of the old weeping willow provided shade and a subtle camouflage for the front porch. Rose added her personal touch when she'd planted the African violets and red and pink impatiens in the flower beds. Marli gazed over at the picturesque scene early Monday morning from a chair in front of the trailer, while drinking her coffee. All was quiet, except for a few cicadas, and the cool moist air enveloped her. This had always been Marli's favorite time of day.

Later, the four of them traipsed over to the house with color swatches from the hardware store. Today was the day they would decide the color for the exterior of the house. As if following directions from within, each of the four women went wordlessly to different areas on the porch and held up her own personal favorite.

Marli said, "I want the house to blend in, as much as possible, to the woodsy surroundings. I've always liked dark brown because it doesn't stand out much, at least in our canyon area."

"But it's so green here," Tilda reminded her.

"Well, that's true. Maybe we could try mixing brown and green together and see what happens," Marli suggested.

"You're gonna end up with the color of shit, sounds like to me." Jody appeared from the side porch with a can of wood putty and a knife.

"You mean more like sick baby poop," Travis added, joining Jody.

"Oh, gross," said Carol. "But—it may not turn out as bad as you think."

"Now wait just a minute! Let's go back to the hardware store and have them mix a few colors and see what we like best." Once again, Rose worked to keep the peace.

The women agreed to do just that and returned later with three small cans of varying shades of greenish-brown.

Marli, Tilda, and Carol each stepped up onto the porch and brushed paint onto the side of the house. Rose stood back giggling. Each of them performed her own brand of salesmanship to promote her chosen color, and it resembled an advertisement bordering on performance art, complete with laughter and applause. Tilda painted a picture of a violin along with a bow and musical notes. Marli danced around hers—curtsying to each side. Carol reached and stretched with huge, long brush strokes. The guys had taken seats on the front railings. Travis crossed his arms over his chest and Jody removed his cap to wipe his brow as the noon train whistled in the distance.

Jody shook his head and chuckled. "Well, I don't know, Travis. Which shade of poop do you like best?"

"Oh, he probably likes the artistic, musical one," said Marli, side-stepping what she really thought. She couldn't help but notice his and Carol's natural attraction to one another.

"Hey, we're all artists here," Tilda said.

"Well, what do you know?" said Carol. "Did y'all hear that? She says we're all artists now." Tilda *was* rather particular about who she considered to be an artist or not.

"Woo hoo!" Rose shouted, her laughter adding to the chorus.

Travis nodded toward Carol's. "I think I like the big rainbow brush strokes at the end there."

And that's the one everyone finally agreed upon: the medium poop color.

———

The next morning—another hot, sticky day, Carol decided to stay and help paint the house instead of going to visit the neighbor with the others. After all, painting was practically her favorite pastime. And she had lots of experience with painting the walls of her own house—over and over and over again. Just for the fun of it. Picking intriguing colors, brushing new paint on interior surfaces, standing back and imagining the aesthetic possibilities— each provided her with stress relief. And then, when the stress level rose again, or she just got sick of looking at *not quite the right colors* anymore, she'd start the process all over again. This way, she was never finished. Her house seemed to reflect her own unsettled, unfulfilled inner state. She always appeared to exist in a constant sea of chaos. Some people thrived like that. Marli worried one day she might pay the price for it, but for now it just made her more entertaining to be around.

The others left Carol to indulge in her "paint therapy" and walked down the road to take Rachel two of the watermelons Joe had brought over. They didn't need all four.

"Hello ladies!" Rachel called from her front porch. Her faithful old dog, Rusty, was by her side. "It's so nice to see y'all again." Her house was attractive, architecturally, but could definitely use a fresh coat of paint.

"We brought you some watermelons from Joe's mom's garden," Rose said, holding up one of the medium-sized beauties.

"That's mighty kind of you," Rachel said. "They're lovely. Now come on up her and sit a spell, won't you?"

"Thank you. I don't mind if I do," Tilda answered and set her melon down on a small wooden crate, next to Rose's.

Rachel continued snapping beans into the bowl in her lap and the visitors settled into the old eclectic chairs.

"Here, let me help you with those." Marli picked up an empty bowl. "I was wondering if you'd had a chance to look over those oil papers?"

"A little bit. From what I could tell, it seems like a decent enough deal. I wondered about the location and the piping though, and all that." Rachel tipped her full bowl of green fragments into a larger dish and began again. "But my son has a lawyer looking over it for me. I'll keep you posted."

They spent the morning snapping beans and talking about the past. Marli was happy her friends were getting to experience this Mississippi pastime firsthand. It was good rural Southern conversation at its best. She looked up from her bowl of green beans. "You know, Rachel, my dad used to talk about these three boys who lived in town when he was a kid. He insisted their names were Boy, Man, and Pig. And those were actually their honest-to-goodness, real names. It sounds so strange. Could it possibly have been true?"

Rachel stopped mid-snap. "Oh, I don't know. I know folks were real poor back then, what with the Depression on and all. Kids had all sorts of nicknames—and some families were pretty large. But it was before my time, though." She shook her head and smiled. "But who knows? I suppose it could've been."

Marli began again. "He also told us he had a friend who everybody called Six-Toed Joe. And he really did have six toes. What do you make of that?"

"Six toes on one foot? On both feet? Or six toes all together?" Rose asked. She leaned over to pick up a bean she'd dropped and Rusty ambled over to sniff the area.

"Well, I don't rightly know," Marli mocked in an exaggerated Southern accent. "I suppose he meant on each foot, but it was before my time, too."

They sounded like a bunch of cackling hens, all excited over a nest of bugs or something.

Rachel's mother, who'd been taking a nap, shuffled out the screen door. She wore an old, rumpled house dress and dark brown loafers.

"Did you have a good rest, Mama?"

"Well, I sure 'nough did," she said, nodding to the company on the porch. "I'm Ruth." She sat down heavily in the rocking chair next to the door.

Rachel introduced her new California friends. "And this is my mother, Ruth."

"They already know that, dear," Ruth said. "Did you introduce old Rusty, too? He's gettin' mighty old. Just like me."

"Yes, I did, Mama. Marli's grandma was Martha Jean Vernet. Do you remember her?"

"Hmm. My memory ain't what it used to be. Weren't she a schoolteacher over in the Pickens school?"

"Yes, she was," Marli answered excitedly.

"Yes, yes—I do remember now. She was right nice. Everbody knowed her. Ethel will be here soon to git me, Rachel. Ya know that ear that's been troublin' her? Well, the doctor put some stitches in it, which will hopefully hold it closer to her head. You know, after that dawg gone and bit her. It looks better now."

Marli glanced at her friends, checking out their shocked expressions. She was familiar with this kind of banter back here, but they were not.

"Yes, she told me about that, Mama."

"That sounds awful." Rose shifted in her seat. "Is her ear going to be all right?" A noisy crow landed in the grass, under the laundry hanging on the clothes line.

"Mm hmm. It'll be all right in the end, I s'pose," Ruth drawled.

Marli grabbed more beans from Rachel's bowl. "My grandma told us when my dad was a baby his ears stuck straight out. So every time she held him she'd have one hand behind his little head, reaching around with her fingers to hold his ears down flat against the sides of his skull. That seemed to straighten his ears right out, according to her."

The group snickered with the direction this conversation was taking.

Ruth chuckled and leaned back to rock. "I s'pose any mother might do that."

Marli snapped her last bean and dropped the two halves into her bowl. Curiosity burned as she wrangled the courage to ask Rachel and Ruth, two black women, or *colored* as they were referred to in these parts, what life was really like for them here in the Deep South. These were women who continued to live in the center of the Confederacy, as descendants of slaves.

"When my sister and I were kids, and came here to visit our grandparents—" she began. "There was usually a black woman cooking in the kitchen."

There was a long pause as Marli attempted to collect her thoughts.

"Yes?" Rachel asked, breaking the silence and looking over her glasses.

"Well, a lot of houses seemed to have—um—maids, I mean—" She wasn't quite sure of how to phrase things.

"Yes indeed. They still do," Ruth affirmed. "My grand mammy mostly raised me and my two sisters, 'cause Mama worked for Mizz Parker over in Jackson. She'd get home ever Saturday evenin' and have Sundy's off with us. She'd leave early Mondy mornin' to start it all over again."

Marli was surprised Ruth opened up so quickly. Tilda and Rose bent forward, obviously uncomfortable, to concentrate on their bean snapping.

"When my chillun come along, I made sure they wouldn't have to be maids like my mama and me. Yes siree, they both went to college. They made me right proud." Ruth leaned back and smiled at the memory.

"That's wonderful. How'd you manage it?"

"It was awful hard, but my husband and me did without and scrimped and saved and just put one foot in front of tha otha."

"It must have been very challenging. You know, with the attitudes around here. It sure didn't seem fair," Marli said.

"No, it sure wasn't. In fact, it still isn't." Rachel turned to look at her mother. They both glanced downward.

Marli began again. "I remember one time when we were heading off to church with Grandma, walking down the front steps in our new flowery dresses. Gloria, I think that was her maid's name, came up the walkway toward the front door and told us how adorable and cute my sister and I looked. That woman smiled so big and seemed so happy. But now that I'm older, and trying to understand some of this, I can't help but think she was just putting on a face. She probably couldn't stand any of us white folks, after what we put them through." Marli shook her head and thought of her dad.

He'd told her that as a kid, they'd gone to church every Sunday. His little town of Pickens was unique. On one Sunday a month, his Baptist congregation would go over to the Methodist church for service and on another Sunday they'd come over to his. He'd even go to the Presbyterian one week and on the fourth Sunday everyone went to their own church, where they were members, for business meetings and to get together with their pastor. He told her he'd never seen that anywhere else, and that it was a wonderful thing. He said he didn't think it mattered what church you went to, "as long as you believed on God and the teachings of Christ." Evidently, he even went to the "colored" church, a couple times. He'd sit outside and just listen to them sing. Marli could almost hear his voice. He'd come a long way in his attitudes. The guy probably had to when he moved to California after growing up here. He'd become more open-minded, but had still remained too biased for her comfort.

Marli mumbled, "I'm sorry—for all those entitled white folks. As if it does any good."

"It's not that simple," Rachel said. "That maid woman probably really did love your family. With all the brainwashing and segregation and trying to keep us ignorant, it's hard to say what each one felt independently. Attitudes are not changing very quickly around here. There's still so much conflict."

"And we've even seen Confederate flags flying around here," Tilda said with a frown.

A car pulled into the driveway and honked, scaring a stray cat up onto the porch. Ruth got up, excused herself, and the black kitty bolted around the corner. Rachel helped her mother down the steps and talked to her sister, who was taking their mother back to Yazoo City.

The women stayed and had dinner, complete with the watermelons they'd brought, and spent most of the afternoon in Rachel's air-conditioned house.

"It feels wonderful in here." Tilda sank into the large, comfortable couch to sip her *ass tea.*

"As my grandma used to say, 'I'm thoroughly enjoying this.'" Rachel's warm hospitality reminded Marli of those long, languid afternoons in Grandma's house. The musical cadence of that Southern accent lulled her into a safe cocoon of comfort.

On the short walk home, Tilda said in a hushed voice. "I wonder what Carol and Travis are up to."

"Why, they're painting, of course." Rose snickered.

"Yeah, right. Don't tell me you haven't noticed the chemistry between those two." Tilda turned around and walked backward, ahead of them.

"Of course, we have," Marli said. "But we oughta cut 'em some slack, don't you think?"

"No way! This is way too much fun. I kind of hope she gets some, you know?"

"You're so crass, Tilda." Rose shook her head, but grinned.

"So, you want to take bets? I say they get together before we leave Mississippi. How about you guys?"

Marli turned thoughtful. "As much as I'd like to, I don't want to feed it one way or another. Let's just hang back, give them space, and see what happens. It's none of our business, anyway."

"I know," Rose said. "But I'm betting on it, too."

They arrived back at the house as Carol and Travis came walking up the path together. Tilda gave Marli a knowing glance and Rose smiled.

Jody came around the corner. "Y'all are here just in time to see the brand-new, poop-colored house. It's the *in* style, you know. The latest rage. How do you like her?"

Marli wrestled with her own natural attraction to Jody, especially when he raised his eyebrows specifically at her.

"Ooh, I think I like it," Rose said.

"Me, too," Tilda and Carol said, almost in unison.

Marli looked at the house and then at the surrounding woods. "Yes! It blends into the canopy so nicely. I do believe this color will really catch on here," she joked. "It's just that it may not be very popular with the folks who want to stand out and be noticed."

"Nuh-uh," Travis interrupted. "I think this here house is gonna be one of a kind."

"Yup." Jody laughed. "Poop color and all."

Joe just stood back and smiled and in his quiet manner he began cleaning the air compressor hoses.

"One more coat," Jody said. "We'll do that tomorrow, if it doesn't rain. And then we'll paint the trim."

That evening, the razzing began.

"So, Carol. What did you do today?" Tilda prodded, emphasizing the word *you*.

"I helped paint the house. What do you think I did?"

"Well, you did show up with Travis from who knows where," Rose teased.

They were sitting around the picnic table in front of the trailer, drinking wine.

Carol got up to pour herself a glass of water. "Well, if you must know, I helped paint this morning and then I made lunch for all of us. Travis offered to help clean up afterward and Joe and Jody went back to painting."

"And?" Tilda pressed.

"Then he wanted to take a walk when we'd finished putting the leftovers away and washing dishes. I pointed out how hot it was, but he persisted. You know, to get away from the paint fumes," she said, making quotation marks with her fingers, grinning.

"Just a walk?" Rose asked.

"Yes. Just a walk. We went out to the oil well, which isn't pumping, by the way. Did you know that, Marli? The ground all around it is just bare gravel."

Marli recognized the attempt to avoid the subject and went along with it. "That's probably so the trucks can maneuver when it's muddy."

"Anyway, we followed the dirt road back to the soybean field at the edge of the woods and then wandered toward the pond. Have you seen that crumbled-down brick hearth over there? Travis said it was probably an old servant's cabin."

"I think it was." She remembered coming across it with her sister last year.

"Come on, Carol. You're holding back," Tilda sung.

Carol blushed. "He kissed me. Okay? Y'all happy now?"

"I knew it!" Tilda gleefully shouted.

"Aw, I hope you guys go out," Rose said. "I think that would be a good thing for you, Carol. Don't you?"

"I don't know. My life's so screwed up right now. And I'm rusty. I mean really rusty. It's been a very long time since I've been—uh—*with* anyone. And I'm a little nervous."

"I know you feel that way. But you're both adults. It doesn't have to mean any more than it does right now. And it doesn't have to last forever." Tilda refilled Carol's wine glass and added, "But it might make *now* just a little bit better. That's all."

Not bad advice at all, Marli thought.

24

A NEW SKIN

Ellie

llie kicked off the duvet for the umpteenth time, frustrated by her lack of sleep for the past two hours. Lying awake, hot-cold-hot-cold, she couldn't help but stew over the messed-up oil deal. She'd been so excited by what this new drilling could offer them. Why did Marli have to go and complicate things?

She had predicted her sister would not be too keen on an oil well sitting right next to the new house, but they weren't ever actually going to *live* there, anyway. She was hoping that, as a rental, it wouldn't matter so much. Knowing Marli, she had asked Watero if there were any other options and they'd informed her about the neighbor's location. They had already researched that, just in case, even before Ellie had asked. But, obviously, they preferred the simpler option, as did she, and were pushing for that one. She wished Marli had simply signed on the dotted line so they could be done with it and be $20,000 richer—with the promise of more healthy profits to come. Ellie's thoughts drifted back to Christmas morning, three or four years before, at Marli's house.

Dad had been leaning back in the recliner with his eyes closed. When Marli brought him a cup of coffee, he'd smiled, just sensing what she'd done. He seemed so comfortable there and would show up often, unannounced according to her sister, and putter around the place and visit. It was like a second home to him. He'd even eat Marli's quasi-vegetarian fare. Things like tofu mess, Swiss chard tacos, wild miner's lettuce salad—things he normally would have avoided.

Marli had a way of making him feel welcome and comfortable. He hardly ever just dropped by Ellie's house. But then, she was rarely home, and always busy even if she was. She and Bob didn't have time to make dinners together or simply hang out with the old man.

She got up to get a drink of water and use the toilet. She watched the water swirl down the bowl and pictured their oil money doing the same. And Dad. And Mom. Everything seemed to go down the toilet in the end. She looked in the mirror while washing her hands and noticed the gray undertones in her bangs. Ugh. Time for another touch-up already?

She returned to bed and pulled the covers up over her again, laying back onto her pillow. Bob was snoring, so she moved her leg against him so he'd roll over onto his side. What if she'd taken more time off to do fun things? Perhaps worked less? Or spent more time with Dad? She could have known him better than she did. But Bob had insisted that she earn her potential. That was the lifestyle they'd have to live if he was going to stay married to her. It hadn't seemed like much of a sacrifice in the beginning. It simply evolved into how they were now. But at what cost? She wondered.

At 6:00 a.m., the alarm went off and her hand swung at it several times before she hit the snooze button. Bob was already gone. After the second alarm, she threw off the covers and stood up, ran her hand through her hair, and looked back at the rumpled silk sheets. Thankfully, the housecleaner was coming today.

———

After a morning of showing houses, she met Bob at the attorney's office. They'd made the appointment to add some things to their trusts. One of them was her half of the Mississippi property.

"Of course, this will go into your separate trust, Ms. Vernet," said the thin woman in a gray suit. Both she and Marli had kept their maiden names.

Bob had pushed her to get the property into the trust soon, before any encumbrances, such as a finished house, could affect the status of the estate. But Ellie wanted things to be clear, so she explained the building situation to the lawyer.

The lady turned in her swivel chair and peered over her glasses at Ellie, then Bob, then back to Ellie. She cleared her throat and reiterated what she'd just heard. "You'll need to discuss this with your sister and have your percentages of ownership, house versus land, and whatever else there is, legally documented so we'll be able to reference this in your trust."

Ellie felt Bob's eyes practically burn a hole into her. He shook his head disapprovingly. At that precise moment, it felt like he was a mirror reflecting back to her, the person she had become. Greedy. Self-centered. Chasing the almighty dollar. She was shocked. What had happened to her?

"Excuse me," she said and stood up. "I have to go now." She grabbed her purse and the folder of papers. "I'll let you know when I figure it out."

Ellie hurried down the stairs and out to her car. She was shaking and pulled out in front of another car. She slammed on the brakes when a horn blasted behind her. She looked back, took a breath, then accelerated. She felt the ice-cold air conditioning blast onto her wet face. It felt like she was in an icebox. She hadn't even realized she'd been crying. Wiping a finger under her eye, to make sure they were tears, she wondered how she could be this out of touch. With herself. With Dad. With Bob. "Bloody hell!" She cried all the way to the coast.

Ellie took the Pacific Coast Highway north; it hugged the shoreline most of the way. This was as close as she could get, in her car anyway, to massive amounts of water. She loved the beach and the calming effect it often had on her. She rolled down the window and breathed in the salty ocean breeze, slowing down now on that Friday afternoon. She needed to be alone with her thoughts and emotions, so she continued to drive—with no destination and no radio. She reached down and turned off her cell phone. She wanted time for inward reflection with no distractions.

She began to think Marli might be right. She *did* need a break. Probably from herself, but how was that possible? She thought back to when she'd taken off on a trip to Europe, right after college. On a whim, she'd joined Marli and spent the summer staying in youth hostels and getting around with a Eurail pass. She'd met Bob almost as soon as she'd returned. Then their life together, on the treadmill, began. The future looked bright and promising, so she'd jumped in, no questions asked. But now she dreamt of that earlier carefree time again.

She paid for her Starbuck's coffee at the drive-through window and got back on the PCH, heading north. Once again, the ocean breeze caressed her face. All of a sudden, she felt she had to get back in touch with that other person. The one she was before she met Bob. Instantly, she knew what she had to do. She had to go to Mississippi! Join Marli and her friends and share the expense of the house! It was *her* money. Not Bob's. Life was too short to just save for more, more, more. Her sister was right, doggone it. Enough is enough! Her mind became crystal clear, as if a heavy fog lifted. Tears streamed down her face and this time she was fully aware of them. What an epiphany! She turned around and headed home to pack.

25

A SURPRISE VISIT

After breakfast, Rose and Carol began installing outlet cover plates. Tilda and Marli were going to hang wallpaper in the two bedrooms upstairs. Tilda had done this before and Marli was eager to learn how. She had picked the flowered print after seeing the same pattern in Rachel's house.

"It's a good thing we're getting an early start. This'll take all morning." Tilda groaned as she carried the bag of rolled wallpaper up the staircase.

Marli lugged the five-gallon pail of adhesive up after her. "Yup, it's just a hair after 7:00 a.m. now. I think this'll be beautiful." She set the bucket down under the tall dormer window as Tilda began removing the plastic wrap from the rolls.

"The rose pattern is for this room, isn't it?"

"Yeah, the ribbon design is for the other one."

Tilda had chosen the ribbon one when they'd ordered that rose pattern. Marli spread newspapers over the floor while Tilda read the directions.

"I want to make sure I remember all the details of hanging wallpaper before we start."

"Good idea." Marli was glad her former college roommate had done this before so they wouldn't both be novices at this tricky task. She poured the adhesive into the tray and scrunched her nose. "This is pungent stuff."

Tilda squatted with the first eight-foot-long roll. "Here, you hold the end while I paint this on. We need to try to keep it even, okay?" Tilda looked up at Marli and handed her the roll.

Together they unrolled, brushed, hung, smoothed out wrinkles and examined the results over and over again. Column by column, red and pink roses sprouted onto the room's walls, concealing the drab sheetrock.

"This is going to be nice. Way better than the hideous wallpaper in that one house we rented during our senior year. Remember that?" Tilda asked.

"No doubt. And hopefully this wallpaper will stay. Unlike that lovely mustard-colored junk you couldn't stand. By the way, I didn't think the color you painted over it with was much better, though."

"Yeah, but it was free. A different era, you know?" Tilda pulled another sheet up on the wall. "Hey, do you think that oil deal you were talking over with Rachel is going to work?"

Marli held the bottom of the strip away from the wall. "I don't know. I hope so. Better than a smelly monster right outside the front door."

Morning sunlight shone through the filter of leafy trees outside the window and danced on the newly decorated walls.

"It's lovely, don't you think?" Marli asked.

Tilda moved to the center of the room and looked around. "Yes, it most certainly is."

They moved their operation into the second bedroom and began the process all over again, but this time with the multicolored ribbon-design wallpaper. Halfway through, the top edge of one of the columns began to roll down. Marli lunged over to grab it with her left hand as her right remained on the piece they were working with. All of a sudden, a third set of hands appeared and pushed the paper back up.

"Ellie? Oh my God!" Marli yelped. "You're here! You're actually, really here! How on earth?" She stood there holding up the wallpaper, frozen, with her mouth agape. "Oh, my goodness alive!"

"Yay! To the rescue," Tilda said. "I didn't know you were coming."

"I didn't either, until last night." Ellie pressed the paper under her hands. "But I couldn't resist. I should be here. I didn't want to miss all the fun."

"Good for you. It means a lot." Then Marli mocked in a Southern accent, "We were doin' so well up 'til that last piece." She sensed a possible change of heart in her sister. A lighter mood maybe? She decided to put her misgivings about the oil well business aside and give Ellie the benefit of doubt and try to move past it for now. "It's good to see you."

"Is this right?" Ellie asked, pressing the sheet upward and smoothing out the bubbles.

"Yeah, that's perfect." Tilda stood back and crossed her arms.

Ellie finally let go and hugged her sister. After the long embrace, she studied the four walls of the room. "You guys are doing a great job. I'm impressed."

After finishing the last section, Marli hugged her sister again while keeping her gooey palms turned outward. "I'm so glad you got here. Let me give you a tour." She wiped her hands on a rag and led Ellie down the stairs to the kitchen, pointing out the porcelain enameled sink. "How do you like it?"

"It fits perfectly here. And what a nice view out this window."

"What made you change your mind about coming here? I mean, really."

Ellie turned and walked over to look out another window. "I guess I just wanted to see things for myself. And you're right. I need an adventure, too."

Marli sensed there was more to it, but her sister looked drained. More drained than she should've been from just the flight and the drive up in the rented car from Jackson. But then she realized she must have taken the red-eye. She decided not to pry.

"So, what do *y'all* think about Mississippi weather?" Ellie asked, after the other women joined them in the kitchen.

Carol wiped the sweat off her forehead with the back of her hand. "It's *downrat* lovely."

"Oh, it's not so bad once you get used to it, I guess," Rose admitted with a warm smile.

"How'd you manage to get away, anyway?" Carol asked. "I thought your summer was booked up."

"Well, I rearranged my schedule. I figured I could spend a few days with *y'all* and see how you're doing. Besides, Marli, your husband suggested I come since I'm quite a bit ahead of him sorting through Dad's stuff. He said a getaway might be good for me. And plus, Maddy doesn't have any cheer competitions for a couple weeks. I'll drive back to Jackson the day after tomorrow, Monday, to catch a flight home."

"I'm glad it worked out for you." Carol held up the spray bottle and gave Ellie a surprise squirt.

"Hey! What's that for?"

They all laughed together.

"It's our poor man's personal air conditioner," Marli explained.

Rose added, "But we share."

Ellie rolled her eyes. "Oh brother. You guys are too much."

The five of them made sandwiches, *ass tea*, and sliced dill pickles for a late lunch. Since it was Saturday, the men were off early for the day.

"How 'bout we all go swimmin' this afternoon?" Marli suggested.

"I'm for that," Ellie answered.

"That'll feel great." Rose started gathering the dishes. "I'm so sweaty."

They all changed into swimsuits and walked down the trail to the pond, towels thrown over their shoulders or wrapped around them. With shrieks and laughter they eased into the water and swam toward the middle, except for Carol who went around to the dock to untie the boat.

"This is just what the doctor ordered." Tilda rolled over and kicked into a backstroke.

"I sure wish we had something like this at home," Ellie said, before ducking under the water. They all agreed.

Carol paddled over to the group and was finally coaxed into the water by her friends.

"Don't you feel better now?" Marli gently splashed her hair.

"Yes ma'am," Carol said, before sending a wave over Marli's face.

"Hey! You better watch yourself, girl," Marli teased. "Anybody want a beer? I can go grab a six-pack out of the reefer."

"Reefer?" Carol laughed. "I thought you said you were getting beer."

"I am. It's just what Ellie and I grew up calling the refrigerator. Our parents called it that." Marli grinned at her sister. "Remember?"

"Yes, I do."

"Okay, whatever you say."

"It's true," Ellie insisted. "We didn't know any different."

When Marli returned, she gave each of them "a cold one" on the dock. They were busy diving and cannonballing into the refreshing water, acting like children.

"What a great way to spend the afternoon, huh?" Tilda clinked her bottle against Marli's.

"I agree," Rose said as she spread her towel on the end of the dock and lay down on it.

"Hey, Ellie?" Carol asked. "It's nice to be away for a while, huh?"

"It sure is. It was tough to get away, though. Bob doesn't understand. He thinks I'm having a nervous breakdown. Maybe I am."

"Me, too," said Carol.

"I hope it's not a trend." Marli kicked her dangling feet in the water below.

"Yeah. That could send us all into early retirement." Ellie closed her eyes and tipped her head back toward the sun.

"Or an insane asylum," Tilda countered.

"I guess it would have to be the institution for me since I'll never be able to afford to retire," Carol claimed.

"Ain't that the truth." Tilda sat down next to Marli. "I don't know what I'm going to do."

Ellie climbed into the boat and arranged her towel.

Rose suggested they talk about something more fun than their insufficient retirement funds, which seemed unavoidable since the recent economic downturn.

Marli drew circles in the water with her feet and sipped her beer. "And you know what else? This Southern weather sure doesn't help any with the hot flashes."

"I find them annoying no matter where I am." Ellie reached over the side of the boat to splash water onto her face. "About a month ago, I woke up drenched in sweat. I got up and opened the back door and just stood there. It felt like I was going to burst into flames. I stared at the pool and thought of jumping in, but then I figured that would wake me up even more and I'd never get back to sleep. And, of course, I had to get up early the next morning for work."

Carol laughed. "I know it. Sometimes, I'll be at the front of my class, feeling the sweat ooze out of my pores, knowing my clothes are getting completely drenched, and hoping the students don't notice."

"I must throw the covers on and off twenty times a night," said Rose. "I try not to wake John with my tossing around, but it gets unbearable sometimes."

"Yeah, poor Richard must think I don't love him anymore. Sometimes he'll reach over and just put his hand on my back. But it feels so hot it burns, and I can't wait to get away from it. I feel bad, but it's like Ellie said. I'm an inferno, ready to self-combust." Marli shook her head at the thought.

Tilda stood on the corner of the dock and looked out over the pond. "I haven't had many hot flashes. It hasn't seemed that bad to me."

Carol and Marli looked at each other, stood up, and walked innocently toward their pre-menopausal friend. They locked arms behind her and nudged Tilda over the edge. The resulting splash sprayed everyone, which reminded Marli of the special bond they had with each other.

Rose giggled. "You deserved that, you know."

"I guess I did," Tilda gasped. She swam around to the shallow water to climb back onto the dock.

"I'm glad I got to come out and see *y'all*," Ellie said. "This is fun."

"I'll drink to that," said Marli. "Cheers, everybody. Bottom's up."

Refreshed and relaxed, the group gathered the towels and empty bottles and wandered back up along the path. Ellie and Marli turned right to walk around the pond.

"What really changed your mind?" Marli asked, ducking under a wispy limb.

Ellie stopped as if examining a leaf. "I've decided it's not about money." She turned the slender leaf over in her hand. "You're right, you know. Enough is enough."

"Yeah?" Marli gave her sister an acknowledged silence.

"I've decided to split the cost of the house with you. Would that be all right?" she asked, finally looking up.

Marli reached for her sister's hand. "That's wonderful. Thank you. But is everything okay?"

"Yes. And no. I kind of left in a huff and Bob really resents my change of heart. But we've been married a long time and I've let him call the shots, for the most part. But this is *my* money. Not his. And it's *my* decision what to do with it."

"That's a big move on your part."

A long, black snake slithered toward them.

"We better move!" Ellie yelped and the two quickly jumped out of the serpent's path. "I think we'll need counseling, but at least it's a start."

Marli watched Ellie's eyes pool up, but that was it. She was glad her sister had come, even if it was only for a couple days.

As they headed back to the house, Marli's cell phone rang. It was Rachel. After the usual pleasantries, she stopped. "My sister's here. Can we both come over?"

After they went back to the house and changed into shorts, they walked over to the neighbor's house. Marli knocked on the front door and introduced Ellie, and Rachel invited them in.

"Would you like some *ass tea*?"

That was how Marli always heard it now. *Ass tea*. "Yes. Thank you."

Rachel sat in the light-blue wing chair after serving her company the traditional Southern beverage.

Marli described the black snake they'd seen and Rachel laughed.

"It was most likely a black racer—not poisonous."

"That's good to hear," Ellie said.

Rachel smiled and set down her glass on the coffee table. "Well, my son's lawyer gave me the go ahead on that oil deal if y'all are still interested."

"That's great news." Ellie smiled. "And you're right, Marli. This can be a win-win for all of us."

Marli was deeply touched by Ellie's turnaround. She was proud to be in the same family, and happy her sister had joined her in Mississippi. Plus, she even agreed to financially share in the house project! And now, it looked like Ellie could actually see the bigger picture regarding the oil deal. She couldn't ask for more.

That night, all five women went out to a local restaurant for supper. Each drank more than her fair share and they slept late the following morning. It was good to have a down day. More swimming. And eating. And drinking.

On Monday morning, Ellie took one last walk through the house before driving down to Jackson to catch her flight home. A gentle breeze danced through the woods and reminded Marli of her dad and why she was here.

26

GOING OUT IN DIFFERENT
DIRECTIONS

*T*he drone of the cicadas gained in decibels as the morning wore on. Tilda batted at a mosquito buzzing around her ear and replaced the bow on the fourth string of her violin. Under the large oak tree behind the house, she studied her music on the stand in front of her and continued to play. After repeating a passage, she quickly tucked the instrument under her arm and scribbled new notes onto the staff paper. After telling Marli she wanted to capture these "Mississippi woods" in musical form, to take home with her; she added, "This could well be the only time I'll ever visit this neck of the woods."

Rose came out the back door of the house with a newspaper. She stopped on the steps, where Marli was sitting, to listen to the emerging composition, before approaching the artist at work.

"Hey Rose," Tilda said. "What's up?"

"Your music sounds nice. I was wondering if you'd like to go hear the Mud Rucks play at Gator's tonight? Check this out. It starts at

7:00 p.m. over in Yazoo City. Would it be okay if we take the car, Marli? Did you still want to stay here?"

Tilda grabbed the paper, smearing pencil lead from her fingers onto the edges.

"See the ad right there?"

"Hm. It looks good. Sounds like fun." Tilda agreed. "Hey, where's the spray bottle?"

"Right here." Marli sprayed her own face and handed it to her. "Yeah, you can have the car. I won't need it. I just want to hang around here tonight."

Tilda spritzed her neck. "Oh, that feels better. I should be done with this by early afternoon and then I'll need a shower. What about Carol?"

"I think Carol is going to dinner with Travis," Rose answered.

"Woop-dee-doo. What do you know?" The musician laughed.

"You know, this is beautiful, Tilda. You playing your violin here in the woods like this." Rose stood back to enjoy the scene. "I wish I could play like that." After Tilda ran through the segment again, Rose cleared her throat. "You know, I'm a little worried about going back home. I mean, I do miss John and all, but I'm enjoying this so much. It's been nice not to have chores I absolutely have to do, you know?"

Tilda brushed her bow across a string. "Yeah, I hear ya."

"It is nice, huh?" Marli agreed.

"I do miss home, though. But then there are all the expectations and stuff that go along with that. I don't know. John's pretty needy. I don't think he has any idea how much I do to take the pressure off him. I keep the house clean. I tried my best to have the kids behave when he was home. I cooked three meals a day. He did the job and I did everything else. Now that the kids are grown I need a break. I don't know how I can keep doing this anymore." She wiped her eyes. "I'm just gonna try not to think about it for now."

"It'll be fine, Rose," Tilda assured her. "I'm actually looking forward to getting back home and starting my lessons again. And to tell you the truth, I'm a little horny." She swayed her hips and shrugged her shoulders. "I think I just need a good fuck from my lover. Just so you know."

Marli and Rose cracked up. Their friend was so candid, and sure didn't beat around the bush—at all. She just said what was on her mind.

"Well, there is that," Rose finally responded.

Tilda added, "This has been great, but I think I get too lazy without a routine."

"Yeah, I guess I just feel a little lost these days," Rose said. "John's a wonderful husband and he's provided well for the kids and me. But now that the kids aren't around and he's busy with work, I just somehow need more—or something different. At least that's what it feels like. It's complicated. I'm kind of floundering."

"Well, I don't know what to tell you. I never had kids. Thank God!" Tilda chuckled and played a quick little phrase. "What do you think of that?"

Rose rubbed her chin in thought, while Marli continued to sit cross-legged in the grass, twirling a dandelion between her fingers. Tilda looked at them quizzically. "Well?"

Rose scratched her head and stepped forward. "Well, it reminds me of what I seem to be becoming—" She looked up into the trees. "Kind of like those little surprise notes you just played. I don't seem to be who I used to be. It's doubtful John knows quite what to do with me anymore. Even before we left on this trip, I wasn't always doing what he wanted me to. In the past, if he didn't want to go somewhere, we wouldn't go. But now, I just go by myself if I feel like it."

"Seems healthy to me." Tilda moved her eyes away from the music stand and focused on Rose.

"Even over the phone, just the other day, he said he wants me home by Wednesday. But I told him he'll just have to wait. I said I'm not sure when I'll be back and then I hung up on him."

"Really? That's pretty bold of you." Marli smiled at her friend, thinking that maybe Rose was finally coming into her own.

"I called him back later, though, and apologized. But I held my ground. He'll just have to deal. This trip has helped me a lot. To get braver around him and stand up for myself."

"You've come a long way, Rose," Tilda counseled. "He's a good guy. He'll come around. You two are just figuring out your new phase of life, now that the kids are grown. I think it's a good thing." She smiled encouragingly and turned back to her music stand.

Marli wandered toward the house and called home. Her son answered.

"How'd you do in your race yesterday? Wasn't it a 10k? … Second place? Wow, that's terrific, TJ. I'm so proud of you. … Okay. You have a wonderful day. Can I talk to Dad? … Hey there to you, too, stranger. … Well, it won't be that much longer. Just a few more days here. I miss you, but it has really gone by quickly. I'm so glad I got to do this. It means a lot to me. … I love you, too. Bye for now."

They talked every few days or so. She and her husband were close, but hardly smothering. Richard traveled to academic conferences frequently, and occasionally Marli's performances would take her on the road. Both actively pursued their own interests while settling into a comfortable coexistence.

———

That evening, Tilda and Rose got gussied up to go to the café concert, while Carol changed her clothes to go out for a casual dinner date with Travis. She wore the new outfit she'd bought during the shopping spree with the ladies. She looked good in the floral-patterned skirt and sleeveless blouse. She had one of Rose's handmade barrettes in her hair, accented by a turquoise stone that Marli thought highlighted her blue eyes. Travis came by at 7:00 p.m. to pick her up.

"You look nice," he said, as they met at the door of the trailer. They were driving over to Canton to a place that served catfish, hushpuppies, and fried crawfish. "Their specialty is a gator margarita, whatever that means. It's good, though."

"You guys have fun," Marli called from the flower bed, where she was kneeling, pulling weeds.

After they'd gone, Marli went over to the pond for a float in the old aluminum boat. She let it drift, content to go wherever the breeze and water took her. She lay on her back, looking up at the overhanging branches and changing cloud shapes. She got lost in memories of Dad.

She had booked his memorial service at that Baptist church near his house. He'd been there numerous times, but had not been a regular. Nonetheless, he preferred it to the other church down on Woodview Avenue. She and Ellie gave the preacher Dad's list of favorite Bible verses. During the eulogy, the pastor managed to highlight the best of those messages without coming down too heavy-handed on the small audience. The sisters had gone into this church venue with a bit of trepidation, not really having any idea how loving and forgiving this House of God was or if it was one of those "fire and brimstone" churches. But there had been nothing to fear. The guy did a great job. Jasmine, Marli's oldest daughter, had a beautiful soprano voice and sang "Simple Gifts" and played "Ashokan Farewell" on her violin. Her boyfriend, an opera tenor, bellowed "Zion's Walls." His voice echoed throughout the building. The entire congregation rocked with "When the Saints Go Marching In."

A few of Dad's old buddies had come to the service. One of his best friends, Ted, was closer to Marli's age than his own. She and Ellie joked that he was their adopted brother. The three of them each stood up front and told about the special moments they'd had with Dad. Afterward, they went over to Manny's, Dad's favorite pizza joint, and socialized.

Above Marli, in the twilight, a mockingbird hopped from branch to branch, carrying on in sharp, staccato tweets.

She thought again of her sister. How difficult it must have been to let go of her half of the Franklin Fund to allow Marli to pursue their father's dream. Ellie had sacrificed a lot. A wave of gratitude washed over her.

Suddenly, Marli felt a bump and the boat veered sideways. She jolted upright and immediately got soaked. Lifting her arms to protect her face, she shook her head like a wet dog, and then saw him.

"Jody!"

He had come up from behind, in the other boat, and used his oar to send a wave of water her way, which, of course, had startled her. His engaging, warm smile took her by surprise.

"Just what do you think you're doin', mister?" Marli panted and quickly grabbed the sides of the boat to keep her balance. She was drenched.

"I was ready to go home and couldn't find you. So I came down here to look. Are you okay?" he asked, pulling her boat closer with his oar.

"Yeah, I'm fine," she admitted. "I was just off in the land of memories. Mostly about my dad."

"Reminiscing, huh? I do that, too, sometimes. My mother passed over ten years ago and Dad lives by himself, over in Durant. I see him every so often." He looked up into the trees. "Hey, remember when you told us about that little interaction your dad had with your son? How'd that go again?" Jody asked.

Marli scrolled through their past conversations. "Oh, that time TJ hit Sage when he was around eight, and Dad put the fear of God in him? He'd yelled at him, 'You never EVER hit a girl! Do you understand? NEVER!' You mean that time?"

"Yeah. I thought that was such a good response, and good timing, and an ideal situation to instill that in a young boy."

"Uh-huh. It was."

"He sounds to me like he was a mighty strong influence on you guys, Marli. You're lucky. Most people don't have anything like that. I hope I manage to convey some semblance of that to my own son." He took off his cap and wiped a sleeve across his forehead.

Marli watched his brown hair fall to the side. "Yeah, he was something else. You know, when we bought our house it had a condemned sign on the front door. The place was in shambles, and there was an open pit out in the front yard for a cesspool. My dad built us an outhouse to use while we put in a septic tank and fixed up the property."

Jody laughed. "Wow. A real outhouse with a hole in the dirt and everything?"

"Yup," Marli said, giggling. "And we still use that thing to this day! It comes in real handy sometimes when we're working outside." She pivoted on the bench as the boat slowly turned.

"You know, Marli, you seem to be right at home here, out on the homestead," he said, gazing at her. "You've got a real knack for visualizing this project from start to finish. If I didn't know you better, I'd almost venture to say you might could live out here." His focus remained on her.

She paused in thought. "Well, I do like it here, this place and my new friends and all. It's peaceful and away from all the modern city crap. The canyon where I live is sort of like this, too." The crickets and frogs, one by one, joined their voices into the chorus of the approaching twilight. A fish plopped nearby and she heard the faint whistle of a distant train.

Jody splashed her again. "How 'bout a race?"

That brought her back. She shoved a wave of water at him. "You're on!" Marli dug her oars into the water and powered past him. She beat him to the edge and beamed. "That felt great! Thanks for the invitation."

He helped her pull the boats out of the water and onto the shore. She became aware of his physical proximity. His musky scent from working outside all day aroused her. Walking out of the brambles, Marli stumbled over a vine and Jody caught her, pulling her up off her knees. They stayed briefly in each other's arms. She finally whispered, "Thanks." His strong hands grasped her shoulders and she reluctantly pulled away.

"I'm really gonna miss you," he said, before releasing her. She turned slowly and led the way up the dirt ramp as they moved away from the pond.

Marli liked Jody and he liked her. At least, it sure seemed like it. They had a great rapport with each other. It was almost as if they'd grown up together. Or known each other for a very long time. They understood one another. It was almost like being brother and sister, except for the obvious chemistry between them. If they hadn't both been in stable marriages, one or the other might have been tempted to stray. But Marli knew, deep down, it wouldn't be worth it. Wrecking two good marriages would be stupid. They knew better. Their heads were screwed on pretty tight. The two of them enjoyed a beer together before he left for the night.

⌒

After midnight, Rose and Tilda were sound asleep in the trailer and Marli was rocking on the front porch of the house, unable to catch any shuteye. A beautiful full moon lit up the woods all around. The trees cast eerie shadows in mystical patterns. It felt rewarding to be here, witnessing the night. Headlights announced Travis's truck pulling in front of the trailer.

Marli could see just enough, through the branches, to watch Travis walk over to the passenger door and open it for Carol. He stood there for quite a while. What were they doing? She felt like a voyeur. Marli tried not to watch, but when he helped Carol out they embraced and kissed—for a long time. She couldn't really make out their muffled conversation. Nor did she want to. It was their business, not hers. He eventually drove away and Carol sat down at the picnic table outside.

"I'm over here," Marli called. "At the house. I couldn't sleep. You want to chat?"

Carol got up and shuffled over, her steps looking tentative in the moonlight. She was carrying something.

"So, how was your date?" Marli smiled in the semi-darkness.

Carol sat down in the other chair. "It was interesting. You know what? Travis has this amazing genealogy he showed me. It says he's related to General Lee and all sorts of important historical figures. But that's not why he dug it out. He just thought I might want to look at it, since I'm interested in that sort of thing." She handed Marli a bound notebook.

Marli took a small flashlight from her pocket and shined it onto the fraying yellowed pages, reading little quips of information out loud, here and there. "Wow. This is amazing. Who put all this together?"

"His grandfather did. He spent close to ten years working on it."

"That's impressive. It says here that his great-uncle, no, great-great-uncle owned a cotton plantation in Hattiesburg. The Vernet genealogy looks similar. Did you know that?"

"No. But I'm learning all sorts of things on this trip." Carol shifted in her chair. "You know—about a mile or two from here—Travis pulled over on a side road that overlooks the river and stopped the truck. It's such a pretty night. The warm night breeze came in through the open windows."

Marli closed the pamphlet and placed it on the small side table. She looked up at the moon hanging in the sky.

Carol continued. "I told him genealogy is really something to treasure. Not many families have their history that well recorded. He's lucky."

"Did you guys just talk?"

There was a long pause. "No. Not exactly," her friend began. "I'd leaned over to kiss his cheek, just as he turned his head toward me. So we ended up kissing on the lips. Kind of accidently." She giggled.

Marli smiled and patted Carol's knee.

"Then he hugged and kissed me deliberately. Things started to get a little steamy in that truck."

"Good for you, Carol."

An owl flew by in front of them.

"Holy crap!" Carol barked. "I think that owl followed us from the riverbank. It kept dive-bombing the truck. Like we were disturbing his place, or something."

"You probably were." Marli snickered.

Just then, raspy shrieks came from the weeping willow and the owl careened by again.

"Wow! I guess we really did piss him off."

The women laughed and the frogs and crickets contributed their own expressive sounds to the beautiful symphony in the swamp.

27

THE LAST SUPPER

*J*oe and Travis were upstairs, putting the finishing touches in the bathroom. Jody worked outside, fixing one of the front steps. Marli walked over from the trailer, carrying two steaming cups.

"Here you go, Jody. How 'bout some coffee?"

"You bet." He pushed up the bill of his cap and stood, taking the mug from her. "Thanks. This'll keep me going."

She looked around, taking in the unique brown clapboard house; the grey slate roof with its pleasing pitch and dormers; the square panes gracing the windows that reflected the vibrant hues of the surrounding woods. How absolutely amazing it was, that all this had come together so beautifully. It would be sad to leave it all behind.

"You guys are still coming for supper tonight, right?"

"Yup, sure are. Wouldn't miss it for the world." Jody squatted to drive in a screw with his power drill.

Rose, Carol, and Tilda pulled up in the car and started unloading groceries into the house. Marli opened the screen door for them.

Jody stepped aside so they could get by. "Hey, what are we havin' anyway?"

"That's going to be a surprise." Rose laughed. "No peeking!" She hoisted one of the bags higher on her hip and went into the house.

"Well, I guess that's my cue," Marli said. "I better get to work."

She watched from an open window as Harold, from the hardware store, pulled up and honked. Travis came down the stairs and went out to meet him.

"I brought you that bracket you wanted, Travis. It just come in this mornin'."

"Thank you, sir." Travis took the small paper bag from him.

"Hey. Weren't that your truck I saw down by the crick last night? What were you doin' down there? Fishin' in the dark?" Harold raised his eyebrows in that knowing way.

"Oh, nothin'." Travis walked back toward the house, stopped, and turned back. "Couldn't have been me." Marli noticed him smiling when he ambled toward her.

Harold grinned and backed the car, shaking his head.

My foot, Marli said to herself. *Nothin'? Boys will be boys, I guess.*

The men finished up what they could get done that morning and took off for the afternoon. The women got busy in the kitchen and started to prepare their "farewell dinner." They would be leaving the next day. The house began to fill with delicious aromas as ingredients were combined and then boiled, sautéed, or baked.

Marli stirred a pan of warm milk heating on the stove. On Rachel's recommendation, she'd bought some raw goat milk from a girl across town. She couldn't wait to have fresh ricotta for the lasagna.

"The milk's 195 degrees, Marli," Carol said, adding the apple cider vinegar Marli had measured out for her, which immediately caused the milk to coagulate—separating curds from whey. She poured the contents into a colander lined with cheesecloth and let it drain for a few minutes.

"I'll do the rest." Marli scooped out curds with a slotted spoon and added butter and baking soda. She was teaching Carol how to make the cheese. "Voila. The ricotta is ready." Her skirt flared as she turned around.

Carol rinsed her hands in the sink. "That was quick. The noodles are done and the mozzarella is grated."

Tilda reached over Marli's creation to dump potato peelings into the coffee can on the counter.

"How about the spinach from Rachel's garden? Let's put that in, too, along with the meat," Marli suggested.

"Speaking of which, Carol—" Tilda teased. "Did you, you know, have a good time last night?"

"Meat? Really, Tilda?" Marli grimaced.

Carol's cheeks flushed red, but she was grinning when she turned away to face the window over the sink. "None of your damned business."

Rose sprayed water at Carol. "Oh, come on. It's just us. You know we all have your best interest at heart. After all, we're your friends. If you can't tell us, who can you tell?"

"Yeah," Tilda egged on.

Carol continued to look out the window above the counter.

Marli leaned over and whispered, "You don't have to say anything if you don't want to."

Carol was quiet for a minute, spread both hands and leaned over the sink. She started giggling. "Of course I did. What did y'all expect?" she drawled, and grabbed the spray bottle to squirt Rose.

Tilda gave Carol a high-five when she turned around. "Well, good for you!"

Whew, that cat's out of the bag. Now Marli wouldn't have to worry about keeping the secret, if it actually ever was one.

"It doesn't mean anything, though. We both know we have our own lives 2,000 miles apart from each other. It was just nice to feel wanted again, that's all."

"I'm happy for you." Rose walked over and hugged her.

They carried on, razzing and joking all afternoon. Rose made gluten-free bread and Tilda prepared a salad. The lasagna baking in the oven made everyone's mouth water.

Tilda tossed a dish towel onto the counter. "I'll head over to the trailer now for my shower."

"I call second." Rose pulled a golden brown loaf of bread from the oven and closed the door quickly before any more heat could escape.

"Wow. It's beautiful. A true work of art." Marli leaned over the pan to get a good whiff. "Mmm."

Around 7:00 p.m., Jody drove up in his dusty old Ford pickup. Marli peered out the window and watched him start to open the front door, as usual, but then knock instead. She answered the door wearing a square-necked blue sundress. Her long, blonde hair was scooped up and held by one of Rose's Tigers Eye barrettes.

Jody, in clean blue jeans and a long-sleeved, paisley Western-style shirt, handed her a bottle of Merlot. "Boy, Marli. You look wonderful tonight. You've got the greatest shoulders."

"Well, thank you, Jody." She couldn't help but feel herself blush. "You look good, too. Hey, I thought Fran and Eddie were coming."

"Nope, not tonight. They left this afternoon to go spend the day with Fran's mom. She had a procedure done at the doctor's office. It's no big deal, but she wanted to go be with her. They'll be back tomorrow."

Travis and Joe pulled in together and came up the steps with two six-packs of Budweiser. Rachel walked in with a strawberry rhubarb pie she'd just made. She set it down on the old dresser in the corner.

"So, what can I do to help?"

"It looks like you already have, Rachel." Marli gave her new friend a quick hug.

"Wow! This is going to be some feast," said Tilda. Travis walked by Carol and squeezed her hand.

Marli pointed to two chairs on the far side of the table and said, "Why don't you two sit over there?"

The guys had put together a makeshift dining table by resting a sheet of plywood on top of two sawhorses. A sunny yellow bedsheet served as a tablecloth and an assortment of wine glasses and plates from the thrift store made an attractive table setting. It wasn't anything fancy, but it served its temporary purpose, along with the folding chairs.

Marli picked up the dish of lasagna and passed it to her left. Jody dished up and then handed it to Rachel. Traditional Southern style. After all the courses had made it around the table, Jody stood up.

"I'd like to make a toast." He raised his glass and looked around. "To the best lady friends on the planet. This has been the most enjoyable job I've ever had, by far."

Marli rose to her feet and clinked his glass. "To the best friends in the whole world. And to the most fun, hard-working, intuitive crew ever." Travis and Carol toasted each other. "And cheers to you, Rachel. You've been a good friend to all of us."

After the toasting, everyone dug into the meal. Carol set down her glass. "Did you guys know Travis is related to Robert E. Lee? He's got pages and pages of his family tree all bound up into a family genealogy. It's quite impressive."

"That's the historian in her talking," said Travis. "I heard Marli has a genealogy book, too."

"Really?" Rachel asked. "Is that so?" She dabbed the sides of her mouth with the cloth napkin.

"Yeah, there's documentation that we've been in this area at least since 1733. I'm related to those rumrunners in Georgia. Evidently, old Mr. Vernet got in a tangle with Oglethorpe back in the 1730s over his illegal spirits trade."

"Oglethorpe? I've heard of him," Tilda said. "Pass me some more of that *ass tea*, please."

Jody shook his head. "You ladies and your *ass tea*."

"Would you please pass the salad, Rose?" Travis reached toward her.

"You probably heard of Oglethorpe in school history books." Carol began to inform the group. "He was James Oglethorpe Esq. There was some mention of him in Travis's genealogy, too. He was a British general and he founded the colony of Georgia. He had negotiated with the Creek tribe and set up a series of defensive forts. You know what's really interesting, though?" She laughed. "He returned to England, briefly, to arrange to have slavery banned in Georgia! He wanted it to be a debtor's colony!"

"Who wants pie?" Rachel asked. There was a show of hands from everyone. She got up and walked over to the counter.

"What's a debtor's colony?" Rose asked.

"Well, Oglethorpe thought British debtors should be released from prison and sent to Georgia. That would theoretically rid Britain of its so-called *undesirable* elements," Carol explained.

"What do you know?" Rachel said, cutting the pie. "I never knew all that. What do you know?"

Carol continued. "They didn't end up with many debtors coming over, though. Oglethorpe eventually saw the wisdom in recruiting those with some kind of skill, Britain's *worthy poor*."

Rachel served slices of pie. Murmurs of appreciation were heard all around.

"Mmm. This pie is absolutely delicious," said Jody.

"Indeed, it is." Travis scooped some ice cream on top of his extra-large piece. "And thank you, Carol, for the great history lesson."

Carol nodded with a smile, as the others' eyes darted back and forth around the table. A hush fell over the room. Utensils scraped against plates. Glasses were lifted and set down.

Travis broke the silence. "I'm stuffed." After finishing his last bite, he laid his fork across the plate.

Rachel stood and pushed her chair in. "Well, I've really got to get back home and check on my old dog. He's not feeling too good. He's just getting old. Like the rest of us." She leaned on the back of her chair. "I'm sure gonna miss y'all. I've thoroughly enjoyed your company. Write me once in a while, ya hear?"

"Oh, I will," Marli promised. "We'll miss you, too. It's nice to have a friend here, so close, just down the road a bit." She stood up to collect the pie pan and server.

"You take care, Rachel," Tilda said. "I hope your dog will be all right."

"And thanks for everything. And we do mean *everything*," Rose added with a hesitant chuckle.

"You betcha." Rachel winked at her. "Call me before you leave tomorrow, okay?" The women each hugged her goodbye and Marli walked her out the door. "This is way harder than I thought it would be. This whole thing was supposed to be just a little adventure, but it's turned into so much more."

"I know what you mean," Rachel said, turning to go. "Y'all have been a real bright spot around here. And that oil deal will help me out, too."

"I'm glad it worked out for everybody." Marli watched her walk away in the moonlight. She was reminded what beautiful country it was and got an inkling of why Southerners seem to prefer one another's company and way of life. This had been a truly remarkable experience and made each of them a little more daring.

She came back in through the screen door, where good food, camaraderie, and drinks were still providing a wonderful, entertaining evening. Good-natured humor, coupled with raucous laughter, filled the house with warmth—the kind that permeates the soul and sticks to your ribs. Complete with the sweet dessert that lingers on your tongue and changes the way you remember things.

"Are you sure you can take care of getting our camping trailer returned, Jody? I know it's a lot to ask."

"No problem at all. And we oughta have this place ready to rent out in a few weeks."

"Thank you so much. You know? We're very lucky that everything's worked out so well, considering all the details."

"Won't it feel a little weird having other people live in this house, Marli?" Rose asked. "I know you have to do it and all, but doesn't it feel strange?"

"Of course, it does. But my life is in California, not here. I've got to be somewhat practical, don't I? And I still can't believe my sister agreed to all this. She's a bigger person than I'd ever realized. When I get back home, I'm going to treat her to a nice supper and tell her how truly grateful I am."

"Well, we're gonna miss y'all. I can tell you that right now," Travis said. "I hope you ladies will come back and visit us again, real soon."

Marli's eyes welled up. "I want to thank you—all of you—for helping this dream of mine come true. If even one of us had not been able to come here—*this* may not have ever happened." She opened her arms wide and looked at each one of them. "I'm just so grateful to all of you. My best friends."

"And talk about timing," said Tilda. "This was one of those rare synchronicities in life, eh?"

Marli couldn't help but notice that her friend had softened a little during this trip. She was more willing to just hang with the group now.

"Or maybe," Marli said, "this was just one of those crazy ideas that never ran into a wall."

28

ON THE ROAD AGAIN

*T*hat July morning dawned sleepily for the travelers. They'd been up late washing dishes, packing, and getting organized for their trip back home. Marli started gathering the bedding to put in the roof carrier on the car. She moved Tilda's pile of clothes off the pillow and accidentally dropped a pair of underwear on the floor.

"Hey! Watch it! Those are clean," Tilda snapped.

"I'm sorry. I'm just trying to get packed, is all."

"I just don't want my clothes on the floor."

"Someone woke up on the wrong side of the bed this morning," Carol ventured as she came out of the bathroom.

"Mm hmm," Rose hummed, matching a far-away train whistle.

Marli took the load out and Carol and Rose followed. They decided to give Tilda a wide berth for the time being. Marli looked up when she heard a dog bark and saw Rachel walking up the driveway holding a paper sack, with the old mutt ambling behind.

"Top of the morning to you. I see Rusty's feeling better."

"Yes. He seems to be having a good day today. I made you ladies some pimento cheese sandwiches for your trip."

"Why thank you, Rachel." Marli stood at the door of the car, stuffing excess bedding into the roof compartment, and finally managed to buckle the latches. "My grandma always made pimento cheese sandwiches when we left here each summer, too. How'd you know?"

"Oh, they're pretty common here."

"Wow. Check it out!" Marli shrieked, pointing toward the house. "The Naked Ladies are blooming." These particular flowers didn't give much advance notice.

"Why sure enough," Rachel said. "Will you look at that? It's still a bit early for 'em."

"Aren't those the same ones you transplanted last summer?" Carol asked, bringing a pair of sandals out of the trailer.

"Yes, they are." Marli walked over to bury her nose in them. How fitting, she thought, that they flower on the day she was leaving. As a kind of goodbye from her Mississippi ancestors. She got a little teary.

"They're beautiful." Rose touched a long pink tubular flower and ran her fingers along its length. There was a shared reverence between the two gardeners.

Tilda came over after putting suitcases into the back of the car. "I'm sorry, guys," she said. "I didn't mean anything. It's just sometimes it's a little challenging for me to change gears—and that's what we're doing right now, you know? Besides, I'm *not* a morning person. Hi, Rachel. How are you?"

"I'm fine, Tilda. Well, y'all have a good trip back, ya hear? And write me often." She looked directly at Marli. "I don't want to delay you further."

After more farewell hugs, Rachel turned to leave. She waved a hand over her shoulder, without looking back, and headed home. The dog lagged a few paces behind. The travelers lugged the rest of their belongings out to the car and packed them in.

"I think we're leaving with more stuff than we brought," Carol said.

"Ya think?" Tilda responded.

They took a last look through the trailer while Marli went over to the house by herself. She wanted one last walkthrough alone. She slowly climbed up the stairs, taking one mindful step at a time. She thought it was important to feel fully present, to be able to absorb the essence of the house that had become her friend. This could be the last time she'd be here for quite a while. She placed her hand around the smooth, black knob of the screen door and turned it, pulling it toward her. Once inside the kitchen, she let the door close gently behind her, slowing it with her hand. Aromas from last night's farewell dinner reminded her of the special friendships she'd made here. The borrowed cast-iron skillet sat beside the porcelain enameled sink, a blue-flowered dish towel draped over the handle. Each chair sat at a different angle and distance from the table, which created a sense of movement. She could almost feel the party still going on.

Marli walked through to the living room and stopped to lean against the staircase. The rose wallpaper and wainscoting covered two walls and the others were painted antique white and sun cup yellow. The room appeared larger than it actually was with the morning sunlight pouring in. It felt familiar. Almost like Grandma's sun parlor. Chills shot up Marli's spine. *This* was what she'd wanted. To honor the ancestors who came before.

The downstairs bedroom didn't have a door yet and she stood, peering in. A single bare bulb hung from the ceiling, waiting to be replaced by a ceiling fan. A bathroom took up one corner, which made for additional right angles. She pictured a wrought-iron double bed with a puffy floral duvet; an antique dresser with a scalloped, beveled mirror; and lace window drapes. She could feel the comfort this room could offer.

Upstairs, she lingered in the two bedrooms, and imagined children's furniture and wooden toys from a bygone era. She wanted to go back. To then. When generations lived and worked together and furnishings were made to last. Like family.

She sat down on the floor with the sun at her back and closed her eyes. Visions of Dad and Uncle Parker came to her. The cousins running up and down the stairs. Grandma cutting a piece of cake for Grandpa. The clatter of women in the kitchen preparing dinner, the big midday meal. Everyone sitting, talking, or reading in the sun parlor. Tears flooded Marli's eyes and she smiled, glad to have these memories. She would take them with her.

She walked out to the car to join the others. "I think I'm really going to miss this place." She looked around at all they'd done, and tears, once again, filled her eyes.

"I think we all are," Rose said, rubbing Marli on the back.

The women got in the car quietly, solemnly. Marli eased out the driveway, wanting to absorb every last detail of the place and remember it all. The tires rolled over the gravel, as if in slow motion, crunching and displacing each granule individually. She breathed in the warm, humid air and pulled it deep into her lungs—so she could take it with her to help carry her through whatever might lie ahead. Turning the wheel to the left she looked right, across the meadow, at the border of trees on the far side. Farther along, she turned right onto the paved road and then drove over the bridge. There, on the side of the road, was Jody's old red truck. He was standing outside the cab leaning against the door. She slowly pulled the car over behind his truck.

"What are you doing here?" she asked, leaning out her window.

Jody walked over and braced himself on the car door. "I had to say goodbye again, you know. Besides, Fran made oatmeal cookies for y'all."

"Oh my," Tilda said. "Tell Fran, thanks. We appreciate it."

"Yes. Please do. Thanks for everything, Jody. I really appreciate all you've done for us."

He reached out and squeezed Marli's shoulder. "I'll take good care of the place for you and make sure we get decent renters in there. Y'all have a good, safe trip." He tapped the door twice. "We'll keep in touch." He looked at Marli. His eyes, too, brimmed with moisture. She smiled at him, nodded, and gradually pulled away. She watched him in the rearview mirror, standing by his truck, staring, until her car was out of sight. Silence permeated the inside of the car as their summer adventure began to burn into memory.

Marli turned south onto the highway. They passed old wooden bridges that spanned the river, little rickety shacks in the distance, and caught glimpses of muddy swampland between the edges of woods—all amidst the dark green of rural Mississippi. Long streaks of lightning jabbed between overlapping clouds and the sky darkened. Large, heavy raindrops fell onto the windshield and became more and more regular. The cloudburst turned into a deluge, sending any hovering particles in the atmosphere down with it. A major cleansing was taking place all around them, bringing with it a chance for new beginnings and an opening for miracles.

ACKNOWLEDGEMENTS

My work on this project spanned a decade—on and off again—and changed directions multiple times. *The Old House in the Country* is an attempt to honor my dad who had deep Southern roots. In order to navigate this complex terrain, I felt it needed to become a fun story of fiction.

I'm much obliged to my sister, Bo Varnado, and the friends who read early versions of the novel and provided feedback: including Susan Nelson, Debbie George, Beverly Silvers, Sheri Gaarder, Helen Wilson, Heidi Moore Schlotfeldt, Lynne Hamburger Shevinsky, and Candace Wright. For the business of getting this book published I'd like to thank Monkey C Media.

I couldn't have possibly persevered through this endeavor without the continuous encouragement and support of my husband, Kent Richardson. And thanks for being who you are—my children: Jessie, Kali and Chance.

ABOUT THE AUTHOR

Chi Varnado lives in the backcountry of San Diego County with her husband and a menagerie of animals. She's published three books (two were finalists for the San Diego Book Awards) and a series of three YA novels about ballet. She's also written for *The San Diego Reader*, Patch.com, *The Ramona Sentinel* and *Home Journal*, *The San Diego Poetry Annual*.... After retiring from her dance studio, she spends more time hiking, writing, and working on their rural property.

Learn more at ChiVarnado.com and DanceCentrePresents.com.

REQUEST FOR REVIEW

Dear reader,

If you enjoyed *The Old House in the Country*, please consider giving it a review wherever you review your books. Amazon.com and Goodreads both accept reader reviews. Every little bit helps.

Thanks for reading.

—Chi Varnado